Especially for Trane & Taye!
— Helen

Helen Taylor Andrews

# The Gifts of Joy

Helen Taylor Andrews

Cover photo: "Cathy's View to Georgia" by Helen Taylor Andrews

Author photo by Patsy Taylor Dunn

## Dedication

This story is dedicated to those folks I've known and loved over the years who make music and sing on their front porches, like my daddy and my mama, or those who go to barns, living rooms, or community centers , to make music on a Saturday night. My sister, Patsy, Raymond (her late husband), and I have sung in community centers, and many living rooms. We played the piano growing up and often our house rang with music, Daddy on his guitar, and Mama on her accordion. We sang the songs we learned from the radio or from church over the years. I can still hear my daddy playing "Under the Double Eagle". I'd give anything to hear him play it one more time. Patsy's son, Lee, continues the music tradition with his gifted guitar playing, like his father, and his grandfather, my daddy.

I would like to dedicate this to my mama who was an artist at heart but never had art supplies to work with until later in her life. During our growing up years she made our clothes without benefit of a pattern, and did embroidery, and other crafts, as money afforded. My sister and I have a few of her paintings that we will always cherish. I always wonder what Mama would have been able to accomplish if she had the art training and supplies that I now have access to in life. Everything I paint, or write, or every craft I do, I do in Mama's memory. Mama always told me that I got my 'talent from her'.

I hope so, Mama. My life is richer because of you and Daddy.

For

John David Andrews

April 17, 1946 - May 7, 2015

&

Judge Val L. McGee

October 15, 1920 - December 6, 2015

# Prologue

Over the water to the east, on the Georgia side, Fred could see lightning streak the dark sky. Thunder sounded to the south, booming long and loud. Across the lake, lights blinked and suddenly his electricity went out. The power would probably be off for a while so Fred picked up his guitar, Maybelle, he'd dubbed it, and went out on the screened-in porch of his house, on Lake Eufaula.

The guitar was named in honor of Maybelle Carter, of A. P. Carter family fame. 'Mother Maybelle' revolutionized guitar picking, as well as country and folk music, with her unique thumb-picking style. Fred's Maybelle, however, was not worth the $575,000 that Maybelle Carter's 1928 Gibson L-5 guitar was valued.

He'd only paid $5000 for her but in his way of thinking, she was worth more than her weight in gold. He had other guitars but when he bought her he'd fallen in love with her rich tones and knew he would have paid fifty times that much. It was in excellent condition and had not been mistreated or played a lot. No scratches marred its silky beauty and it fingered like a dream. It was made during World War II when metals were rationed. The fact that the guitar had survived over seventy years was amazing since the man who owned it had once traveled all the time. The guitar was valuable, but Fred never bothered to do any research on it. It played and sounded good, and that was all that mattered to him.

Tonight, like other nights, Fred was alone. Maybelle and a supply of his favorite beer were his only companions. White sheets of rain hid the world from view, adding to his sense of isolation. He'd never felt so alone. Lonely. Nights like this caused him to drink himself into oblivion. Not every night, but more than he'd admit.

Fred Garrett didn't like rain. It messed with his mind. The years had not lessened the pain, the agony of remembering. He'd lost one, and should have been two, of the most important folks in his life on a stormy night, much like this one.

He thought of his best friend, Hart Wakefield, and Hart's wife, Ginger. How happy they were. Fred envied them, because with all he had, he was unhappy. Sometimes he felt sorry for himself, even though he had anything that money could buy. Hart had a family while Fred had his parents and a grandmother, who'd all moved to the beach, leaving him alone.

Fred drank from an open bottle, savoring the coldness as the liquid flowed down his throat. He put the bottle down and strummed a minor chord. Thunder continued to rumble, an accompaniment to the deep drone of heavy rain falling on the metal roof. Rain sounds were amplified on the porch which had a vaulted and beamed ceiling. In the yard, rain fell into a few bait buckets and a wheelbarrow, loudly, then more softly, as the driving rain slowed and settled into a steady downpour. Lightning, thunder, raindrops and the blowing wind through the trees blended, adding background tones to Fred's guitar chords.

Fred noticed a rhythm as the sounds and forces of nature came together in his outdoor amphitheater. He felt around on the sofa to find his cell phone to record the music. He strummed the same A minor chord, timing the beat. Surprisingly it all soothed his uneasiness and he began picking out a melody. Tears ran down his cheeks as the tune, and the rain, reminded him of a little dark haired girl.

Katie had loved playing in the rain, splashing and getting muddy. She would have been eight tomorrow. He still had dreams of her calling him 'Dad-dee'.

He wished he'd had children—a little boy he could teach to fish or play a guitar, and a little girl with golden hair. Most of his friends were married with kids. They had someone to be with on lonely rainy nights. That's what he wanted, too. "God, please send me some peace, love and joy," he whispered. "That's all I want in life."

*Does God listen to drunks who cause themselves to stumble?* Fred pondered the question, but doubted that He did.

The rain slowed and the plinks, tinkles and splats of the raindrops could be heard, individually. The symphony would soon be over. Thunder rumbled off in the distance now, the storm moving on. Fred continued playing, not wanting the music to end. For the first time in years Fred had embraced the rain, hearing the musical notes as the water poured from the heavens, adding his own soulful riffs and chords. He was glad he'd recorded the rain song. He would have to play it for Hart. Perhaps Hart would understand what he was feeling when he played it.

*"Rain is the tears of angels in heaven they say.*
*Somewhere in heaven my Katie will play.*
*Come to Daddy, baby...I love you..."*

The words were almost there, just out of reach—too far away for his alcohol-numbed brain to pull them in.

The lights blinked on once, twice. The power was back on and it was getting late. Tomorrow was another day. Fred took his guitar and walked inside.

# Chapter One

Six weeks later.

Joy's car died in the road and she steered it to a stop on the shoulder of the narrow road. Down the hill she could see the marina she was looking for. And the hope of a job. Most likely with minimum wage, minimum insurance, minimum outlook. As sad as that sounded it was better than no job, no insurance and no outlook. Joy had been there, been doing that.

Her shorts were stuck to her body, her tee shirt wet from top to bottom with the sweat that ran down from her hair which was pulled up in a messy top knot. One hundred degrees in Eufaula, Alabama.

Joy knew she smelled, having had no bath for two days. Dirty clothes, bedding and an assortment of books filled the back seat and the trunk of her car, which had become her home. She grabbed her purse and left her car on the side of the road. She'd have to ask someone to tow it someplace if it didn't start.

She'd run out of cash a couple of days earlier. Hungry, tired and heartsick. Pick any of those adjectives and it would fit her at the moment.

Down the hill, the marina was bustling. Despite

the low water level and high temperatures, the boaters and fishermen were out in throngs, filling their gas tanks and filling their coolers with ice, drinks and snacks.

Set amid tall pines, the low building was mostly metal. A little brick veneer added a touch of color to the otherwise gray structure. Docks, gas pumps and boats made the place look like a piece of abstract art. Folks were everywhere. It was a busy place and on the hottest day of the year so far. And it was still May.

Joy opened the door to the marina snack bar. A guy was busily working the cash register.

"Is Mr. Garrett around?"she asked, as one customer finished their sale.

"He's around. What can he do for you?"

Joy didn't want to talk in front of people, all of whom were dressed much better than she. Most of the women were in bikinis or tank tops, short shorts and flip-flops, the men in swim trunks and tee shirts. She looked down at her sweaty clothes and worn tennis shoes. Her toes were poking through on the left one.

"I need to talk with him. It's important. Tell him I'm here about the job opening. Mavis Duncan said Mr. Garrett—"

He cut her off, told the next customer he'd be right back and waved at her to follow him.

"Come on back. He's real busy and has paperwork to get out today."

The man stopped in front of a closed door and

knocked.

A terse, "Come in," came from inside.

"Fred? Mavis sent somebody here to see about the job." Joy noticed the inflection on the last two words and knew something was not quite kosher.

"I don't have time to fool with it, Sol. Can't you handle it?"

"No, sir. I think you need to, *Mr. Garrett*."

Joy was scared to enter the elegant office. It seemed too nice for a marina, but what did she know. The room was enormous and paneled with real wood. A large executive desk sat near the back wall with a credenza behind it. The man, Mr. Garrett, sat in a leather chair, his gaze locked on a computer screen. Joy's eye went to an assortment of art work that covered much of one wall. One wall was lined with wood-toned file cabinets that matched the paneling. Another wall had a plate glass window overlooking the lake. Everything in the room seemed so intimidating. Even the man behind the desk was large and overwhelming. A sense of dread hit her.

She shivered inwardly from the coldness of the air-conditioned space, and from fear of not getting a job. She needed to work. Today. Right now. She stepped inside the room.

The man kept his attention glued to his computer screen, never looking up.

"I'm...I'm Joy Smith...Mavis Duncan said...said you might have a job opening. I sure could use a job...my car broke down and I...don't have the money...to have it fixed or towed. I know I'm not dressed well enough, but could...could I start today?"

Once she'd started talking, she couldn't stop. *God, why am I so nervous?*

The man never lifted his blonde head. He had a George Hamilton tan and wore a turquoise-colored polo shirt with an emblem on it. He looked arrogant and Joy wanted him to just look her way, to acknowledge her by looking her in the eye.

"Nope. I already got somebody coming in. He's got experience working the cash register. The job's filled. Besides, don't you need to be in school?" he snapped but still not bothering to look over the rims of his reading glasses. "Go on. Get out of here before I call the law to you," he said when he realized that she was not moving.

He was rude, and made her feel less than human. She wanted to crawl into the carpet. *Arrogant ape!*

"Sorry I bothered you, *sir*," she said, emphasizing the last word on purpose. She hung her head and turned away. She left the door open and walked out the front door, back up the long hill to her car. There was no sense standing around if there was no job. She wouldn't beg. Not now. She had, but never again. She wiped a tear that made its way down her cheek. The older guy who'd taken her to the office had seen her wipe her eyes and looked away. *Who cared? He worked for that jackass!*

*****

Fred shook his head and grimaced a little as the teenager left his office. No one would hire anyone

14

dressed like that: wrinkled and smelly clothes—and totally inappropriate for work—a scrawny little ol' gal with filthy, stringy hair and an accent so thick you could cut it with a knife. And from the looks of her she was on drugs. Kids her age needed to be getting an education, not out working to buy drugs or booze. She wasn't old enough to buy alcohol, anyway.

When Sol opened the door and called him 'Mr. Garrett' Fred knew something was going on.

*Hell, I don't have time to fool with it.* Today is the mother of bad days. His accountant had called at 7:00 a.m. and told him that someone in their office had made a mistake on the estimated taxes last quarter and it had gone downhill from there. A gas tank had overflowed while a customer had distracted one of the guys. The credit card reader stopped working for almost twenty minutes. A string of curse words from Fred were interrupted by yet another phone call on his private line.

Twenty minutes later, Joy was sitting in her car, tired and worn out from struggling with the battery cables and spark plug wires, wiggling and moving them about. There was something wrong other than the battery she thought, but whatever it was beyond her expertise. She could clean the battery terminals, add oil and water. Not even a click sounded when she'd try the ignition. It did have gas in it, that she knew since she'd put thirty dollar's worth in when she'd left Talladega. *It couldn't be out already, could it?* The fuel gauge usually worked. It showed a quarter of a tank.

She'd left the marina mad, and hurt, tears slipping from her eyes before she could get out of the place. She wiped them away as she passed folks headed inside. Maybe no one had noticed. Her face flamed with shame, as she thought of the man's cruel words.

As she worked on the car again the tears ended.

No one had stopped to offer help. This was the South and southern folks were nice and helpful, weren't they? No one had even slowed down to see if there was a person in need, although there had not been many to come by. A lot of the business came from the water obviously. What was wrong with these people? *Had the heat robbed them of their humanity?*

Joy kept moving around in the car, seeking the shade offered by the car roof. She supposed she could walk on into town, but, she hated to leave what few belongings she had. *Get real, Joy.* She realized with a sickening turn of her stomach that no one would steal any of this junk. She had nothing of value. Nothing.

Joy's stomach growled and gnawed. She had the headache from hell on top of everything else.

What a predicament she found herself in—broke, hot, and dizzy from lack of food. She'd endured many things in her life, but this was a new low. Sitting and waiting just wasn't going to work. She didn't feel well. Her tongue and lips felt numb, her legs trembled with the least effort. Maybe moving around could remove the fog that was creeping into her brain.

The air was so hot and stifling that Joy was forced to leave the confines of the car, or pass out. She was having trouble breathing. Taking her purse and a gym bag filled with a few clothes she set out back to the main road, U.S. 431, a major highway that ran through the heart of downtown Eufaula. Maybe she could hitch a ride with a trucker to a restaurant that needed a dishwasher or a waitress. Joy crossed the north lane and walked south on the south-bound lane. She had no idea how far it was into town. It had been years since she visited Eufaula and she'd not been driving so she had not been paying attention to road signs or distances.

Fred Garrett noticed a car left by the side of the road near the marina's entrance. The Chevy was a rust bucket, perhaps twenty years old with primer paint and a dent in the driver's door. He slowed down enough to see that no one was in the car. It probably belonged to that girl who had left his office earlier.

He drove through the intersection, under the stop lights and proceeded into town. He needed to take a deposit to the bank and he was due a haircut as well. He was taking off a little early to do both. He was so ready for this day to end. About a tenth of a mile from the intersection, he saw someone walking by the highway. It was the girl who came to his office earlier. It was hotter than hell today. He didn't know why, but he did it just the same. He pulled over to offer her a ride. Maybe he felt sorry for her. He hit the button that lowered the window on the passenger side.

"Climb in," he yelled, over the sound of traffic

speeding by.

Joy looked up into the fancy pickup truck to see the face of the man who had refused to hire her.

"Uh…no thanks. I'll walk," she said and backed away from the truck.

"I'll give you a ride into town. Get in," he demanded in his booming voice.

"No, sir. I won't ride with you." She lowered her eyes and turned from him. *I'd ride with the devil first! Big-headed jerk!*

She moved further away from the edge of the pavement, her back stiff, her eyes straight ahead. Tears filled her eyes. *What a nasty attitude. Who ate his lunch?* She'd rather starve than work for someone like him. *How did Aunt Mavis work for him all those years? She was always talking about how nice he was. Man, what a lie! Wanting to call the law to me like I was a criminal. What did I do to him? I guess my smell offended him.* Joy had used the last of her deodorant a few days back and deodorant was the last thing she needed to buy as broke as she was. She trudged on, stumbling more than once on low spots. She didn't look back but knew he sat in his truck staring at her walk away.

*Who cares? He probably thinks I'm a hooker or worse anyway.*

She dressed for comfort since her car's air conditioner had never worked. She knew she looked rough to the casual observer, not that she cared at this point.

After waiting for a stream of traffic to get by the man drove away, spinning the truck tires, slinging gravel and dust, gunning the engine as though he was irritated.

Tears seeped from Joy's gritty eyes and she wiped them with her arm. No one slowed to offer a ride. Hitchhikers scared people these days, even female hitchhikers. Joy understood. She wouldn't pick up hitchhikers herself.

Teenage boys in an open convertible slowed and yelled obscenities toward Joy as she walked on. The boys had laughed after calling her names, making vulgar gestures, and speeding away. They were probably on their way to the beach. She remembered Aunt Mavis saying that U.S. 431 was a short-cut to Florida for folks coming from Georgia.

Joy didn't have enough energy to respond to their ugliness. It didn't matter. She'd been called all those names before. Yes, the words hurt but as she'd found out early in life that people were cruel. Maybe one day in the future she'd be a lady of leisure, with money to buy anything she wanted and have a place in the world where others wouldn't look down on her because of how she looked, where she came from, or how she talked. *Someday, someone will love me, bring me flowers, candy, and whisper sweet words... Another pipedream, Joy.*

Each step was torture. Her feet felt like lead and her legs were cramping.

*Put one foot in front of the other. Keep going.*

She didn't remember when she'd had anything to eat. Not today. *Was it yesterday?* It could have been the day before. She'd bought gas, and had paid for a flat being fixed, using the last of her money. Her

19

spare tire was in the trunk, flat as a flounder, too. Just her luck.

*Take another step. Keep going. Keep thinking. Move.*

The man who'd fixed her tire wanted to sell her a new tire but she didn't have money for that. She had just enough to get a pack of crackers and a bottle of water at a discount grocery store. She remembered now. She knew that a grocery store was cheaper than a convenience store.

*Another step, a few more. Keep on, Joy. Don't stop.*

Now, a day later she walked beside this four-lane road. Five minutes had elapsed and she'd not gone over a few hundred feet. The heat from the asphalt and cars passing added to the sun's broiling rays. Heat shimmered on the road and it looked like objects were melting into the black asphalt and she saw mirages—one of a huge white horse—come and go. In a minute, another mirage appeared in the distance. It looked like a castle that then morphed into a white cottage with pink roses on the picket fence.

*Am I going mad? Prince Charming will appear next I guess.*

No. The castle turned out to be an eighteen-wheeler on the other side of the four-lane. And there was no Prince Charming. Not for her.

*I'm hallucinating now. Why can't I think? My mind is...so... weird...slipping...like I'm fading away into a fog. What's wrong with me? Jesus, help me, please.*

The weeds crunched beneath her shoes and she

fought to avoid the fire ant beds that dotted the side of the road. Still ants bit her ankles before she could brush them off, though. She concentrated on the fence to the right, knowing she had to keep moving. She felt queasy, on the verge of throwing up and black spots swam in her vision. Her eyes were dry now, no moisture for tears. Bile rose in her throat. Why was she so sick? She hoped it wasn't some bug going around. The last thing she needed was to be sick.

*****

Fred pulled over again. He stopped on the road right-of-way and put his truck into park. He kept looking into his rearview and side mirrors. He changed the music on his satellite radio. He looked at his nails, checked his email on his phone, and fiddled with his rear view mirror. After watching the girl's agonizing journey he blew out a breath and shook his head in disbelief. This day was going from worse to terrible. Why in hell had he stopped?

"Jesus H. Christ! Damn teenagers!"

Fred had no patience when it came to certain folks.

She was walking, but so slow he was having to sight her by a fence post to see if she was actually moving at all. He'd seen her wipe tears from her eyes. She had been crying and God, he hated a crying female, all needy and whiney. He hoped she wasn't drinking or on drugs of some kind. That was probably why she was so thin: buying drugs instead of food.

When she stumbled, he turned the air inside his

truck blue with a string of virulent curses, put his pickup into reverse, backed up a short distance, stopped and slammed his door as he exited.

In seconds he reached her. Grabbing her gym bag from her slack hand, he hollered at her, "Girl, are you crazy? Don't be stupid! I offered you a ride! It's a hundred-damn-degrees out here! Come on, you can ride as far as downtown."

Joy couldn't answer him. Her mouth was dry and her ears were buzzing. She did not understand a word he was saying. His voice was annoyed, far away and far above her.

*Am I in hell? The devil has come after me for sure!*

She was burning up, exhausted and so thirsty. All she wanted was a gallon of cold water and some place soft to lie down. So she staggered a few feet to his pearl white truck which shimmered, wavering in her vision like that mirage earlier.

Fred threw the gym bag into the truck bed and watched as Joy swayed and struggled to pull herself into the truck, using the hand grip and the chrome-plated running board. He slammed her door as she slumped inside. He had not offered to help her. Truth be known he didn't want to put his hands on her.

"Are you all right?" he asked as he signaled to get back on the highway. He looked into his mirrors and pulled out on the road, not noticing that she didn't respond.

Joy's thoughts were of new leather and cedar as her vision tunneled and shrank. Her eyes rolled back and all went black.

"What are you doing out walking in this heat?

Why aren't you in school? I know school isn't out yet, is it? What are you doing out hitchhiking? Don't you know how dangerous that can be?"

He paid no attention for a while that she never answered.

Fred thought she was asleep, or sulking as teenagers do, until he reached over and shook her and got no response.

# Chapter Two

Two hours and two bags of intravenous fluids later, Joy was awake and feeling somewhat better. Her eyes searched the ER cubicle for her clothes, and she saw a plastic bag on the visitor chair with what looked like her things stuffed inside, along with her shoes. She wanted to get up but had wires, tubing and needles attached to her.

\*\*\*\*\*

"What's she on, Doc?" Fred asked the emergency room doctor, who happened to be one of his golf buddies. They stood a few feet away from the small cubicle where Joy had been placed.

"Nothing. Not a damn thing. Her blood work is clean as a whistle. No signs on her anywhere. There are calluses on her fingers and palms, and she said those were from working. No drugs, no alcohol, no STD's, either. Talked out of her head there for a while. Of course, her blood sugar level was down to 36, so that's expected. She said something about

24

seeing a castle, a white horse, and roses on a picket fence. She asked me if you were Prince Charming, too. She was *really* out of it."

Fred had walked to the lobby for a few minutes and had missed part of the doctor's earlier examination. He'd called Sol to come pick up the deposit and take it the bank for him. The haircut was forgotten.

"What did you tell her?" Fred asked, noticing the doctor's obvious enjoyment with the direction of the conversation.

"I told her your white horse was a Denali, and that you might be the Prince of Darkness, Hoss, but you damn sure ain't Prince Charming!"

"You're just pissed because I beat your ass the other day. Want your money back?" Fred reached for his wallet.

Doc Parker laughed and told him, "Just keep your ill-gained money."

"I told you to quit betting with me. I'll whup ya' every time." Fred played golf as well as he did everything else.

"Yeah, I know. I'm a sucker. What can I say? I like a challenge. Nobody else in this two-horse town to play with. You do know that she has no insurance and I doubt she has any money. I'd let her go home if she had *someplace* to go and *someone* to look after her." The doctor smiled a boyish grin as he looked up at Fred expectantly.

The woman probably hated his guts. After all, he was not that nice to her earlier, but guilt ate at him now that he'd been told how sick she was. He

25

couldn't just walk away, could he? No, his conscious would not let him rest. He reluctantly nodded in acquiescence. Mavis couldn't look after her, he reasoned. Doc Parker would be on his ass about this forever. *Maybe if I let him win a couple of rounds he'll forget about it. Nah...Man, I am such a sucker for strays.*

*****

She had never been so humiliated in her life, except one other time. The ER physician at this small hospital, Medical Center Barbour, had looked under her arms, crook of her elbows, between her toes and fingers, intimate places, looking for needle tracks and asking her about sexually transmitted diseases, her sexual activity, and drugs. He thought she'd overdosed. She didn't take drugs. Never had, never would.

She really needed to get out of this place. She didn't have the money to stay here. Not for a minute. The curtain swished aside at the same time she reached to pull herself up to make her escape. The man from the marina, her rescuer, strode in like he owned the place. His presence was more overwhelming as he stood at the end of the bed. Six-four, six-five, wide shoulders, and handsome with turquoise eyes that almost matched his shirt. There were storms in his eyes, though, and she wondered what, or who, had put them there. Those eyes were

26

piercing and he reminded her of someone.

"They want to keep you overnight, but the doc said you don't have any insurance and that you need someone to stay with you if you went home. I'll take you home with me and see that you get some food in you and some rest. He'll be here in a few minutes to cut you loose."

He left just as quickly as he'd come in.

*Home with him? I'd rather stay here but I can't afford that.* He—that man—was too arrogant and hateful for her to want to stay around for any length of time. She'd escape at the first opportunity if she had the energy.

Dr. Parker and his nurse made their entrance within a couple of minutes and the nurse removed the IV from Joy's thin hand.

"You could stand to gain some weight, Ms. Smith. And stay out of the heat. Fred's taking you home and he'll answer to me if he doesn't take good care of you. Here are some prescriptions. You're anemic and need to rest for several weeks. No work of any kind for at least a month."

"I don't take drugs, Doctor."

"I discovered that, Ms. Smith. You were unconscious for quite a while and unresponsive when Fred bought you in. He didn't know what was wrong with you and you talked nonsense for a while. Drugs are the first thing we look for these days. Fred's a good man—he'll take care of you. Your blood sugar was down to 36, and by the way, you aren't pregnant. We did a pregnancy test to rule that out and no sexually transmitted diseases. You really need to take care of yourself, though. I suggest you see your family doctor for a follow up within the next couple of weeks. Eat better. Regular meals, with proteins. You want more juice? Crackers? Can you dress yourself? Carol can help you, if you need it."

He looked toward Carol. She offered Joy more apple juice and cheese crackers, but Joy shook her head. Joy just wanted to get out this place that reminded her of a bad time that she couldn't think about now.

"I don't...have any money...to pay for this," she stammered, once again ashamed of her circumstances. And she knew she wasn't pregnant, like that would happen. She seldom had a period. That had mostly stopped two years ago.

"Don't worry about that," he said, winked at her and left.

*****

Fred's house, a cabin by his terminology, was not at all what Joy expected to see. Perhaps one of the antebellum homes in the historic district, but not this rustic, yet elegant, structure of cedar, stone, and glass. It had a steep gray metal roof and blended well into the wooded lot.

Joy liked it despite its size. It was too small for more than one or two bedrooms and already her thoughts ran to sleeping arrangements. She could sleep for a week on a soft bed. Joy looked around in awe at the nice home as Fred brought in the grocery bags. There were not many interior doors she noticed.

28

She made the mistake of looking up and the movement of her head and the height of the cathedral ceiling made her sway and grab unto the couch for support. She was still a little woozy, she had to admit.

He was not talkative as they had driven into a secluded area so she didn't know what to expect when she got to his home. His cabin. This was the nicest cabin she'd ever seen. Maybe there was more than one bedroom. *Or I can sleep on the couch.*

As though reading her mind, Fred offered the solution.

"The couch makes out into a bed. You can sleep on that. It's not big enough for me."

He had brought in all the bags after he'd helped her down from the truck. Before she realized it he was preparing their supper in the well-appointed kitchen. After Joy was released from the emergency room, he'd stopped at a grocery store and left the truck running while he shopped. Four plastic bags were full when he came out less than fifteen minutes later. He didn't waste any time, she'd give him that. And he'd never asked her what she wanted to eat.

She knew she was spending the night with Fred. He'd told her so, like a general giving orders to lowly troops. Like he'd demanded that she sit in the truck, not get out or try to walk around. He'd meant escape but that part was left unsaid. She was too weak to walk far anyway, she found that out right off. And he'd left the keys in the ignition if she wanted to leave but she would never steal his truck. No matter how desperate she was, stealing was not in her vocabulary.

"I'll go back later and pick up your prescriptions. I know you don't have the money. I looked in your wallet. All I could find was a nickel and four pennies. Did you know your driver's license is expired?" He'd looked in her purse and hadn't asked her permission.

Joy didn't remember seeing him do that, but then again, there was a period of hours that had disappeared. She didn't remember getting in his truck or how she got into the emergency room. "Yeah, I know...I can't afford to renew them until I start work and get some money." Story of her life. Nine cents. She'd had less.

Grilled rib-eye steaks, baked potatoes piled with butter and sour cream, and a ready-made spinach salad with a bottled dressing were eaten on a table that had seen better days. Joy figured the table was a refugee from a garbage dump. It was scratched and appeared to be homemade. One leg was gimpy and every time she moved, the table rocked a little. It seemed out of place since the large galley-style kitchen was nice with its dark wood cabinets, granite countertops and stainless appliances. The living room had a huge stone fireplace. A western-looking leather sofa and two matching club chairs sat in front of it. She'd seen the style referred to as lodge. Besides, the island had leather and steel stools and could seat six. Why not use that?

"You could fix this table, you know. It would be simple." *Or we could eat at the island.*

"It's fine like it is. Doesn't bother me," he said between huge bites of his food. He was drinking beer while Joy was drinking sweet tea that he'd bought ready-made.

*What a waste of money.* A gallon of tea cost no more than fifty cents to make from scratch. This guy had paid several dollars for something that she could make in five minutes with eight tea bags, a gallon of water, and a cup and a half of sugar. He's never been short of money. *Don't judge, Joy.*

"Can I take a bath? Or a shower?" Suddenly she was feeling bad, achy all over, and knew she needed to take a bath before she passed out...again.

She looked around the open kitchen and living space with its vaulted ceiling covered in tongue and groove planks and exposed beams. There were four interior doors and one of them had to be a bathroom.

"Knock yourself out. There are clean towels and wash cloths in the linen closet. Right inside the door. Holler if you need any help. You done with your supper?"

"I might eat some more in a little while. I'm dirty...and I know I stink..."

"Yeah, I noticed. Leave your clothes in the bathroom and I'll throw them in the washer. I'll wrap your supper for later, too, while I'm at it. I ain't got anything else to do at the moment." He pointed toward a door to the left.


*How charming this man was. Not!* Dear Lord, she hoped they threw away the mold when they crafted this dude. The world doesn't need another one like him. He was not ugly, far from that, but his attitude sucked big time. Maybe he didn't realize how he came across, how rude and condescending he seemed—almost cruel. As though he was looking down on her, like she was something dirty on his shoe.

Joy opened the door to the left and stopped in her tracks. What a luxurious bath! There was a whirlpool tub, a separate shower stall of ceramic tile with a built-in seat, a long vanity of granite with double sinks, and a toilet hidden in a small alcove. It was a girl's dream. Actually it was beautiful with an artful use of earth toned ceramic tile. Joy had seen similar baths in Architectural Digest and Southern Living magazines when she worked with Sarah Wentworth. Mrs. Wentworth's own bathroom was a large and ornate confection of ivory and gold. Joy's thoughts momentarily ran to her former employer. How she missed the grand old lady.

This bath had a huge floor-to-ceiling window over the whirlpool tub overlooked a small garden that was surrounded by a high wall of cedar boards. Interesting rocks, moss, raked sand and pebbles made up a Zen-like space. A pruned Japanese maple in a gigantic blue pot was placed just so. The guy may be a jerk but he had great taste in baths and gardens. The design allowed the bather to look out from either the tub or the shower and enjoy the garden, but no one could see in.

Joy looked into the huge tub, saw that it was dirty and decided to take a shower. She undressed, found towels and a wash cloth. The linen closet was stacked with white towels, wash cloths and bed linens. A dirty clothes hamper at the bottom was running over with tee shirts, underwear and jeans.

Joy turned on the shower, adjusted the stream and turned to see more shower heads, two on adjacent walls, a hand sprayer, and a rainfall shower head hung from the ceiling. It was a good thing she'd turned on the correct one right off. Wow! Did the luxuries not end? The man probably didn't not realize, or care what he had in this house. Or how blessed he was to live in a nice home with a clean shower. The last shower stall she'd used was in a women's mission in north Alabama and it was so rust stained that she'd been scared to touch anything and water bugs had crawled about. This shower was at least five by seven feet and seemed clean. There were no water spots on the two glass walls.

An assortment of high-end shampoos, conditioners and body washes were placed on a niche. Joy selected a body wash, lathered up twice, sat on the shower seat as she shampooed and conditioned her dark hair, and finally wrapped herself in a huge towel. Sitting on the toilet, she toweled her hair until it was no longer dripping.

Her arms trembled from the effort by the time she finished and wrapped herself in a huge towel. She walked into the living area and asked Fred about her gym bag. He told her it was in the bedroom and pointed toward a door next to the bathroom. She went in to dress. All she managed was a well-worn sleep shirt before she fell onto the king-size bed. She was asleep within seconds.

## Chapter Three

*He liked big busted blondes in five-inch heels and short skirts—not someone who looked like they'd escaped from a concentration camp.*
~insight on Fred

Fred wondered what was keeping his wacky guest and knocked on the door before entering. Joy was on his bed dead to the world. Dark circles purpled her eyes, her long black eyelashes brushed her cheek like a child's and her thin arms looked like a child's, too. He'd easily carried her into the emergency room, bypassing the wheelchair offered by the security guard at the door. She probably weighed no more than eighty-five pounds. On a five foot- three frame.

He picked her up and moved her to one side of the bed. The covers were half on the floor where he'd thrown them this morning, so all he had to do was pull the sheet and a light blanket over her. She never moved or acknowledged him. She was out and down for the count. She smelled good, like his shower gel. He picked up the towel she'd used and threw it in the washing machine along with her discarded clothes. He put them in the washing machine, poured in detergent, and for good measure added bleach.

Fred went out on his porch and played one of his guitars until eleven p.m. and pulled out the sofa bed. After tossing and turning, he got up and crawled onto his king-size bed. Joy had not moved from where he had placed her. He noticed her breathing was steady as sleep overtook him.


He woke at his usual time, 6 a.m., showered quickly and made coffee, eggs and toast. As he ate he thought of his houseguest. He'd studied Joy's driver's license. She looked like a teenager, but was in truth thirty-two years old. Less than five years younger than he. He was fast approaching the big four-oh.

Fred left her to sleep, leaving a note that he'd be back after work and would bring food, and her prescriptions.


When he returned the house was silent and Joy was still asleep in his bed. She'd turned and was wrapped around his pillow, hugging it for dear life. He noticed a large bruise had blossomed on her left hand.

She'd told him that had she no money, no bank account, no credit card, never been arrested, that she'd held down a number of jobs including waitressing, working in a laundry, a motel, short order cook, maid, and a house cleaner until a while back. Joy had moved around the state, changing jobs erratically. She'd been married at one time, divorced for six years, no children. The clunker car belonged to her, free and clear, she'd said and she'd told him of having the tire fixed and the spare being flat, too. She'd talked like a wind-up toy on the way to his house. Fred knew she was nervous and talked too much because of it.

He knew a lot about her, yet knew nothing. Everything she told him sounded plausible. *How could she endure so much and still keep going, working? Why wasn't she on welfare? Or food stamps? Why was she so thin?* Did she have something really bad wrong with her that Tom Parker's ER exam didn't show?

His mind went back to the emergency room events. He'd looked his fill as the ER team had worked with her, bringing her from unconsciousness. They had asked him questions about her but he'd had no answers. She was so thin, almost skin and bones. Like she'd been on a starvation diet or was a druggie. He was afraid that's what was wrong with her when she passed out in his truck. And he was relieved when Doc Parker told him he could find no evidence of drugs, and her blood work came out clean except for the low blood sugar, anemia, and assorted vitamins that she was deficient. And she wasn't pregnant. Joy was not a fashion plate and a more than little rough around the edges. Even in her license photo her hair needed styling, her face had not seen makeup or lotion in years, and her skin was pale, sallow-looking, as though she had been sick for a long time. Her fingernails were rough and broken, as were her toenails. She'd never seen the inside of a beauty parlor nor a nail salon.

She had told him that Mavis Duncan had told her cousin, Nora, about the need for a cashier and general helper at the marina. Joy was kin to Mavis and they'd kept in touch over the years, sending cards and photos. When Joy had been able she called Mavis, she said.

He knew he was wrong for doing so but he searched her purse. Joy didn't have a cell phone that Fred could find. Her purse and wallet were cheap, maybe second-hand, with little in either. There were no cosmetics, no lipstick, no gum, no lip balm or lotion. There were no pictures of kids, or a man, or family, just her expired license, nine cents and an old embroidered handkerchief. A hair brush, two car keys, one for the ignition, another for the trunk or doors, a pencil and a small note pad completed the contents of the denim purse. The note pad had a few phone numbers and Mavis's address in it, the marina's name, but nothing else. There were no email addresses. Nothing personal, none of the feminine products Fred knew women kept in their purses. She was the least vain woman he'd ever encountered. Even Mavis wore that bright red lipstick that bled into her wrinkled skin.

Everything about Joy looked—he searched his mind for the word—cheap. His mother would take one look at her and put Joy in the white trash category. Fred couldn't do that, nor think that. He now knew some of her situation and could understand, for perhaps the first time, how a woman could find herself in this predicament.

Fred was of the opinion that everyone deserved a chance. He'd hired men over the years who were down on their luck, like Solomon 'Sol' Burgess, who had been in prison earlier in his life. Joy was certainly down on her luck. He would do a good deed and help Joy to get on her feet and she'd be on her way in a few days.

He let her sleep and returned to town.


He later went to Hank's Garage where he cleaned out all Joy's belongings and stuffed them into the back seat of his truck. Most were dirty and needed washing. All her clothing would have fit in three Wal-Mart bags. She'd been on the road for a few days from what she'd said, but she was neat, having left no food wrappers or drink bottles in the floorboards as he'd expected.

Her car was twenty-two years old, dented and rusted, but the interior was immaculate, which he found amazing. It smelled okay, the seats weren't torn and the carpet was relatively unstained.

He'd gotten her key from her purse to get her belongings. He'd opened the trunk, too. Two pillows, an old quilt and a couple of dingy sheets were in it, and the spare tire which, as she said, was flat. He found a small assortment of used books in a plastic crate, mostly romance novels by well-known female authors. There was also a stack of coloring books, each page colored and Fred wondered if a child had colored them. Except that these were meticulously done, expertly shaded. *An adult did them,* Fred finally decided as he stacked them back together.


*****


Joy had slept for fourteen straight hours and was

starving when she got out of bed. After rummaging in the refrigerator she found her supper plate with the food still intact, plastic wrap covering it tightly. Joy removed the salad, and popped the plate into the microwave and was soon smiling at the taste of the delicious food.

She sat at the island and thought about where she was and where she'd been.

She'd not had a steak in a long time until last night. Ramen noodles, cheese crackers, and boxed macaroni and cheese made up her diet. She'd stay in the cheapest places she could, working at whatever job she could find. She knew how to live cheap and eat cheap. Her car was paid for, and she'd slept in it more times than she cared to remember. She'd saved her money for months to buy the thing three years back but it ran well and was fairly dependable. Until now.

Six weeks ago she'd found herself in Talladega, Alabama, not far from where she'd been raised. She'd stayed with a second cousin until Larry had called Nora, wanting to know if Joy was there. Thankfully Nora had thought on her feet and lied to Larry, telling him that she'd not seen nor heard from Joy in years. Joy knew this to be the truth since she'd been standing right by the phone when Nora answered it. That very minute, Joy packed her few things and spent the night at a Christian women's mission in another town.

Joy wouldn't tell Nora where she was going, only that she had to, and immediately. She'd left her last job after her boss had offered his services since she seemed lonely. Of course, the language he'd used indicated to Joy what his real intentions were. She'd heard it before. Divorced did not mean easy, available, whore or prostitute. The man had hired Joy to clean his house, cook light meals, wash clothes for his invalid wife and himself, and do a few other chores. Sweeping the kitchen was not what he had on his mind, when he propositioned her. He'd not paid her for last week so she left, glad to get away from the man.

She'd felt sorry for the lady, who was a prisoner in her own home, with no one to look after her except her husband and a few hourly workers throughout the week. She left without looking back other than being sad about the poor woman left alone with that terrible man.

Nora told Joy about Mavis's stroke and speculated about the possibility of Joy replacing her on the job she'd had for almost twenty years. The job was at a marina down in Eufaula, Alabama, a beautiful old town with historic mansions sitting among dogwood and azaleas. Joy had visited the town with her mother many years before but had not seen Mavis in years. Joy's mother had been dead for years, succumbing to heart problems. Joy had called and written Mavis all along, but long periods would pass between contact.

Mavis had told Joy that she could stay with her but now she was in re-hab and her circumstances were uncertain. Joy was welcome to stay in Mavis's small apartment but it would have to be a temporary arrangement.

Joy cleaned her plate as she reminisced. Tea was

left in the refrigerator and she'd poured two large glasses and enjoyed the view that Fred had from his front porch with a third glass. She was still parched and her skin felt dry.

The cabin had a huge screened porch, almost as large as the whole house, and a multi-level deck out from that with wooden stairs winding down to a large dock and pier on the water. Joy knew that she was looking at Lake Eufaula, formed by the damming of the Chattahoochee River, which ran between the Georgia and Alabama border.

Fred's land sloped from the street level down to the water, but there was no beach, as such, just the dock. The water level looked to be four or five feet below the dock floor. A pontoon boat was tied to the dock. At the cabin level, a garage was built, almost hidden from view. Four bays with doors faced the water side and Joy could see a paved turnaround and parking pad. She'd not noticed much about the place when Fred had driven up and practically hauled her inside, along with the groceries.

A meowing got Joy's attention and she looked toward the side deck to see a large yellow cat coming toward the screened door. The cat sat and stared at her, meowed again loudly, asking to come in, she supposed. She opened the door and 'Big Yeller' as she quickly dubbed him, strolled into the kitchen area and went right to a bowl already filled with dry cat food and water.

Fred had a cat.

*Maybe he wasn't such a bad man after all.* Lots of men hated cats, and dogs, too, for that matter. If a

41

man hated animals, Joy was wary of him.

The kitchen was a mess and Joy began picking up dishes and glasses, filling the dishwasher, as she cleaned up the countertops and the table with the rickety leg. She'd fix that table later, when she felt better.

The living area was as messy as the kitchen, so Joy picked up fishing magazines, beer bottles, pizza boxes, food wrappers, dirty socks, and a pair of huge and heavy cowboy boots. The place smelled like a poker party. She'd cleaned up after a few of those over the years as she worked for various individuals. She had been a nanny and housekeeper for one doctor but that job didn't last long since the doctor's wife was insanely jealous. Not that Joy ever had any romantic inclinations toward the poker-loving ER doctor. She wasn't looking for a man, then or now. Period.

The house had a washer and dryer located in a closet right by the back door Joy discovered and soon she had a washer filled with Fred's laundry. It was the least she could do. He'd rescued her in his own caveman way, so she figured she owed him. This cleaning would be a down payment on what she knew she owed him, just for the ER bill and prescriptions.

There was no carpet in the house since the floor was made of stained and scored concrete. Joy found a broom, mop and pail by the washing machine and soon the whole cabin had been swept and mopped. She'd already found fresh linens for the bed and she washed the sheets she'd removed. No telling when they'd been washed, but they were not dingy.

She found her clothes in the washer where Fred had left them. He'd forgotten to put them in the dryer. They smelled like bleach.

*He thinks I have germs, huh?*

Dust coated every surface in the place. The man obviously never had anyone in to clean. Joy ran her finger over the TV screen. It was gigantic, one of the biggest flat screens she'd ever seen, seventy inches, maybe larger. She turned the TV on and dusted while The Barefoot Contessa cooked chicken cordon bleu. Within a few minutes she'd dusted the living room and bedroom. She rested a while, ate some cheese and crackers before scrubbing the toilet and the huge whirlpool tub. It had been a while since anyone had cleaned it. She hoped no one had actually sat down in that…goop. Joy didn't want to think of whatever germs were growing and what Fred's girlfriends would say if they'd seen that black stuff growing around the drain that matched the black ring around the tub. She left the shower for another time since she was too tired to move any longer. The shower was so large it would take half a day to clean.

The bed was remade, the kitchen spotless, floors gleamed, the cat fed and Lordy, was she exhausted. She should sleep on the sofa but that bed was so comfortable. She went into the bedroom, grabbed the quilt she'd found thrown in the corner and had put on the bench at the foot of the bed. She got in the bed, snuggled into the quilt, turned on her side, and was instantly asleep.

The cat jumped up on the bed with Joy, and found himself a place close to her warm body.

*****

Fred returned home at six, his usual time. He put in long days and was at work more than he was at home. His employees kept things running, gassing boats, keeping the snack bar and bait store operational. Fred did whatever needed doing and he stayed busy doing it. He ran several businesses from the marina office.

He carried a bag of KFC takeout and set the bag down on the counter. He sniffed the air. He realized his house smelled and looked clean. His damned house smelled clean. Like pine cleaner. Somebody had come in and cleaned his house. If Sol had sent someone over he'd fire his ass. Fred didn't like strangers coming into his home. Not even to clean.

Where was his house guest while this was going on?

The bedroom door was slightly ajar and Fred peeked in. Joy and the cat were asleep right in the middle of his freshly-made bed.

Fred poked her shoulder, none too gently, with a large forefinger.

"Who in God's name did you let in to clean my house? I should have known better than to go off to work and leave you sleeping!"

He was hollering. Joy rolled toward him. Sleep mussed her hair and the side of her face was wrinkled. The cat was asleep on top of the quilt and she could barely move.

"What did you say, sir?" she croaked. Her words came out like a creaky door. She rubbed at her shoulder where the crazy giant had poked her.

"I want to know who in the hell you let in this house to clean! I don't like folks coming in my house when I'm not here. Don't ever open the door to anyone if I'm not here!"

He stormed out of the room, back into the kitchen.

Joy managed to get out from under the cat who had gained a hundred pounds after he climbed on the bed with her. She padded barefoot to the kitchen stopping a couple of feet away from Fred. *Why is he so upset with me?*

"Mr. Garrett, I didn't let anyone in. I woke up, ate and cleaned your house. It needed it. And I owe you money so I started cleaning...I wrote down my hours...over there on that notepad..." She pointed to the counter by the refrigerator. "Sir, if you'll please take me to Mavis's house, she told me I could stay there. I won't be bothering you..."

Fred had his back to her, fuming as he stared out the window over the kitchen sink.

"You mean to tell me that you got up—as sick as you are—and cleaned this whole damned house while I was gone? Are you crazy?" he yelled as he turned, his right arm swinging toward her, his finger pointed in her direction. "You are. You're crazy as a damned bedbug!"

His voice had risen to another level and Joy visibly cringed, waiting for the blow that she felt was coming. She backed away from him, her arms

45

automatically raised to cover her face and chest. Her face was white as a sheet and she trembled from head to toe.

Fred stopped his ranting as he saw what was going on. She is a victim of abuse he realized in that instant and he was acting like he was going to hit her. And he had poked her roughly on her shoulder. He'd hurt her. Someone had been beating this woman, or worse. Guilt hit him like a ton of bricks.

Tears trickled down Joy's face and she quietly asked, "Will you please, *sir*...take me to Mavis's house? Mr. Garrett, I can't stay here...I won't have you hitting on me, too...If you won't take me, just tell me how...how to find her apartment. I'll walk there if I have to...I have the address but I don't know how to find it from here. It's been a long time since I came here to see her."

She was afraid he was going to hit her. How could he have been so stupid? Why didn't he see the signs? It made sense now. *She was on the run.* He had hollered and yelled at her. It didn't matter about the cleaning. Not a word could pass the lump in Fred's throat. He'd never thought a woman would ever be afraid of him, but Joy was afraid of him. He cleared his throat before he spoke.

"Look...I'm sorry, okay? I apologize. I don't usually yell or hit folks. And I'm not going to hit you. I've never hit a woman in my life and I'm not going to start. I just didn't think you'd be strong enough to clean the house. Not after being passed out from heat exhaustion and malnourished. Doc said you need lots of rest and good food. I'll take you to Mavis's when

46

you're ready and you're not ready. I don't want you cleaning or cooking or anything, you understand? You're practically dead on your feet. And do not call me sir, or Mr. Garrett. I'm Fred."

"I'm okay now."

"No, hell, you are not," he said louder than he intended pointing with his forefinger toward her, again. She focused at the finger pointed in her direction and he lowered it, realizing that even that posed a threat to her, in her mind. He was chastising her.

"I brought all your belongings in from your car. It's all out in my truck. I'll bring it in...not you, understand? You sit, you rest. And I promise I won't yell again...well, not at you, anyway. And I'm sorry for hurting your shoulder. I don't know why I did that."

Yes, he did know, too. She irritated the tee-mortal hell out of him. His body went into full alert in her presence. No woman had ever affected him so. He certainly didn't understand that since there was nothing attractive about her, all bird- thin and flat-chested. He liked big busted blondes in five-inch heels and short skirts—not someone who looked like a refugee from a concentration camp.

He pointed toward the KFC bag.

"Let's eat and then we'll sort out what we need to do about you."

She stared at him, not believing her ears. He was talking about her like she was a child, not a grown woman. Something raised itself within her—an anger she could no longer contain.

"Sir, do you know how old I am?" she asked, putting plates down on the table. She'd had her fill of this—over-grown turkey— treating her like she was a child. "I am not a child," she said quietly, reining in her emotions, pushing down the anger that made her want to rail at him.

"Yep, I know. You're thirty-two, but you look about fifteen. And your weight on your license is wrong. You don't weigh near that much. You've lost twenty-five or thirty pounds, at least. Mavis said you'd worked your fingers to the bone and she's right. I can see your bones everywhere. You need to fatten up, just a bit. You're a little...um...flat...in front. And your legs look like a bird's."

*How dare this yoyo make fun of my flat chest, or my legs. Count to ten, and keep your cool, Joy.*

"I know I'm flat. That's what happens when you lose weight. When you don't have money, you eat when and if you can. Sometimes I have to buy gas, not food." She stared at him, defying him to come back to that.

"Oh," was all he could manage to say. Her words knocked the wind, and what was left of his anger, out of him.

Fred had never been hungry. Never had been without food, nor money to buy whatever he wanted, whenever he wanted. He had to admit that he'd actually given little thought to those who didn't have money, or food, except when the local charities started hitting him up every year for donations. This woman had not had a decent meal in months. Maybe years. Her clothes were rags. He wouldn't use any of them to wash his truck. Was Joy here to teach him a lesson in humility? If so, she was making her point.

She could see the expression soften on his face. Maybe he wasn't as violent as she'd been imagining. He'd calmed and she thought he was thinking.

"Are you going to give me a job at the marina?" she ventured. If she had a job, she could leave, find someplace to live, be independent.

"We'll see. Doc Parker says you're bad anemic and need iron and supplements and lots of rest, to gain some weight. Your car is a wreck. The damned tires on it are bald. The steel belting is showing on every one of them. It's in the shop and will be for a while, from what Hank says. Mavis's in re-hab and can't look after you so, looks like it's up to Fluffy and me."

His words lightened the moment, and Joy chuckled.

"Fluffy? I was sure he'd have a macho name like Big Yeller or Jake...Fluffy?"

"He was just a tiny bit of yellow fluff, probably weighed just a few ounces when he showed up one day, just like that. Somebody threw him off up at the road and he's been here ever since. I had him fixed, although he didn't like that too much, not that I blame him. Makes me cringe every time I think about it..."

"He came right in the house and loved all over me. Like he knew who I was. I figured your lady friends must be in and out a lot..."

"Nope. No lady friends..."

"I'm sorry, I just... assumed. Men friends, then?"

She knew someone, or several folks, had used that

whirlpool tub many weeks or months ago. There had been a ring around it, along with the black goop.

"No. Hell, no! I ain't gay!" He was yelling again. "Sorry. I have men friends and some gay friends, but, no, I'm not."

"I'm sorry, I didn't know. I figured you either had a lot of girl or boyfriends from the looks of that whirlpool tub. It was really dirty."

"Don't tell me you scrubbed the damned tub, too! What am I going to have to do to get through to you?" His voice was rising again, but he stopped himself in before he got to the yelling stage. *The woman would make a man drink!*

"I need a beer. Want one?" He strode to the French-door stainless steel refrigerator and reached inside for a Corona, his beer of choice.

"No. No thanks, I've never liked it. My ex drank enough for a boatload of folks. He broke me from ever wanting to drink. I've cleaned up enough puke and urine at home, and at my jobs, to fill that lake out there."

"Look, you need to rest, eat better, gain some weight. Stay here for a while and we'll go from there. Your car won't be ready for at least a week or so. You're broke. I saw your wallet. I had to. You were passed out and I had to fill out all that damned paperwork at the hospital. What was I supposed to do? Drop you off and leave you?"

She looked at him and without so much as a blink and said, "It's been done before. You wouldn't have been the first."

She wasn't going to tell him about that. She

couldn't go there herself most of the time. Painful memories.

"I don't suppose you want to talk about it?" he ventured.

"No..."

\*\*\*\*\*

Fred decided to give Mavis a visit and inquire about her kin, Joy Smith. Mavis Duncan had recently retired from the marina for health reasons and was in a local nursing facility for re-hab, having recently suffered a stroke.

"Nora said Joy's been looking for work now for a while. When she worked in Talladega, her boss made a pass at her and she told him where to put it. She can't help it 'cause she's tiny and a divorced woman. No man ought to be hitting on her, just 'cause she's divorced. Besides she was married to one who hit her and threw her around. He's been stalking her again, and that's why she keeps moving around, living in her car a lot of the time. I don't know how many jobs she's had and how many times she's left in the middle of the night. Larry just won't give it up."

The old lady had been a good employee for many years and Fred knew she was telling the truth.

"Joy got nothing out of her paycheck for herself. She could buy his beer and groceries, pay the bills, but if she wanted something for herself, no way! I'll bet she's got the same clothes she did when she married the bum. We all wondered what she saw in him to start with. I guess she wanted to get away from the situation at home, too. Her mama, bless her heart, took the same crap off her old man. He ain't worth the bullet it would take to send him to hell. Treated Rosalie just like Larry treated Joy. Maybe Joy thought all men were the same and one was as good as another."

"Do you think I should hire her? I know you, or somebody, gave her my name. Right now she's anemic and physically exhausted, so it'll be a while before she's back up to snuff. At least that's what Doc Parker told me."

"Y'all still golfing?"

"Yep. I whupped his ass just last Sunday," Fred said, and chuckled.

"How much did you take him for this time?"

"Only a hundred. I told him to quit betting."

"Well, you can bet on Joy. She's been through so much. Losing her baby that way, and then that jackleg getting away with it. She was scared to tell the truth about what really happened."

"She's so small. Why would anyone want to hit her?" Fred asked, curiosity getting the best of him. "Is she crazy? Bipolar? "

"You know how some men are, Fred. They think they can wipe their feet on a woman, beat her up, throw her on the bed and have their way, whether the woman is willing or not..." she trailed off, waiting to see if Fred would ask her the details, but he didn't. It wasn't Mavis's story to tell but she knew Fred deserved to know the details, to hear Joy's side of the story before Larry found her again.

Fred's ears started ringing and his mind went all fuzzy. The rest of Mavis's word never registered with him.

*A man who hits a woman is not a man.* And he didn't like hearing about men treating women like Mavis was saying...*willing or not...*

# Chapter Four

*"You had me at biscuits and gravy."*
~Fred

Joy slept on the sofa bed, Fred in the bedroom. Fluffy slept with Joy, cuddled next to her knees. When she woke the next morning, Fred was gone. It was Sunday and she was hoping he'd stay long enough to take her to see Mavis. He'd left her a note, telling her that he'd return in a few hours and that he had some TV dinners in the freezer and for her to help herself. Even his notes were gruff. He didn't let the niceties, like manners, bother him.

*****

"What happened to your house guest, Hoss?" Sol asked Fred when they had a slow time. Fred didn't always come in on Sunday and his presence had the men wondering.

"She's at the house, resting, I hope. When I got home yesterday she'd cleaned the whole damned place."

"Well, I'll be. You reckon she's settin' you up to steal you blind? You can't tell 'bout folks these days. Even if they are teenagers. You better watch her like

54

a hawk." This was from a man who had been in prison himself. Fred rolled his eyes at the man who was ten years older than himself.

"Oh, she's no teenager. She just looks like one. She's thirty-two. She's kin to Mavis some way. Mavis probably said but I forgot how. She said Joy—that's her name—is a hard worker. She cleaned my place really good. And it needed it, too. That whirlpool tub ain't been used in three years. There was stuff growing in it, I know."

"You could afford to have someone go in and clean once in a while, don't you think?"

Sol talked to Fred like he was his parent, not an employee. Fred sometimes thought that he got no respect. The man was a diligent worker, though, and kept going when Fred was often tired himself. Fred loved Sol, too. Fred had hired him after he had been released from prison and had come back home to Eufaula. No one would hire him, but Fred had and Sol had been a trusted employee for years.

"You might just let her work there, doing your housework and I'll keep doing what I do and Johnny, Nelson and Alec can hold down the fort. We were all doing Mavis's work for her most of the time, anyway. We don't have to have Joy work here at all. Alec's working out good. He knows how to work the cash register. Nelson's got the snack bar, me and Johnny… we've got it handled with the gas and bait. You don't have to work so hard yourself, Hoss. Give it a rest once in a while. How many hours a week you putting in? Sixty, seventy? It ain't worth killing yourself over, you know. It ain't like you need the money."

That much was true. He didn't need the money. Had never needed the money. His daddy was rich, and his before him. Old South rich. His mama was rich when she married Fred's dad—the old money attracts money routine. John Fredrick 'Fred' Garrett, IV, was born with a silver spoon in his mouth. And was an only child. If he had lived someplace else he might have been a playboy. Eufaula, Alabama had little need for playboys and little for playboys to be interested in. There was some industry, but the lake was the main business of the area. Fishing tournaments, the Spring Pilgrimage, and the spring and fall arts and crafts shows were the main attractions for the town. The historic mansions were visited by many tourists during the spring and the fishing tournaments brought in folks from around the world.

Fred enjoyed boating and working at the marina came naturally. There was money in boat storage, too, so Fred had built a huge metal building where boats could be repaired and stored over the winter months, or for those who lived in other areas. He owned properties that were developed on the lake and had interests in area banks, the music industry, a real estate company, and owned several rental buildings in the quaint downtown area. He had investments in stock and made money without even trying. He chose to run his businesses from the marina because he felt at home there although his late wife and his mom frowned on the idea.

Sol might be right. Joy could keep house for him, and she could help Mavis, too. There'd be things that

Mavis would have to have done for her. He'd get Joy's car going and give her a salary. And Joy needed new clothes. He'd seen what she was sleeping in and had given her a pack of gray tee shirts that he'd never opened. They were 2XL and came to her knees but they were not holey, or stained and thread bare. She had accepted the tee shirts with real gratitude even though Fred had done it just to see what she'd say—a test. Lori wouldn't have worn anything like that and would have thrown something so cheap back in his face and told him where he could stuff them. *What made him think of her? Damn it!*

The phone rang and Fred answered it. He knew who it was from the caller ID. He'd forgotten the monthly Saturday night sing down at Hart Wakefield's. Hart was calling to see what was going on. Fred had not missed going in almost a year.

Fred told Hart some of what had transpired, giving Hart the basics only, like Joy's name, but not much else. He'd been busy rescuing her and had forgotten it was time for the sing, as it was called.

Fred knew Joy's full name: Joy Ann Smith. He also knew that it was not her real name, as Mavis, herself had blurted out the truth when he'd visited her.

"She was born Barbie Joyce Burns, but when she was little she called herself 'Joy' or 'Joyce', never Barbie, which she hated. She told her mama that every little girl's doll in America had her name and she wanted a name of her own. After she divorced

Larry, she had her name changed. Said she didn't want anything of his, meaning Larry, attached to her. In fact, she picked Smith for a last name to help keep him from finding her."

*****

A good house guest, Joy had turned into an even better housekeeper. Fred's house was spotless, the cat loved her and she could cook, he was delighted to learn. He kept telling her not to do anything, but she insisted, so they'd settled on her doing what she felt like doing and nothing more.

Fred liked the fact, too, that she found food in the freezer and knew how to fix it and didn't complain about what was in there. She could prepare homemade macaroni and cheese or stuffed pork chops.

Joy had asked him to bring home flour, sugar, vanilla flavoring, spices, cubed steaks, hamburger meat, chicken parts, fresh and frozen vegetables, pasta and tortillas. His refrigerator and pantry were brimming with staples he'd never bought before.

He'd come home to find smother-fried cubed steak and gravy, with mashed potatoes and steamed vegetables. Another night she'd made chicken and dumplings, and the next night fried chicken and home fries. Her chili was outstanding and she had used no beans. She cooked grits, eggs, biscuits and gravy, roast beef, enchiladas. Fred's pantry and freezer were getting a workout. She made tea as good as any restaurant and her housekeeping skills were flawless.

The junker that Joy called her car was repaired with new tires all around and had a full tank of gas. Fred had Hank to deliver the car to his house and had given him an extra bill or two to keep the information to himself. He didn't want anyone knowing that Joy was staying with him. Eufaula was small enough that folks talked. Joy's car did enough talking on its own with its primer paint, dented doors and cracked windshield.

Hank had watched Fred remove Joy's things from the car as well. That alone, in Eufaula, was enough to set tongues wagging. In a few days his mother would probably get wind of it and call him aggravating the hell out of him wanting to know all about it. If she did Fred would just tell her he'd hired a maid, no, make that 'housekeeper'. That sounded more personal. And sure to piss her off. He sometimes enjoyed doing that to his mother. He wasn't sure why but it was fun to rock the Garrett boat.

His mother was so tight-laced that Fred often wondered how he'd been conceived. Of course, his parents never touched each other and that was something he'd noted, and hated, about their relationship. He always wanted more. He enjoyed folks, being around others, whether it was playing golf, fishing, playing music or having friends. He was always bringing home his friends and his folks never approved of any of them. Thankfully Fred's grandmother was a loving person and showed Fred the attention his parents did not.

59

Joy was slowly regaining her energy each day. Fred had taken her to his own doctor's office and Dr. Bob Latimer had given her a quick exam and did lab work. No one was in the office other than the receptionist and a nurse that asked Joy a few questions after weighing her. Fred had stayed in the lobby playing on his phone.

Joy was pleased to know that she had gained four pounds in the three weeks she'd been at Fred's house. Her face was fleshing out, the angles not as pronounced, her bony hips and tiny thighs were taking on shape. She didn't cringe every time she looked in the huge bathroom mirror. Joy knew she still looked rough but she felt better than she had in months. Good food and vitamins were making a difference.

She worked in the house, tidying, dusting and washing Fred's clothes. She'd never seen so many clothes. He was a clothes horse, an expression she'd heard someplace. Everything he put on looked good on him.

He had a huge walk-in closet and it was packed with shorts, jeans, polo shirts, suits, sports jackets, tuxedoes. Obviously Fred went to enough fancy events to own not one, but three, tuxedoes. Most folks rented them she knew. Shoes were lined in neat rows on the shoe racks that Hart Wakefield, the renowned builder from Henry County, had built on-site. This guy, Hart, was Fred's best friend, as well as the builder of Fred's cabin. Fred said that Hart had also built his father's house over on 'the Point'. Fred talked about Hart a lot and they seemed to enjoy a long-standing friendship, and music, he said. Joy had no idea who Hart was, what or where, the Point was, and didn't care to know how much money Fred's folks had. He was nice to her, and she felt safe for the first time in six years. That meant more to her than anything. Security. Safety.

They talked each night when he came home. But, he had not mentioned about the phone call that had come into the marina today—a man asking for 'Joyce Blackstone' and not leaving a name, nor a number. Sol had answered the phone and told Fred about it but had told the man that there was no one there by that name.

They did talk about the news, the weather, TV programs, and the lake. Lake Eufaula (and the city of Eufaula), as Alabamians call it, was named after a Creek Indian tribe, the Eufaula, meaning 'high bluff'. It is beautiful and impressive, from its size, covering almost 46,000 acres, its 85 miles length, and 640 miles of shoreline. He told her that the Georgia folks had named the lake, 'Walter F. George', after a Georgia U.S. Senator and that there was a lock as well as a dam to the south where power was produced and that Georgia claimed the entire river right up to the banks on the Alabama side. And how everything built on the water had to go through the U.S. Army Corps of Engineers and how dry the weather had been and about the water level being low, and how there had been a battle between Alabama and Georgia for the water that flowed between the states. He was well versed on the subject of Lake Eufaula.

The lake is a beautiful body of water and everywhere there are elegant homes as well as small, rustic cabins and house trailers, and those with water frontage had docks or floating piers. Joy loved what she had seen of the area as they had driven to Fred's home.

# Chapter Five

*"Where flowers bloom, so does hope."*
~Lady Bird Johnson

Joy was a decent conversationalist Fred discovered. She was much smarter, too, than he'd first thought. He'd been too quick to judge her on that front. Yes, she spoke soft and slow, with an accent that was as thick as molasses, but her mind was quick. She didn't have to be told twice about anything, and Fred discovered she was fairly well read. She told him that previous employers had books and she'd read many best sellers, as well as classics, and she also mentioned wanting a library card. Joy had always enjoyed reading but had read the few books she owned, several times over. Fred didn't have many books around, although he had a selection of fishing and hunting magazines, but none that appealed to her.

She cleaned his house like it was a motel room, every day which he commented on several times. She said it gave her something to do, that she didn't like just sitting around. She also said that she was used to working and had done so since getting out of high school.

One day when she got somewhere safe, she was going to get a library card and read all the books she wanted. She'd mentioned that to him last night as they ate supper. And she wanted to buy real art supplies, but she'd never mention that.

There was a great view from Fred's porch that Joy

was itching to paint. There were great views all times of the day. The sun coming up over the water woke Joy as it streamed onto the porch, even into the living room for a while each morning. At night, the lights shimmered on the water and the moonlight, oh, so beautiful. And Fred had a few pots of petunias and geraniums sitting on the deck and birdhouses in the yard. All waiting to be captured with her crayons. *If I had any*. She'd lost them along the way when she'd left a job. The crayons were a cheap way for her to express her creativity without spending much money. She could pick up a coloring book in most thrift stores or missions, for a dime or quarter. Lots of times, most of the pages wouldn't be colored, or she'd color over the page some child had started. And they were easily stowed away for those times when she had been forced to leave in a hurry.

Today, a man had brought her car, and through the cabin's back door glass, she saw Fred hand the guy a wad of money. Fred came in and told her that her car was ready to use but then he didn't give her the car keys. She'd watched him put them in his jeans pocket. She would have to ask him for them since he was adamant about her not going out anywhere on her own.

For now she contented herself by observing the woods, the water, and enjoyed the noises of laughter coming from up the way. Fred's house sat on more than one lot as his nearest neighbor was a few hundred feet away in either direction. Joy could see kids jumping off a dock, and occasionally their squeals of delight could be heard. On the opposite side of Fred's lot, another dock was filled with women sunning in the Alabama heat. The house next door was big, two storied and Fred mentioned that Jack Turner's mom lived there. Jack lived near Ozark Fred told her and that Jack's dad had died, and Mrs. Turner had basically moved to the lake, leaving Jack to run the family farm.

Fred told her that many folks from surrounding towns had lake homes and would travel up to the 'back water' as it was called in the past, for the weekend, or even a summer. Older couples retired to the lake and Fred's realty company had sold the last lot in the subdivision just a few months earlier. Someone managed the real estate company for him she knew since he told her he spent most of the day at the marina, working out of his office there. He was open with his business to a point, although he didn't tell her everything, it was enough to inform her of his goings and comings.

Although today there was a light breeze, Joy knew well how too much sun, and the heat, could harm a person. Maybe she'd try getting some sun one day soon when there was time.


Fred was out of groceries and Joy asked about shopping at the local store. She needed some personal items and hated to ask him to buy them. Fred said he just went to Wal-Mart and reluctantly asked her to go with him. He waited until 9 p.m. to leave the house.

Joy assumed Fred was ashamed to be seen with her in the light of day. She didn't say anything but a

65

couple of folks stopped Fred to talk, as he knew everyone in town. She stood away from him, and slightly turned as he talked casually for couple of minutes, never introducing her to anyone they met. Not that she expected him to, but she did feel snubbed. She pretended an interest in a display of pineapples and cantaloupes.

They filled the shopping cart with fresh fruits, vegetables, beer for Fred, and meats. Fred bought packs of meat that Joy would have bypassed in favor of cheaper cuts. She kept her thoughts to herself. He had money to buy whatever he wanted and thought nothing of it. Joy put in boxes of cereal and snack foods she had not had in a while. She loved yogurt and bought a carton of two flavors. Paper towels and toilet tissue joined the full cart.

She slipped away for a few minutes and returned with personal products that she shyly tucked into the brimming cart. Fred could have hit himself.

"Get what you need and don't slip around, okay? I'm sorry, I should have realized you needed women's…uh…things. Would you like to run through the ladies' section to see if there's anything there you'd like? This stuff will hold for a little while if we hurry."

She reluctantly nodded her head in agreement. She could use some new underwear and her face flamed thinking of someone putting her dingy and holey panties and bra into that bag at the hospital. And Fred touching them. Off they went back to the ladies' apparel and underwear.

Joy waited until Fred had turned his head toward a

66

selection of sleepwear and she put a three-pack of white cotton panties into the buggy, along with a cheap bra.

"Don't you need a pair of tennis shoes, too?" Fred asked. He pretended not to notice the cheap underwear she'd hidden on the side of the cart. He'd noticed the shoes she was wearing but he'd chosen not to say anything. Her toes were showing through the ragged ends. And he'd not found another pair of shoes in all of her belongings.

"Well, I guess. These do look awful, don't they?"

Fred steered the cart toward the shoe racks and asked what size she wore. She told him a size five and before she could stop him, he'd tossed in three pair of tennis shoes, in different colors, flip-flops, and some cute sandals that Joy had been eyeing but wouldn't pick up. And when her back was turned, he threw in a pair of red, open-toed heels.

The shopping cart was soon spilling over with groceries, and the clothing that Fred had thrown on top of everything as they made their way back to the check-outs. Joy kept shaking her head as Fred found one excuse and another to add to the stack. After finding out her shoe size, he asked about her size in tops and pants. "Junior one pants, small or medium top," she said, "but, you don't have to keep buying me things. When you pay me I can buy a few new things. I know my clothes look shoddy. I haven't bought any clothes…in a…while…and I can't afford to pay you back right now for all this."

Fred's heart turned over with those words. That same big lump that bothered him earlier came back.

He hated the words coming from her mouth. Had Larry done this much damage to her? She was as beaten down as any dog he'd ever seen. She had no self-esteem.

Fred used his American Express card to pay for the several hundred dollar purchase and suddenly felt guilty for having wealth. Joy had so little. Hell, Lori would only wear Victoria's Secret underwear and got mad when Fred told her to slow down buying once. Like she needed three of every color they had.

As they loaded everything in the truck, Fred asked if there was anything else Joy needed or forgotten.

She had forgotten something, but was hesitant to ask Fred for it.

He noticed her reticence and asked what she needed. When he got no answer, he pulled out his wallet and gave her a handful of twenty dollar bills.

"Will that be enough? You need to hurry. The ice cream will be melted."

She smiled. *He wasn't worried about the ice cream when he was buying those seventeen bags of other things.* She hurried back into the store to the school supply section where she picked up a pack of sixty-four colors before heading to the toy section where she bought three thick coloring books on a clearance shelf. She practically skipped back to the truck with her secret purchases. Fred didn't ask what she'd bought, but she handed him back all the money, except for about six dollars. She'd spent six dollars of the hundred that he'd handed her. She gave him the receipt and he tucked it into the truck's console.

"Thank you for everything, Fred. I'll keep up with

all of it and I'll pay you back as I can. I hope you'll let me work at the marina and I can pay it back faster, and I can clean for you still, too. I can work overtime...I don't mind."

"Let me worry about this, all right? In the scheme of things, it's not that much. You need new things and I'm able to provide them. It's a gift, okay?" He looked at her and didn't move until she nodded in agreement.

No one had been as kind to her as Fred, except maybe Mrs. Wentworth. Fred talked with her like a friend, not an employee and as much as she wanted to think otherwise, she knew that it would end one day and she'd move on. Something would happen and he'd ask her to leave. Or make her want to leave. Joy was not in his social class and would never be. She was an employee; cleaning his house, cooking his food. A live-in housekeeper, nothing more.

She'd long ago accepted the fact that folks were in basically two groups: the haves and the have-nots. She never kidded herself about ever being in that first group. Joy was realistic. Some folks were blessed to be born into money, or have nice parents. Fred was like Mrs. Wentworth. She was classy, though, and never flaunted her wealth although she dripped with expensive jewelry, and wore nice pant suits or dresses every day, even at home.

Joy remembered something her grandmother always said about folks: "Money can't buy class, good taste or brains. Either you have it, or you don't." Joy had often heard her say, "No class, no taste."

She dreamed of Fred that night, and in it, he had rescued her…again.

*She'd been knocked off the end of the pier, not by accident, and found herself drowning in the lake. Fred had somehow found her, pulled her from the water to the wooden pier, and started mouth-to-mouth resuscitation. She'd coughed and he'd smiled at her, a big grin. He'd held on to her and lowered his head and kissed her—a long, slow kiss that had left her needy and left Fred looking at her with heat and longing in his eyes.*

*She thought she'd never see him again and just as she'd given up, he was there. And that kiss was like nothing she'd ever experienced. She'd been swept away, drowning again in the moment, so intense. It was almost as though there was love behind the heat.*

*A speedboat had pulled up then and a group of women on it were talking with Fred. One woman, wearing a yellow string bikini, got out of the boat and put a rope around a post. She approached Fred and pulled him away from Joy. Fred and the woman started talking in hushed tones and soon they left, arms wrapped around each other. Joy sat on the pier while the other women on the boat laughed and sped away. Fred and the woman had entered his house, leaving Joy alone on the pier. Fred had never looked back.*

She woke at her usual time but the dream was still

vivid in her mind. She touched her lips where Fred had kissed her in the depths of that dream state. She still felt a thrill as her body remembered his touch. How long had it been since she'd been kissed? Years, she realized, but knew she'd never been kissed like that, nor had her body ever responded like that. Heat warmed her face as she got up to make up the leather sofa and prepare breakfast. Fred had kissed her in her dreams but that would never be a reality. The dream had made her question herself, her feelings toward Fred, even her sanity. He'd never do that in real life, in the awake world. Joy would always carry those memories with her. Once, though only in her dream, she had known what it was like to be kissed with desire, and by a man whose fists never hit moments later...

She finished making the sofa and straightened the cushions. The bedroom door opened and Fred would soon be leaving for work.

That dream replayed in her mind as Fred ate sausage, grits, eggs and juice. Joy watched him as he slowly chewed. He drank deeply from his coffee, obviously enjoying the rich brew. She fixed it like he liked it, black and strong.

He looked good in his Levis, navy polo shirt with the marina's logo on it, stretched tight across his broad chest and biceps. She knew that he worked out and from the looks of his muscles those hours in the gym were working. He ate like a horse, lots of food and drink. He enjoyed life.

Her thoughts ran to a place they'd not been in a long time. Fred appealed to her on many levels before; from his regal bearing, to the way he'd treated her with many kindnesses, not to mention being a handsome man. Now, that appeal was stronger than ever. Not that Joy would ever act on it. She knew where she stood. And that dream was just a dream. One that she didn't understand and made her think about him more than was necessary. Somehow her feelings had changed toward him. She no longer resented his presence but looked forward to him coming home, their meals, and his actions showed a tenderness she'd never known in another man.

After he left for work Joy looked at all her purchases. She felt like a princess with new jeans, a few pretty tops and all those shoes. Oh my! She was in love with them. She put on a pair of the bright green flip flops and danced a little happy dance. The colors made her feel good and she began her household duties after she had meticulously noted the price of each, and every, purchase on her notebook where she kept her hours jotted down. She noted the amount of the coloring books and crayons. First business was putting her new clothes and shoes away. She'd borrowed about four inches of Fred's closet shelf and folded her new duds to store there. She put her shoes in a neat stack, away from Fred's shoe rack. She'd move them if he said anything.

There weren't that many closets in this small house. What was she supposed to do with her clothes? Certainly not leave them folded in a stack where most of her old clothes were —on a bottom shelf. She wanted her new clothes separate. She'd found a tiny corner of the room-sized closet where she'd re-stacked some of Fred's storage boxes that contained what looked like more clothes. He was not the neatest person so she had slightly rearranged his closet. Fred had not said anything about her using a space for her clothes, but he might not appreciate her putting her old ratty work clothes, or her new clothes, near his collection of polo and tee shirts.

The closet was completely cedar lined and Joy loved the woodsy aroma and breathed it in every time she opened the door. *It smelled like Fred.*

## Chapter Six

*Joy was an artist—with no art supplies.*
~Fred's observation

*She'd bought color crayons and coloring books.*
That explained the stack of coloring books he'd found in her car. Each page had been artfully colored and shaded with such skills that no child could have accomplished. In some she'd not only colored the figures, she'd colored the background, where there was nothing. She had added gardens with trees, flowers and paths. One was different with abstract colors thrown in and Fred thought that it was interesting that she worked with crayons like they were a fine art medium. Joy was an artist—with no art supplies. His heart pinched and tears burned the back of his eyes, for some reason he couldn't fathom.

He pulled the receipt from his truck console and read the four item list: a sixty-four pack of crayons and three clearance-priced coloring books. He wondered what she could do with real paints and canvas. She'd taken her purchase and he had not seen what she'd bought.

Joy was quiet, yet he sensed a depth to her that her demeanor hid. Maybe she was scared of him still and wouldn't speak up. Most women chattered non-stop. Lori was one of those. Always talking about something she'd seen that she wanted or a party she wanted them to attend, and of course, she was all about clothes, shoes, and makeup.

They'd had huge his and her closets in the house on the Point and she'd filled it to the brim and bought new things almost daily. And the Good Lord knew nothing that she bought had ever come from Wal-Mart. She didn't do the grocery shopping nor the cooking. She said she didn't know how to cook. Fred did the shopping and a good part of the cooking. Lori was used to having 'help' and was not happy to learn that Fred had no intention of hiring a cook or housekeeper.

Lori had taken Katie to day care most days, rarely keeping her at home through the week. Lori's mom, and his mom, kept hinting that she needed a maid but Fred never took that bait. Hell yes, he could afford one, but no, he wanted his wife at home looking after their child and doing what stay-at-home moms did, and learning how to cook. But she never did any of that. Keeping Katie interfered with her social schedule, as she frequently reminded him. She'd once told him that she'd 'had the baby but he surely couldn't expect her to look after 'it', too'. Fred resented Lori's treatment of Katie and they had had numerous arguments over it. In fact, they had words about that very thing minutes before Lori had taken Katie and left. She'd never returned and Fred's life had been turned upside down.

He felt shame that he didn't love Lori but had married her .Yes, he'd had sex with her. Once or twice, but Katie was not his baby. No way. The math just didn't work, unless Lori had the world's longest pregnancy It had been almost fifteen months since he'd been with her. Fred knew for a fact that Lori had dated other men since he'd dated her. Jack Turner, Kyle Laney, and Anthony Walden were just three that he had personal knowledge of or had seen them with Lori.

Lori had set her hat for Fred and Fred had obliged, under duress, and had hated it until Katie was born. He loved her even though he knew that she was not his. Fred's mother would not let it rest and Fred, being the dutiful son, and under threat from Lori, had gone along with the marriage. After all, the whole damn town knew he'd dated her.

It had been a huge affair with scores of bridesmaids and groomsmen, although Fred had had little say in any of it. Lori and his mother had cooked it all up and had it planned and over so fast that Fred barely had time to object—within three weeks. Katie had been born a mere five months later and Lori had laughed, telling everyone that Katie was an 'engagement baby'. It was too late to argue so he kept his mouth shut.

He didn't care, not any more. His mother had pushed Lori into his life and he had pushed her right back out after her death.

He'd cried for Katie at the double funeral and folks thought he was crying for Lori, too. He let them think whatever the hell they wanted. It wasn't known but he'd already filed for a divorce and pressing for custody of Katie.

It was already in the works and Lori was finally agreeable to the divorce but wanted a king's ransom in alimony and child support. He understood to a point. After all, he was rich and she wanted her 'fair share', which meant Fred would have had to sell many of his holdings to meet her demands. She would have lived well at his expense until Katie was eighteen years old at least. Lori was a selfish bitch and had made Fred's life a living hell.

If Lori couldn't have Fred, she'd get enough of his money to hurt him forever. Precious Katie was the innocent pawn in Lori's bid to set herself up for life. He'd told her that the settlement wasn't a done deal per his lawyer, who had an ace up his sleeve he'd told Fred. She'd gotten mad and minutes later she'd silently grabbed up Katie and rushed out into the storm.

Once during a particularly bad argument, Lori had screamed at Fred that Katie wasn't his so he had no say-so in her life. Fred only nodded and replied, "No, she's not mine. But at least I love her. That's more than you can say. She's an inconvenience for you."

They had so many fights, arguments, over money, Katie, partying. Some nights Fred could remember every single word that passed between them. Those were the nights he'd drink himself into oblivion. Could he have said something different and Katie might still be alive? Would Lori have left without Katie had Fred known, interfered? So many scenarios came to his mind. The what ifs and the whys. Guilt ate at him even though in his heart he knew he'd tried to do right by the both of them. He wished to God that Katie had been his daughter. She was beautiful and full of life, with black hair and green eyes.

Fred had a large portrait of Katie in his office and he seldom looked at it without feeling guilt for her death. He had unending night mares about Katie's death, scenarios of how he could have perhaps prevented it. Some nights the alcohol numbed that part of his brain that wouldn't shut down, always dredging up flashbacks of her short life, her sweet smile, infectious laugh and adorable dark curls. Could he have stopped Lori? He'd never know, but it all haunted him daily, and every night. Sol had seen Fred wiping tears one afternoon not long after the accident and had suggested, more than once, that perhaps counseling might help Fred.

Of course, Sol would never mention the tears he'd seen in Fred's red-rimmed eyes. Hell, he'd cried a few times, no, make that a lot, in his life, too. Prison and the stabbing had caused Solomon Burgess to cry. He wasn't afraid, nor ashamed, to admit it. Sol could see the shadows under Fred eyes and the haunted looks, the pain within the depths of those blood-shot blue eyes. But Fred chose to suffer alone and had told his trusted friend, best employee, and confidant to mind his own business. Maybe he deserved to suffer and so the painting stayed. Besides he didn't want to bare his soul, his failures, to a stranger who might pat his hand, take his money, and tell him not to blame himself. How would that make it better? Fred knew it would not, at least in his own mindset and chose to continue condemning himself.

\*\*\*\*\*

Today he was finishing the sales taxes that were due on the 20<sup>th</sup> of each month when the phone rang. He ignored it. He had totals to run, a bank deposit to make, and paperwork to drop by his accountant. John Garrett was mayor when Fred went to college and later a representative for Barbour County. A heart attack had prevented him running for governor two years ago. Fred had a good business head, and had majored in business at Auburn University although his father had wanted him to go into politics. Fred had no desire to be in the limelight that would come with being in public office.

Business was good and always had been. He stayed at work most times to keep from going home. Now Joy was there and the thought of going home didn't bother him quite so much. He smiled to himself and had an idea pop into his head.

The phone rang again and he answered it this time. The caller ID indicated the caller was Jack Turner.

Fred finished his conversation with Jack who told him that Julie Adams was back in town and had asked about Fred. She was one of Lori's friends and Fred had no plans to ever date her again, or anything else with her. He'd made promises to himself and he planned to keep them.

Jack enjoyed singing and often went to the monthly sings at the Wakefield's house in Tumbleton. He was always back and forth to the lake looking after his mom and the lake house. His father had died a couple of years back and Jack stayed busy with his farm just out from Ozark. He had chicken houses and a host of girlfriends.

*Poor Jack,* Fred thought. *Jack's mother lived on a lake and swam in a bottle.* The being that sat on Fred's shoulder reminded him that he swam in a bottle as well.

The next morning, Fred left a note for Joy in the usual place, by the kitchen sink.

*"We're going to Hart's tonight, so don't cook anything. Be ready by six. Jeans and a tee shirt will be OK. Wear those red heels. ~Fred"*

What was she going to do? She did not want to go to Hart's house. Fred had told her about Hart and his wife, Ginger, the ex-model, who had moved back to Alabama from New York. Joy didn't want to have her nose rubbed in her lack of social skills and money, and she wouldn't know how to act around rich folks, especially a model. She had worked for rich folks, as a maid. Fred was different. He'd told her that she was paying for her car being fixed by cleaning his house and cooking his supper each night. She was happy for that arrangement and somehow knew that Fred would give her money if she asked. She continued to keep up with her working hours and had special place for her notebook, and had written down every single item that Fred had bought her, including the colors and coloring books, personal products and clothing.

He'd been the soul of discretion since that first night. She'd slept on the sofa bed, Fred in his bedroom, with the door shut. She knew that. She'd

80

actually heard the lock 'click' more than once. Was he keeping her out? Or him inside? Now he wanted her to go somewhere with him?

Joy took a bubble bath in the whirlpool tub after she'd gotten a call from Fred telling her not to chicken out on him. She was going to Hart's. It was their music night and Hart had invited Joy to meet Ginger.

Joy knew that Fred played the guitar. In fact, he had seven. Along the fireplace wall containing the large screen TV, hung more guitars on metal hangers, and others sat on floor stands or in cases. One was special since Joy could read 'Maybelle' on the leather strap. *Did it once belong to a woman named Maybelle or was it named after someone special in Fred's life?* It was the one Fred usually played. Joy took great pains to dust each carefully without moving them around. They were all in great condition and she decided they were very valuable.

In her cleaning today Joy discovered that Fred had left a considerable sum of money by the sink in the bathroom. She cleaned around it, not even picking up the loose change. She had no desire to steal. It was a sin in her book.

The bubble bath was luxurious and the whirlpool tub eased the tension from her shoulders. She shampooed her hair and dried it with Fred's hair dryer, fluffing it and building volume. She'd lost her dryer years back and never bothered to buy another. Air drying was cheaper anyway.

Fred got home early for a change and Joy was already dressed for the visit to Hart and Ginger's. She was full of questions and trepidation and wanted to quiz Fred but knew that he might get mad with her if she pushed and prodded too much. Men were that way, she'd discovered. They didn't like women who talked too much, asked too many questions. Bothered them.

"They live out from Tumbleton," Fred told her as he pulled out of the drive. "He's a great musician and they have this get-together on the first Saturday night of every month. A bunch of us pickers get to jam and Ginger gets to cook to her heart's desire. You ought to taste her chicken and dressing. So damn good it'll make your tongue lick the top of your head. And cakes! Man—her pound cake with strawberries and whipped cream. That'll put some meat on those bones. Put some on mine. I have to diet after every time I go down there."

"Do they live in a real big house?"

She didn't want to ask if they lived in a mansion. She assumed they did but wanted to be prepared for what she would have to endure.

"Nah, it's not all that big. It's an old home place Hart fixed up before he and Ginger got married. She lived next door and they got acquainted in a 'round about way, sort of through her good cooking. By the way, she's got the cutest little ol' dog. His name is Joey, but Ginger dresses him up with damn barrettes in his hair to keep it out of his eyes. Lord, Hart's foolish about that little ol' dog. And Jimmy, too. That's their little boy."

Fred was on a roll. Joy had not heard him so excited, talking about Hart and Ginger. Their dog and little boy. Joy noticed that Fred had mentioned the child later, almost as an afterthought.

*He reminds him of what he's lost,* Joy thought. During supper a few nights back Fred had briefly mentioned losing his wife and child in an accident but didn't give Joy any details. And she didn't pry.

Fred had put his guitar, Maybelle, into the back seat, safe in its case, even buckling the seat belt around it. He was excited about playing with Hart. That's why he was so happy, high with exhilaration, the anticipation of making music. Almost as happy as she always was to color in her coloring books. She loved her box of sixty-four crayons. *So many glorious colors to choose from.* She felt creative, alive, alone in her own little world, coloring flowers in fantasy colors, layering color over color.

She felt so blessed with new underwear, jeans that fit, a turquoise colored tee-shirt, and the cutest pair of red heels. They fit perfectly, too. Fred hadn't said a word about how she looked when he came home, but she could tell in his eyes that he was pleasantly surprised. Her hair was up in a loose knot with tendrils around her face.

*She looked fantastic.* He could not believe how that sick, dirty, and yes, smelly, person that he'd picked up by the roadside had changed. She was not

Eliza Doolittle and he damned sure was not Professor Henry Higgins, but *Pygmalion* came to mind when he saw her standing there in her Wal-Mart 'finery'. She'd cleaned up well. Of course, she was still rather scrawny and Fred reminded himself that he liked busty women with generous curves.

His eyes had lit up and Joy was hoping perhaps he'd say something. Maybe he hadn't wanted to embarrass her, by comparing what she'd had previously to her new clothing. She felt like a princess and wanted to hug Fred for his thoughtfulness. She kept that thought to herself.

Fred looked nice, too, in his denim shirt and jeans, with ranch boots. He was so big he didn't need boots with heels, although he had a few pair. And cowboy hats, and a ton of baseball caps. A brown Stetson with a leather and silver concho headband was in the back seat along with his guitar, strapped in the seat belt. Maybelle. She thought of Fred wearing a hat, on horseback. He was almost as big as Hoss Cartwright from the old TV show, Bonanza.

*No, Fred was way more handsome than Dan Blocker.* Fred was blessed with perfect teeth and he held himself ramrod straight, and had muscles instead of fat.

The rural landscape kept Joy's attention as Fred drove to Hart's home. Fields of corn, peanuts, soybeans, cow pastures with black Angus cows, distant tree lines and rusty silos would make great painting subjects, she decided and was excited just thinking about them.

She kept quiet allowing Fred to make any

conversation. No one knew the desires of her heart and even if they did, what good would come from it? She'd long ago given up having any dreams for herself. Her spirit was as broken as her body had been in the past. She'd learned not to have any expectations. That way she'd never be disappointed. She was content to feel safe. Being safe was enough.

Fred was an exceptional man Joy thought as she studied him along with the scenery. He was boisterous, even loud at times, thoughtful and courteous at others. He enjoyed his beer and food and always wanted seconds of Joy's cooking. He held doors open for her and had offered her money a number of times. On the occasion that she accepted the cash, she always gave him back the change, along with any receipts. She had told him about the money he'd left by the bathroom sink and he said he would get it. Nothing else.

Metal farm gates and fence lines framed the scenes as they sped along and she saw potential paintings everywhere she looked. She wished for a camera in those moments, but kept silent. How she wanted to save each scene and hold them forever in her memories: the millions of green colors, the grays, browns and tans of tree branches, the deep purple shadows in the gullies and ditches, the red clay soil where farmers had plowed the earth, the old tenant houses with their gray weathered boards and rusty roofs, and the scattering of wild petunias and purple wildflowers by the roadside, 'yard spread', her late grandmother had called it. This section of Alabama was                                    beautiful.

## Chapter Seven

*"Your sleeping-in days are over when a baby comes. Ask Hart."*
~Ginger Wakefield

Joy was in love. Hart Wakefield was the nicest man, and he reminded her of someone famous but she couldn't decide who it was. *Maybe Sam Elliott?* He was not quite as tall as Fred, but he was such a sweet-spirited man. He wasn't good looking in a traditional sense, but was ruggedly handsome, she thought. He held his nine-month old son with a tenderness that Joy found touching. My baby had been a little boy.

Ginger was a surprise. Not only was she the friendliest person Joy had ever met, she was not really beautiful, but rather had an air of glamour around her. She wore her flowing amber top over black leggings and jeweled sandals with wild abandon. Her toenails were painted a sparkly golden tone that Joy loved. And Joy noticed how Hart's eyes followed Ginger's every move. Ginger made the room come alive when she entered it. Joy wanted to be like her—to have a man feel that way about her—and look at her that way. It wasn't going to happen. Joy felt like a brown mouse by comparison. Ginger knew her place in Hart's life and was happily, joyfully, in love with her carpenter husband.

Joy felt so small next to Ginger as Ginger hugged

her, welcoming her. Joy was five-three, Ginger was about five-eleven. She came just past Ginger's shoulder even in heels. Of course, she felt small compared to most folks anyway. Next to Fred, she felt like David to his Goliath.

Fred had introduced Joy as his friend and made no mention of her cleaning his house or cooking his food or washing his underwear. He'd kept his hand at her back, like tonight was a date. Joy knew better, but it was nice to think that, even for a minute. Fred would never think of her as anything other than an employee.

Ginger cornered Fred while Hart had Joy busy, and enchanted, with baby Jimmy.

"Freddie, Joy's a doll. So down to earth and friendly. Um...by the way, Julie Adams is here someplace and I told her you were bringing a date. So don't let her waylay you. Conniving heifer."

"Thanks for the warning, Ginger. Yeah, Julie is conniving for sure. She's not with Jack Turner, is she?"

"No, he came alone this time. I don't think the last girl friend liked the country music too much he told me. He's old enough to have been that one's daddy anyway. I really like Joy, Fred. Seriously, she's a good person. I just feel it in my heart. Don't let her go."

"I don't plan to," Fred replied as he made his way back to Joy's side. Why would he want to mess up a good thing? Joy was a great housekeeper. His house was spotless. His clothes were all washed and ironed. She ironed his shirts. He didn't think that he even had an iron but she'd found one. He normally took his shirts to the cleaners. Joy did it all without complaining and without asking him. And she was a damn fine cook. Maybe she'd make biscuits and sausage gravy for breakfast.

Since Joy cooked for him every day now he looked forward to thinking about the meals she would serve. He'd never done that before, except when he was younger and his Mimi would make chicken and dumplings or banana pudding. Fred's mother couldn't boil water without burning it and always had a 'cook' or 'help' and since they'd moved to the beach his parents ate out almost every meal.


The night was filled with folks, fun, food and music. Joy discovered that Fred was a truly gifted musician, when Hart and the other players began tuning their fiddles, guitars, mandolins and banjos.

Hart Wakefield's monthly Saturday night music fest attracted some of the Wiregrass area's top musicians, amateurs and professional. Night club musicians, college music professors and good ol' country pickers all stood, shoulder by shoulder, tuning their instruments. Not a tuner gadget in sight.

Joy sat with Ginger and Pam, Hart's daughter and her boyfriend du jour (dish of the day), Johnny Robertson. Pam held little Jimmy and played with him like he was hers, despite him being her half-brother. Jimmy was cute as pie, with his reddish hair and coloring like Ginger's. He had Hart's stormy gray eyes, though. He was a happy and adorable baby.

"Ginger said that she wanted Jimmy to take after Dad's coloring, but, bless his little heart, he's as red-headed as she is."

Ginger laughed good-naturedly at that remark and told her that when Pam settled down and had a child, she'd be glad and wouldn't worry too much about what color its hair was—that sleep- deprived mothers didn't have brains enough left to worry about such a trivial thing."Your sleeping-in days are over when a baby comes. Ask Hart."


The pickers were well out-numbered by the audience, the grinners. Fifty or so folk had somehow appeared out here in the middle of nowhere to an open air concert. Many sat at tables on the long screened side porch while others sat on the porch steps, folding chairs, or the tailgate of their nearby trucks, like Jack Turner who kept clear of the crowd. A few had coolers in the bed of their trucks and Joy realized that some had brought their own beer supply but were drinking respectfully from plastic cups.

"Orange Blossom Special"," Mule Skinner Blues", "Faded Love", "Dueling Banjos" and other classic country songs were played and received with enthusiastic applause. A young girl came to the microphone and sang a newer song, one by Carrie Underwood, with Hart and Fred playing along. She wowed the audience with her vocal range. For a twelve-year old, she was good, thought Joy.

Hart played for Jack Turner to sing a George Strait song, then one of the late Merle Haggard's—"Silver

Wings". He had a good voice and the looks to go with it. Most of the singers played an instrument, too, Joy noticed.

Joy admitted to Ginger that she couldn't carry a tune and didn't even sing in the shower. Ginger told her that Hart had asked her not to sing in the shower that it woke the baby. She was loud but could not remember the words to the songs, she admitted. "I'll stick to my cooking. He and Fred can sing. You should hear them harmonize on the old hymns."

Joy wondered how Fred could even fit in with this crowd, but he did. He was in his element, smiling as she'd never seen him smile. He was downright gorgeous when he did. Strong white teeth shone in his tanned face. Fred was one of those lucky blondes who easily tanned. His broad shoulders stretched his denim shirt, and he wore a brown Stetson. He had the looks of a country music star. *And his voice. Oh, dear Lord! It was deep, rich and velvety smooth and so hot it could melt chocolate.* Or a woman's good intentions.

After an hour or so of music and song, it was time for supper. Ginger had put down a spread fit for royalty: roast pork, fried chicken, hot wings, potato salad, green salad, vegetable casseroles, mashed potatoes, rice, and a whole table of desserts: pound cake with toppings of cream and strawberries, banana pudding, peach cobbler and tea cakes. All of it was food that warmed every country boy's heart and stomach.

Joy filled her plate with a bit of each thing, but soon found that she could not eat everything that she'd taken out. Fred made his way to where she was sitting, ate his plate piled with food and bit by bit ate every morsel of what she'd left on her plate.

"You saved me a trip back for seconds, *babe*," he said, with a wink. "You having a good time, *doll*?"

Joy looked around to see who was sitting nearby. "*Who* are you talking to?" she asked, glaring at him.

"*You*. Are you having a good time, *sweetie*?" He pushed for an answer, again emphasizing the endearments.

He was drinking beer and had one with his meal. He didn't bother with the plastic cups most were using.

She'd seen him grab a couple of beers, sipping them between songs. He wouldn't have said that to her otherwise. *Something was up.* He'd never called her anything other than Joy. Until tonight.

"Yes, I am having a good time. You called me 'babe'... 'sweetie' and 'doll'...Are...are you drunk?" she asked, fearing that she'd have to drive back to Eufaula.

"Nah, it takes more than two or three to get me plastered, *honey*. Worried you can't find your way back home, *babe*?" He chuckled and winked boldly at her, with folks watching.

That was exactly what she was thinking. *How did he know? He thought it was funny, the devil! Babe?* Now he was calling her pet names at the end of every sentence.

She hoped he was kidding and shook her head. He knew the answer to that. He'd taken all these back roads and shortcuts to get to this place which was way

91

out in the boonies. This was not a place she was acquainted with, and driving at night, no way. She hoped he was right about his ability to hold his beer, too.

She kept an eye on him and he didn't drink another beer, although she noticed that he sipped on Dr. Pepper the rest of the evening. Somehow she knew that normally he only drank beer at these affairs and that he had driven home drunk many times. Having lived with a man whose life was spent either drinking beer or sleeping off a drunk, Joy knew she'd never want to live through that again and made a vow to make sure it didn't happen. This would be the last time she'd go anywhere social with Fred.


Ginger gave Joy a tour of the restored old home while she took baby Jimmy in to bed. It was way past his bedtime but everyone who came asked about him and wanted to hold him, so Ginger had let him stay up. He'd been so good, being passed around like some toy, grinning at the women and blowing bubbles, displaying little pearl teeth and babbling a few words.

"He's so cute. I know you and Hart are so proud of him," Joy commented as the baby eased right off to sleep. They stood over the crib and watched him breathing for a while and taking in the baby scent. "I was pregnant once, but...but, I lost it...it was a little boy, too. I would love to have kids but it doesn't look like it'll ever happen."

"Oh, you never know. Don't give up. Hart didn't

want a wife, or a baby, and look at him now. He was so lonely and needed a companion. He just didn't want to admit it. I had to do a lot of praying and a ton of good cooking to bring him around," she laughed as she turned out the lamp. The night light gave enough illumination for Joy to take in the old fashioned décor of the nursery, a small bedroom just off the master bedroom at the front of the house.

"Fred might decide he's ready to try the whole wife and baby thing again one day."

"Oh, he's not interested in me. I just clean his house and cook for him. I'm not his girlfriend or anything. I work for him, that's all."

"Really? Well, just so you know, you're the only woman he's ever brought around here since I've been here and Hart said he'd never brought a woman before. Hart thinks the world of Fred. He built Fred's cabin and also his folks' place over on the Point."

"I've heard about the Point. It's like an exclusive area in Eufaula, right?"

"Oh, yeah. Some really nice homes. Fred sold his after Lori and Katie died, according to Hart. Hart said that Fred wanted a cabin just big enough for him and not big enough for a family and that's what he got."

"Yeah, it's not too big but I wouldn't call it a cabin. It's very nice. I sleep on the sofa bed since there's only one bedroom."

"You're *staying* with Fred?"

"Uh…..well…..yes….I…don't have any place to stay right now and I got sick and he took me to his place…and I've…I've been there since."

"Hey, look, it's none of my business. Hart just

didn't say anything about that. Maybe Fred just didn't tell him."

Ginger walked back into the kitchen and changed the subject. "Wow, look at all this food that's left! I hope some of these folks take leftovers home."

"You're a great cook, Ginger. Fred said you'd written a cookbook. That's so neat. You must really be talented to do something like that."

"Thanks. Here, let me give you one. I'll even autograph it for you. Or course, the signature isn't worth a dime, but it'll make it personalized anyway."

Ginger was so sweet, kind and genuine. Joy was impressed with the warmth that flowed from the former model. Ginger signed the cookbook and Joy took it, admiring the cover art, wondering who had painted it. She noticed the name but had never heard of the artist—Helen Taylor Andrews.

"You're so...so beautiful and I love your house, and what you're wearing and that toenail polish. I love that color. Everything looks so...so, 'put together' on you. I can't do that, even if I had the money."

"Sure you can. Just think of colors that you love the best, that look good on you and work with them, like that turquoise top you're wearing. With your dark hair and skin, you can wear all the great jewel tones, even all these browns and coppers that I love to wear. Work with what you have. Lipstick and fingernail polish are pretty cheap. You can buy decent stuff at Wal-Mart. I think this is Maxim's "Golden Passion". It's maybe six bucks or less. And Dollar Tree has polish for a buck. It just takes the effort."

Ginger wiggled her long, elegant toes to make her point. Even her feet were beautiful, Joy thought, ashamed for feeling envious of a woman's toes. Joy had always thought that she'd been standing in the wrong line when God was passing out looks.

Joy stood there taking in all that Ginger was saying. Ginger had no way of knowing that six bucks could feed Joy for three or four days if she planned ahead. Instead of cutting Ginger short, Joy listened as she continued giving beauty tips. Joy would never begrudge anyone for having money. She was a bigger person than that.

"Your hair would look great with a few highlights, maybe layered. And I know this girl in Headland who does a fantastic job with hair. I can give you her name if you want." Ginger clipped on a baby monitor.

"Thanks. I'll keep that in mind. I'll have to save up to have that done one day in the future. I like the idea of highlights. I'm going back out to enjoy the music. Thanks for the tour. You and Hart have a beautiful place. It's not at all what I thought it would be. I asked Fred if y'all lived in a mansion and he said not."

Joy had to get away from the subject of beauty tips and the like. None of it was for her. She'd like to wear pretty things, makeup and such, but that was for later, in her dreams, when she had money. When she got her first paycheck she intended to look for a place to stay or maybe move in with Mavis until she could save enough money for all the deposits and fees that even a cheap apartment would cost. Everything was expensive. So far Fred had not given her a paycheck so she assumed she owed him a whole boatload of money, for the emergency room and for fixing her car, and the tires. She had not been anywhere on the car since the man had worked on it and brought it back, but she had seen the new tires still with the stickers. She owed Fred thousands.

Right before midnight, the music fest broke up and everyone departed. Joy had enjoyed herself having met some really nice people, although some had come in late and she'd not met everyone. She'd listened and watched Fred and Hart perform the last song, the one that they always sang at the closing— 'Amazing Grace'—and wished that the night could have lasted forever.

Just as Fred and Joy got to his truck, a guest, a woman that Joy had seen hanging around in the fringes walked hurriedly forward, stopping just inches from Fred.

"I wanted to see you before you left, darling," the blonde said."I've missed seeing you around. I haven't seen you since our last date. How are your folks? Still loving the beach?"

The woman didn't give Fred a chance to answer before grabbing him, pulling his head down to her level and planting a lip lock on him, right in front of Joy. "Oh, I'm sorry. I didn't see you standing there, "she said, basically dismissing Joy. "Freddie is the best lover ever. I simply cannot resist him. Did you ride down here with him tonight?"

"Yes, she's with *me*, Julie. Do you mind? We need

to get on home. It's past *our* bedtime," Fred said, emphasizing 'our'. He got into the truck. He'd not helped Joy into the truck and he'd intended to do that. Maybe those beers had affected him more than he'd thought.

"Don't be a stranger, darling. We need to get together for drinks, or a little something, something."

Fred slammed the door in her face.

# Chapter Eight

*"What if I have dreams and wishes? No one has ever asked me what I wanted in life."*
~Joy

Fred was silent on the way back to Eufaula. That woman had upset him and he obviously didn't want Joy to know what was going on. *Old girlfriend? New girlfriend?* And Joy was still wondering who Fred's guitar was named after.

Joy attempted conversation after a few miles of stony silence. "Ginger is very nice, Fred. She and Hart make a great couple. That Jimmy is the sweetest thing. I'd give anything to have a child like him. He is so cute."

She tried to be upbeat. After all they were his friends. And that Julie certainly fit in her grandmother's no class, no taste category. What a piece of work.

Fred didn't respond. Not even a nod of acknowledgement to let her know he'd heard her talking.

*So much for that effort*, Joy decided.

She could tell from the tightness of his jaw that he was furious. She'd glanced his way and he never even looked toward her. The dash lights shone a greenish tint on his arrogant profile. He wasn't even blinking. For the first time she felt less than welcome in his

98

presence. It bothered her to no end.

Fluffy had been left in the house and when they got home, he was ready to go outside. Joy stayed up for a while, staring in the darkness out toward the lake. It was so peaceful, the moonlight making little dots of brightness on the water. Lights across the water seemed like tiny fireflies, flickering across the way.

Joy pulled off her new outfit, washed her face and brushed her teeth. She grabbed her sleep shirt, one of Fred's gray tee shirts, and pulled it over her body. The night had been so good up until that Julie person had stepped into Fred's face. *Was she an old girlfriend?* She mentioned their 'last date' and that Fred was a 'great lover'. He had yet to say a word to Joy and, no, it wasn't any of her business. She was nothing to Fred. She knew that. She wasn't in his league, his social class. She knew her place, but being here with him she had to keep reminding herself of that all along. Sometimes this house, Fred's cabin, felt like home.

Fluffy came to the door, scratching and meowing to get in. Joy was the maid so she opened the door. After turning out all the lights, she sat down on the sofa bed. Fluffy drank water and ate a few bites of dry food. She could hear him munching. Soon he came and jumped up to be petted. Joy obliged him, clutching him to her chest. He purred loudly, enjoying the attention. At least the cat liked her. She sat staring out into the darkness.

Fred could not sleep. He owed Joy an apology, explanation—something. He got up from the bed, unlocked the bedroom door to find Joy sitting up on the couch with the cat clutched in her arms. She was upset and he knew it. Tension hung in the air between them.

She saw him standing there but was not going to talk to him. He had exuded anger the entire trip home. Now he was standing at the end of the sofa, like nothing happened. He walked to the French doors and looked outside, ignoring her as though he had not seen her sitting there.

Eventually he spoke. "Look, I owe you an explanation—"

"Don't bother. You don't owe me anything. It's none of my business and I don't care, anyway. You can love whoever you want. Or they can kiss you. It's nothing to me."

"Babe, look." He turned around toward her. He was wearing only white jockey shorts. It was not like him to be almost naked in front of her. Joy averted her eyes to keep from staring. He seemed to fill the room with his presence.

"Don't 'babe' me. If you don't mean the words, please don't say them," she said, her voice stronger, louder than she'd intended it to be. She didn't realize she was so angry with him. *Why?*

She got up from the sofa, and Fluffy jumped off, too, ready to go out. Joy went to open the French door and Fluffy ran outside after Joy opened the screened

100

door.

"I don't—"

"Fred, please, don't start. You've been drinking and I don't want to hear a word you have to say at this minute." She had to be rational. He meant to talk this out, and she didn't want to go there.

"I didn't drink that much. Doll, I—"

She held up her hand but she wasn't sure he saw it since the room was somewhat dark. "You know I don't like drinking, or cursing, or smoking. I'm not a prude but I've been cursed, peed on, and had smoke blown in my face more than enough in my life. If you want to drink, that's your business, but do not ask me to go with you ever again. You can take that Julie person—and quit calling me, doll and babe. Do not say words like that if you don't mean them."

"Your ex peed on you? Why would he—"

"Look, he's a drunk. I've heard it has happened to other women. He's got some mental thing going, and I just don't like—"

He interrupted her this time. "You don't like smoke being blown in your face. It invades your space, right? Like he invaded your space when he hit you. Over the line, like that? You don't think urinating on you was invading your space? That sorry bastard ought to have his teeth knocked down his throat for doing that. If I'd been there, I'd have decked him and asked questions later. Doll, look—"

"Fred?"

"Yes?"

"Are you drunk?" She knew she saw him drink three or four. There could have been more.

101

"I'm not drunk. I told you, it takes more than a few to make me drunk."

"How many?'

"I forgot."

"See, you're no better than Larry. That's what he'd always said. I won't stay around here if you're going to drink like that. I won't stand by and let myself go through that again. I'll leave tomorrow. I'll pack my things tonight. Give me my keys."

She held out her hand for the keys.

"Nope. I'm not going to give them to you. I don't want you to leave. Not now, anyway. I'll let you know."

"So…I can't have my keys? You don't want me to leave? Why? Why didn't you just tell that Julie person that I wasn't anything to you? Why didn't you tell those folks at Wal-Mart who I was? Are you embarrassed for me to be here? I just want to know— I need to know—where I stand in this mess. I'm not your girlfriend. I'm not just a house guest, you know. I clean your house, cook your food. I can find someplace to go, even if I have to live in my car again. I don't have to stay here. You know that. I'll leave so fast it'll make your head swim! Just give me my keys."

"No, doll, you can't leave. You're not well and I need you to work here at the house," he said as he turned toward her. "I can stop drinking and cursing."

"No, Fred, you won't. You won't remember half of what we said tonight—"

"I can hold my beer," he stated with conviction. "I'm not like him. I will remember."

"Fred, I want to believe you. I really do. You've been good to me, but you don't owe me anything. I'll leave in a couple of days and you'll get together with Julie, or whoever, and everything will be hunky-dory. I have no claim on you. I want say-so in my life, for once, Fred. I've never had much of that. I have to do this my way—and move on. I can pay you—"

"Babe, you're under my roof, and I want—"

His words hit her like a dash of cold water. Something deep inside her snapped, roiled up and she lashed out at him. "I don't *care* what you want, Fred. I want my life to be mine. Not one that you choose for me. Maybe I don't want to clean toilets for the rest of my life. What if I have dreams and wishes? Is it okay for me to have dreams like everyone one else? No one has ever asked me what I wanted in life. No one! And quit calling me 'babe'! If you don't mean those words, don't say them! Don't you know how that hurts when you say words like that, and not mean them? It's degrading and I won't take it—any of it— from you. That puts you on the same level as Larry. I'll walk out that door and not look back."

"I'm sorry, Joy. I know you don't believe me, but I am sorry."

"No, Fred, I don't believe you. Why don't you go back to bed and keep that door locked, okay?"

He couldn't argue with her any longer, so he nodded and headed back to his bedroom.

Joy sat back down and was still awake hours later.

*Why did I say all that to Fred? I have never talked back to my employers before—ever. Fred just pushes the wrong buttons with me. I'll have to leave now for sure. He won't allow me to stay after tonight. You blew it, Joy. As usual.*

Something had changed between them and would never be the same. That thought saddened her more.

*****

He felt chastised, ashamed and oddly, needy. Maybe it was the alcohol, but he wanted to take her and call her those names and make her like them. *Nah, she'd never go along with that. Besides she is about as appealing as a doormat.*

He was amazed at her standing up to him, though. In her own way, that had to be a break-through. It had been a revelation for Fred. He was glad.

Her words haunted him for a long time, though, and spoke volumes about her plight in the past.

*"What if I have dreams and wishes? No one has ever asked me what I wanted in life."*

*And I just thought of her as 'appealing as a door mat' when actually she had looked pretty doggone good tonight in those new clothes. And sexy red heels.*

*Sexy? Maybe I have had too much to drink.*

*I need to say something to Mom about telling Julie where I am. Always butting into my life…*

*****

104

Fred was off on Sunday and Johnny was the manager when Sol wasn't there. Johnny called at nine a.m., waking Joy up. *Why didn't Fred pick up the house phone?* How had she overslept? Joy looked everywhere for Fred, even the bathroom. He was up and gone, someplace, but not to work. *He'd been drunk last night. Wasn't he?*

"He's not here. Can I take a message?"

"I guess so. Sol said if a guy named Larry Blackstone called or came by that we were supposed to let Fred know. That guy called, asking for a Joy Smith. Said she was in trouble and he had to contact her. He didn't leave a number and the caller ID said it was a blocked number. Will you give him the message?"

Joy affirmed that she would give Fred the message. She put the phone down. She sat on the bed, shivering, trembling head to toe. Larry knew where she was. Nora had blabbed or else one of her good-for-nothing kids. They were always looking for ways to cause trouble or to make a dollar. Nora's oldest was on drugs and the middle girl was already hooking at some of the truck stops. Nora had laughed and called her own daughter a 'lot lizard'. It sounded awful to Joy's mind that Nora cared no more than that for her own daughter. She could not understand how some folks thought.

As soon as Fred returned, Joy was leaving. She had packed her few belongings and was going to hit the road. South, east, west—any place but here. Larry might already be in town, close by.

Being here, hidden away at Fred's, had been her saving grace, but she wouldn't subject Fred to her suitcase load of trouble. He'd been too good to her to bother him with the mess.

She needed to leave immediately but knew she owed Fred an explanation, and not a note. Surely he'd be home in a little since it was almost lunch. She didn't know what to do, but she wasn't taking time out to cook, that was for sure.

The sound of a truck pulling into the drive made Joy look up from her task as she carried the last of her boxes and bags into the garage. Somehow, someway, she'd pay Fred back for all he'd done for her. She'd find a way to pay him every cent if it took forever. Maybe she could send him money every month. They'd have to talk about that. She needed the keys to leave and he had them.

Fred had left his cell phone in the truck when he'd gone to Wal-Mart earlier this morning. He knew that he'd missed a call from the marina but wasn't worried about it. Johnny and Sol called all the time. It was usually a problem with a credit card not going through or something easily remedied.

He'd been so mad with Julie last night he could have cursed her for those hateful words. God, Joy must have felt awful, being subjected to Julie's actions. He knew he should have said something to her on the way home, but he knew he'd raise his voice and curse—long, loud and ugly. Joy was just beginning to have some light and brightness in her life. Now this. Their talk late last night had been an eye-opener for him. She could stand up for herself. If pushed. Maybe she wasn't the push-over he thought.

Since he was awake at his usual time, he'd quietly slipped out of the house without waking Joy. He'd stopped at a drive-thru and bought a coffee and biscuit and rode around in the early morning quietness of the small town. Not much was going on at 6:30 a.m. He'd relived last night's events in his mind, over and over, until he wanted to just hit something. Or yell.

Julie was not getting into his life and Fred knew he'd never allow himself to date her—ever again. He enjoyed having someone at home, though. Joy was company and he liked her cooking and cleaning, too. She was quiet and didn't get all needy and greedy. *She colored with crayons, for God's sake, and was happy to do so.* So what if she didn't like his drinking and cursing? *Big damn deal. I like to drink. It helps me forget.*

The back seat was filled with painting supplies: brushes, oils, acrylic and watercolor paints, palettes, canvases, watercolor paper and anything he could find in each media that the superstore had in stock. It wasn't what an art store would have but it was more than Joy's sixty-four pack of crayons. He was sure she would learn quickly in each and be making nice paintings right away. He looked forward to seeing what she could do with real art materials.

As he pulled into the garage, he saw her standing by her car, a few boxes and plastic bags lying around her.

"Where do you think you're going?" he asked, eyeing the stack of things around her as he got out of his truck.

"Larry's here. I have to leave. Johnny...from your place...called and said to tell you that Larry Blackstone...was looking for Joy Smith. That's me, you know. And he'll probably kill me if he finds me. I'm leaving right now. I don't want...you in the middle of this...my mess. I need my keys...so I can leave. You locked...my car. He'll find me here...He's crazy—" She was so upset she was stuttering, and he could see her trembling.

"No, wait just a damn minute."

He reached into his truck and retrieved his cell phone. He touched the pad and was soon talking with Johnny Parkman, his manager. He listened for a minute and hung up, thanking Johnny.

He took Joy by her shoulders, holding her gently in place. "First off, you're not going anywhere. If the man shows up, I'll stomp his ass into the ground. I'm big enough to do it, too. You go back into the house and we'll talk about what we're going to do. Help me get all this stuff inside, okay?"

She turned to get her things, but he motioned for her to help get the bags from the back seat of his truck instead.

Fred and Joy pulled bag after bag from the truck before she realized what was in them. She was crying by the time they'd unloaded the truck.

"It's not your birthday yet, but I know it's coming up before long. I woke up this morning, got out early

108

and decided to buy you some art supplies. These are not the best but it's the all we have in Eufaula. I can order you some things online or we can go to one of the places in Dothan if you want better quality."

"I can't...take...all this, Fred," she managed to get out. "It's too much. I can't ...afford to pay you....you...back for all...all...you've done for me...like it is...I can't have this, when I need ...I need to...leave in a hurry." There, she'd said it. "It's the sweetest...thing...anyone has ever done for me...but I can't keep it...I can't."

She was crying in earnest and Fred could not stand to see a woman crying—not her again. It was too much and he gathered her in his arms and held her. Touching his chin to the top of her head, smelling the sweetness of her shampoo, feeling the warmth of her body was an exquisite pain. She felt good in his arms.

"You will take it all and you'll use it and you'll paint lots of beautiful paintings with it. Promise me you'll stay here, with me. Don't leave me. *Please*." His voice cracked on that last word and she cried harder. "I need you here. I need to know you're safe, okay?"

He could not tell her that he liked coming home, knowing she was there. Her cooking and cleaning had been a plus, but just knowing that someone was in his home, a living, breathing human, made going home easier than it had been in years.

"You know about Larry? Aunt Mavis told you, didn't she?" She turned away from his embrace, his shirt was wet from her tears.

"Yeah, she did. Most of it. Want to tell me more?"

"Not right now. I just need to get where he can't find me. He's promised he'll kill me when he finds me and I have no doubt he will. I've got a restraining order against him but it won't keep him away. He can get within five hundred feet of me, legally. What good is that? He could shoot me or run over me walking across the street. It made him mad when I divorced him, cut out his income. He's lazy and is missing his bread-winner, that's all. He's crazy. He wants me to marry him again and I just can't, I won't."

"He wants to re-marry you? Or kill you? I'm confused…"

"Who knows?…Both.. I don't know what he'll do…He's threatened to kill me many times. Among other things. The last I heard from him was that he wanted me to marry him again. Like I would do that…He's crazy. He's just wanting money—that's all he ever wants. He's up to no good. I know that. I can't stay here and put you through his mess, Fred. It's too much. I care for you too much and I owe you too much to allow that. I can't." She looked at him with such sincerity that Fred wanted to take her in his arms again but didn't.

Fred walked to the French doors, his blue eyes glued to the lake, fixed on the Georgia side of the lake. He needed to think. He felt a deep urge to do whatever was necessary to protect Joy.

After a couple of minutes he said, "We'll come up with a plan. I have to make some calls and set things in motion. Meanwhile, why don't we fire up the grill and see what's in the freezer? Then you can look

110

through all your art supplies and tell me what a good job I did."

He was so level-headed. Calm, right now. Just his presence made her feel more secure. He was willing to take a stand with her, for her. That thought brought tears to her eyes and she wished she could quit crying. It made her feel helpless and she didn't like the feeling. She'd always done for herself.

And maybe she needed to leave anyway. Before she fell more in love with this man than she already was. Yes, there it was. She'd said it...put it into words. She liked being in his house, waiting for him to come home, or watching him eat the food she prepared for him and wanting him to compliment her on her cooking, cleaning his house, or washing his clothes. Joy wanted, yearned, for his approval. She loved just being around him. His nearness made her feel safe. He was so protective. She knew she needed to leave, but where in God's name would she go? She'd moved around so many times before. And yes, her car was ready to go, but was she? If she was truthful to herself, the answer was a big no, although she knew she had no future with Fred. There was no question in her mind about that. They weren't compatible and Lord knows she would never be anything to him.

# Chapter Nine

*"You couldn't help it if that woman was crazy as a sprayed roach."*
~Sol Burgess

By Monday morning, Fred had hired a security company to post an armed guard by the road. A fence company was due after lunch to install a tall metal fence with a coded and gated entry, and cameras. From the water side, the security company was installing motion detectors and cameras across the water frontage. He'd called Jack Turner and told him that he was installing security measures and for him to be on the lookout when he was at the lake house. Since Jack lived in Dale County he wasn't at the lake every day but Fred wanted him in the loop. Jack's mom's, next door, stayed drunk more than she didn't, so she would be of no help.

Since Fred already had a security system installed, Fred changed cell phones and house phone numbers, although his number was unlisted. The security company also added additional cameras at the marina. Anyone coming into or out of the store, by road or water, would be filmed.

At a meeting with all the employees, Fred explained the situation in brief, leaving Joy totally out. He'd found a photo of Larry Blackstone, with help from Mavis, and each man was given a copy of the photo. None of the men, except Sol, knew that Joy was staying with Fred. Fred didn't divulge anything about Joy. Her name was never mentioned. No one knew, either, about the motion cameras that Fred himself had set up in various places, not recently, but years earlier. He added one to the pontoon boat that was moored on the water by the pier. The pontoon boat was large and cumbersome to move, so Fred merely left it in place. He rarely used it and found it to be a good thinking spot.

Joy was flabbergasted at the level of protection that Fred had thrown over her within a few hours. He was amazing. He was gruff, tough, and rough as forty miles of gravel road one minute, tender and caring the next. *An enigma, that's what he was—a giant blonde, blue-eyed bear of a man with the heart of a lion and the soul of an avenging angel.*

Feeling some better about her situation, she opened a block of watercolor paper, tubes of paints and started a painting, her first. In school, she'd been a little interested in art, but she knew better than to ask for supplies, content to paint in art class. Her daddy would never have bought her art supplies, or much of anything else. She'd determined to just finish high school. No one else in her family had done that.

Art was something she'd discovered again, after her divorce, while working for a doctor who painted in oils. The paints were so beautiful, colorful, full of promise. Like the pot of gold at the end of a rainbow, it was something Joy wanted to pursue. But, with her limited funds, art supplies were the last things she'd ever buy. Gas, food and basic living essentials were

113

all she could afford. Many times there was no money for even the essentials. She'd gone to sleep many nights in the backseat of her locked car, with a heart as empty as her stomach. Each time Larry managed to catch up with her, she'd escaped with the clothes on her back, more than once. She'd been lucky.

The screened back porch beckoned her and she set up her paints, water container, brushes and watercolor pad on the outdoor sofa and coffee table grouping. Fred sat there to play his guitar and now it was the place for new beginnings for Joy. She had no idea where to start, so she closed her eyes, said a little prayer, swished her brush into water, and wet the 'sky' area of the potential painting. Touching her brush into cerulean blue and then the paper, Joy watched as color exploded through the wet areas. She was as fascinated with the process of painting as she was the first time she'd tried it in high school. Watercolor was not the easiest medium but she loved seeing what would happen as she worked with her own paints for the first time in her life.

Soon she was so engrossed in her work that she had not heard Fred come in. That was a scary thought and she told him so.

"You sneaked up on me! I didn't know you were on the place."

"I'm sorry. Let me see what you're working on. I wondered what you'd paint first."

She held up her first painting—a good rendition of a nearby scraggly tree with Spanish moss, depicted with the lake behind it. She'd hyped up the colors, making for a happy painting which appealed to Fred.

"It's good. No, it's great. I love it! I knew you could do it. I'll take it into town and have it framed. What color frame should I put on it? Will you let me have it? Or I'll buy it." He sounded excited and made Joy feel like a real artist. She was euphoric.

"It will have to have a mat," Joy told him and he nodded. "It's yours." She could have kissed him for his reaction to her painting, but she kept her thoughts to herself.

Fred had bought several paintings over the years from the artists who brought their works to the annual spring and fall art festivals held in the Randolph Historic District in Eufaula. His mother had a collection of art he'd given her. His grandmother collected local art, as well.

With some basic training, Joy would go far.

*****

Fred had a plan. He knew that Joy would not like it. He'd given it a lot of thought himself, even going so far as to call Hart to seek his advice. Fred had told Hart everything he knew about Joy and her situation with her ex-husband. Hart had not laughed in his face, rather, he told him that if it worked, it could be a good thing in his opinion, but Hart asked Fred if he loved Joy and if she was okay with his plan. Fred never answered him. *What did love have to do with anything?* And he could sweet talk her into most anything he had no doubt. Joy hung on his every word. He was well aware of that and could use that to his advantage.

His conversation with Sol had gone differently than he'd expected.

"You gonna what?"

"I'm going to ask Joy to marry me. That way that low-down bastard can't get back in her life."

Fred had confided in Sol and told him almost everything that had happened with Joy, day by day— meals she had prepared, how she'd ironed his shirts, cleaned this, scrubbed that.

"You shore you want to do that, Hoss? She's a scrawny little ol' thang. 'Course I only seen her that one time. She looked like she was 'bout fourteen and jail bait."

"I know. I would have never thought how this would turn out myself. She's turned out to be more than I ever expected. She's a fine cook—great around the house—"

"Prob'ly in bed, too," Sol interjected.

"I don't know about that. She sleeps on the couch and I sleep in the bedroom with the door locked."

"You keeping her out or keepin' yo'self in?" Sol asked, scratching his graying goatee.

"Huh! That's a real good question. I never thought I'd ever look at her…like that. But she cleaned up really good…damn good, Sol. Damn it, there's something about her… I want to protect her."

"Protect her my ass!" Sol said and laughed, shaking his head. "You want her, period. You always talkin' 'bout her. 'Joy done this. Joy said this. Joy cooked this. Joy wore that'. Don't tell me you don't. I know I'm the onliest one you told, but I can see it right now. She's got you hooked. I know for a fact

116

that she's the onliest woman who's ever slept in your house."

"Is that a bad thing, Sol? I like her...hell, I might even really care for her. She stays on my mind a lot..."

Sol knew Fred well. No, he'd never taken a woman to his house, nor allowed anyone to spend the night with him—even in a motel room. Not since Lori.

"Hoss, you ain't tellin' me nothin' I ain't already noticed. I seen you all lost in space there starin' out that window. I know what you got on your mind. Most men would, too. I ain't sayin' that. I know how long it's been. At least she don't seem to be like Lori, from what you told me. You know how I felt about her."

Sol had never liked Lori and Lori treated Sol like hired help. Old South hired help. Demanding this, ordering that. Fred had reprimanded Lori numerous times for making demands on his employees. She was not their boss.

"I know, Sol. Lori was prejudiced. You know that. Everybody knew it. She thought she deserved maids and housekeepers and 'help'. Hell, I wasn't about to hire a maid to do what she could have been doing. She wouldn't lift a damn finger if any work was involved. She just wanted to party...and hell! Why did I start talking about her?"

"So, you gonna marry Joy? What then? You gonna let her come down here and work? She wanted a job, so she knows how to work, I guess, from what you told me."

117

"No, I won't let her work here. I want her at home, painting and raising some kids maybe..." He'd not given that part much thought—until lately and the idea had set seed, taken root in his mind, and wouldn't let go. He didn't intend to say it out loud but he had confided in Sol for years and trusted him. Thinking of having kids—that's what kept him staring out the window. Little blonde kids played through his mind lately—most of the time. Maybe one with dark hair, too, like Katie's, and Joy's. Joy would make a good mother, from what he'd seen. She'd given him no reason to doubt her or not to trust her one hundred percent.

"All she's ever known is hard work, Sol. She deserves a better life— a second chance. We all deserve a second chance, don't we?"

"Hoss, you talkin' 'bout *me* or *you*? You done give me a second chance already, and Nelson. You talkin' 'bout givin' yo'self a second chance, too? If that's the case then, yeah, you deserve one, too. You done what was right by Lori, and Katie. You couldn't help it if that woman was crazy as a sprayed roach."

Fred burst out laughing at Sol's very apt description of Lori. He shouldn't laugh at the dead but he needed a good laugh.

Sol had no problem talking with Fred man to man. Fred was a good man, a great employer, and a true friend. Sol was welcome in Fred's house or vice versa. Race had never been an issue. They played poker every other Friday night together, with their friends, Nate Turner and Artis Brown.

Nate and Art were real characters. Nate drove a

propane gas truck and talked on CB(citizen band) radios. He went by the CB handle, Natural Blue Flame, a reference to his job. When propane burns with the right amount of oxygen, it has a clean blue flame. Nate was an older man, a widower, who lived in a travel trailer out in the middle of nowhere Barbour County.

Art was married to Rosie, with six kids, and worked at the Piggly Wiggly as a butcher, like his father before him. Art had one eye that turned outward and had a bluish-white color. On a huge black man, it looked scary to some, so his job allowed him to stay out of the public eye most of the time, although most folks loved him after being around him more than five minutes. He was the salt of the earth. Art weighed about three-fifty and stood as tall as Fred. He'd played football with Fred in high school and they were the same age. Art had been with Fred the night Fred wrecked his Jeep and ruined his knees, and also his college football career. Beer had been involved as well as an amorous bull that had been standing in the middle of the country road at two o'clock in the morning. Art suffered minor injuries but Fred ended up in the hospital with multiple fractures and a dislocated shoulder.

The foursome had not played poker since Joy had come into Fred's life and they had all made remarks about that. Sol relayed some of the remarks to Fred, laughing as he did.

"The Blue Flame said to tell you to hurry up and git hitched, or kick her out so we can git back to playin' poker agin. Art is 'bout like me. Marry or do whatever it is you need to do—unlock that bedroom door—just quit starin' out that window. L-o-ove is interferin' with our poker games."

"Love? I don't reckon I know what love is, Sol...I don't think I've ever been in love."

"You so in love you can't stand it, Hoss. You might as well do the deed. Ain't none of us gonna have no peace 'till you get yo'self all fixed up."

Sol winked at him.

"I hear ya', Sol."

"Do somethin' 'bout it, Hoss. Don't waste time. Life's too short. Enjoy it while you can. It don't last forever. You know love is just a word until that special person comes along and you'll know it. It'll bring you to your knees. She makes it all worthwhile." He laughed and walked off, mumbling under his breath about 'gettin' lucky'.


Nope, no love involved between Fred and Joy. He knew she liked him and might be just a little in love with him. But not enough to matter. And he knew he might care for her, have feelings for her, but there was no way in hell he was in love with her. But she was the perfect person for his plan. With Joy there were no expectations on her part. She was glad for anything. Anything he gave her was fine.

Sol was wrong. Lori ripped his heart out and practically killed it. There wasn't enough left of it to love anyone. Besides, in his experience, most women were all the same—a bunch of manipulative, conniving bitches, out to get what they could from any available man. His grandmother, Mimi, was an exception, but most times Fred even put his own mother into that same category. He'd watched her conniving ways enough to question his father's willingness to stay with her and go along with her wishes. Fred didn't think his mother had cheated on her husband, but he'd been witness, and victim, to her manipulative ways.

Sol was living with a woman named Rachel, but they had never married and had no kids. He professed to love her, too. Sol loved children but had been stabbed multiple times while in prison and could never be a father. Sol had almost died and his life had turned around since. Fred had offered to help Sol adopt a child but Sol was content to help raise Rachel's sister's four kids. Each one had a different father and Denisha spent more time working at getting up more kids than she did taking care of the ones she had, Sol had told Fred many times.

"I told her, over and over, to keep her knees together and she'd finally figure out where them rug rats come from. 'Course she always finds some new thang to fall in bed with. Ain't none of them got a job, a ride, a house, or want to settle down with that bunch of younguns."

Fred had laughed at Sol's words but knew Sol would have been a good father. *Some men wanted the fun without the responsibility of the consequences. It took a great man with strong moral fiber to help raise kids that belonged to another woman, another man— other men.*

# Chapter Ten

*"Gerard Butler, eh?"*
~Fred

"We're going to get married," he stated. He stood there expectantly, waiting for her meek reply. She always was so respectful and guarded with her words around him. She was a pushover where he was concerned, whatever he wanted. *This is going to be a piece of cake,* he thought.

"We're going to do what?" Joy stared at Fred like he'd sprouted horns. She thought for no more than two seconds before she lit into him. She was baking bread and had flour on her chin and on her shorts. Her homemade bread was Fred's favorite, along with her biscuits and gravy, and seeing the flour there reminded him of that.

*No, "I love you. Will you marry me?"...nothing.*

She went off like a rocket. " You're as crazy as you said I was! Have you lost your mind? I can't believe you said that to me! You don't even like women! I've heard you talk about how conniving and manipulative women are...You don't love me...You don't even like me! And I'm not sure I like you... You're gruff and rude and won't speak half the time. You never even looked up when I went in to ask for that job! And you said some awful things to me that day. How can you say this to me now?" she railed at him with her hair flying all around. Today she was wearing it pulled into a low ponytail. The shine in her almost- black hair and her olive skin gave her an American Indian appearance.

He stood there transfixed by the sudden change in her. He'd sparked her temper and he was liking it. She needed to get mad, stay mad and stay sharp. Larry was a very dangerous man. Mavis had confirmed his suspicions: Joy had been beaten for years, abused, raped by her own husband. He'd later beaten her until she'd lost the baby conceived during the rape. Fred wanted to kill the bastard with his bare hands. Joy was so tiny, so vulnerable. *How could any man, who called himself a man, raise a fist to such a mite of a woman?*

"If you'll marry me, you'll be under my protection. He can't make you marry him if you're already married to me. It's the perfect solution. We can run to the courthouse, get the paperwork done, do the deed. Wham, bam, thank-you-ma'am."

*Whoa, that didn't come out right,* he thought, immediately sorry that he'd said it that way as her expression changed from his last hurtful and insensitive words.

"Look, I'm sorry. I shouldn't have said that. Pay no mind to my tongue, doll. It gets ahead of my brain and this whole deal with Larry makes my blood boil. I can't think straight. I just know I have to do something to make this right and this is the only way I know to fix it, permanently. Look, later on, if things don't work out, we can say 'adios' and split the sheets. And I'm sorry I didn't look up when you walked in. You struck me as being about fifteen and I knew damn well I wasn't going to hire a teenager.

124

Even Sol said you looked like *jail bait*. How was I supposed to know you were thirty-two and been around the block?"

The second his words registered with her, Fred knew he was in for a tongue lashing. Joy's expression changed from hurt to rage.

"Been around the block? You jerk! You cynical...chauvinistic...egotistical man! Ugh! How could I marry you after you stand there and insult me to no end? Like I enjoy hearing myself being talked about like I was the town whore? Yes, I was married, but I've never been with a man since that jerk and from the looks of things, I won't ever! How dare you! I wouldn't marry you for all the cows in Texas! All the fish in that lake out there! I may be just plain white trailer trash from the wrong side of the tracks, but I have my pride. That's all I have left. That's the only thing Larry didn't knock out of me or take from me! I don't need, or want your pity. Anyway, everyone would think I just married you for your money...like that Julie."

Her face was flushed and tears brimmed in her eyes. She was hurt, and so mad. When she got mad, she cried. She felt the need to explode. She had so many words bottled up inside. Years of holding them in. She had to stop him with his wild ideas. Absurd, crazy ideas.

He looked at her like every word she said had wounded him.

"Does this mean we can't go get a license?"

"You have not heard a word I've said! I won't marry you. You'd be miserable and I'd be out on my butt in a couple of weeks when you decide you had made the mother of mistakes. Besides... have you looked in the mirror? Look at me! Look at you!....You're...you're a blonde...Gerard Butler... and I look like a freaky scarecrow. Those boys called me a skank ...and...the four-letter 'c' word. Larry called me... that...while....he was...hurting me...I...hate it."He was silent so she continued. "I've been called it all before. We don't belong in the same social circles, Fred. We have nothing in common...I've lived out of my car, eating cheese crackers for supper because I didn't have money left after buying gas to go to work. You're wealthy. You drive a Denali, a Shelby Mustang and a Harley. I have nine cents to my name. Anything I have now is what you gave me...my clothes, my tires!...I work for you. I scrub your toilet and your underwear. I'm the maid – "

"What if we draw up a pre-nup agreement? We get married, you get my name, and if it doesn't work out, I'll give you a certain sum and you can drive off into the sunset. Gerard Butler, eh?"

"You overbearing...jackass! You think you can buy me, now? Like rent-a-wife? What next? Rent-a-baby?"

He didn't answer but that was exactly what he had in mind. Only he'd never tell her.

"Look, it'll help your situation. I'll have a live-in housekeeper with fringe benefits and Larry can see he's left out of the equation.

"What kind of fringe benefits are you talking about? Bedroom privileges? Forget that, buster! I'd

126

rather sleep with Fluffy! You're—".

She stopped in mid-rant. He was looking at her with those blue laser-like eyes and she forgot what she was going to say next. He was staring at her mouth and she wondered if she had spinach between her teeth.

Once during her ravings she'd crossed her arms under her breasts, pushing them up into a semblance of a bosom, with real cleavage. That held his attention for a while, too. *What was going on?* Maybe she was a witch. She had cast a spell on him surely. Or put something into the tea besides sugar.

He was really into her anger. It did amazing things to her. She was like a tiny warrior, a miniature Valkyrie, with her hair flying about, eyes blazing, shooting green fire directed at him. The anger made her cheeks turn a pretty rose pink. He liked that she was calling him names. That was encouraging and she had an extensive and creative vocabulary and none of them were curse words. She looked him square in the eye when she said each one, too. Didn't cower one bit. That anger turned into passion would be…wanton, and wild…wonderful.

"Fluffy could be part of the fringe—"

"Fred….Fred…look, I like you…sometimes, but I don't know if I could live with you. Not like that…I'm not sure I can…. be… with a man again…you don't know what he did to me. How he hurt me… Anyway, I'm not sure I want to try. Won't that Julie be really upset if you get married?"

"Yeah," he grinned, seeming to like that idea. "That would be really great. She thinks she's got me hog-tied. My mom likes her and is always trying to get us together. Mom would go ballistic if I took you home." His eyes twinkled as he said that.

The rascal was enjoying this.

"Are you out of your ever-loving mind? I know, I already asked that. You're taking this way too far...this marriage thing. You want to marry me to make your parents mad? That makes no sense. Are you sure you thought this up by yourself? Aunt Mavis asked you to do this, didn't she?"

Aunt Mavis was a romantic old soul. Joy knew that for a fact. She wouldn't put it past Aunt Mavis to sic Fred on her. Mavis kept stacks of romance books that she read constantly. The books in Joy's car were for Mavis.

"Lord, no! I did talk with her, though. I asked her about Larry. She gave me an old photo of him to pass around to the guys at work. Don't want him sneaking in on us."

*He seems way too happy with this whole deal. Like he really wants to get married.*

"Fred, I've been married. I don't think I ever want to get married again. It wasn't pretty. It was never what I dreamed marriage would be. When I was growing up I dreamed of romance, the whole package: pink roses on a picket fence, a white cottage, a couple of sweet babies...a shaggy dog...and a loving husband, like Prince Charming, happily ever after—the fairy tale. I wanted the fairy tale...I got a drunk and a no-good excuse for a man who beat me for the hell of it whenever he felt like it, or I made him mad. He's broken my bones, bruised

128

and abused my body, knocked me unconscious and raped me when I wasn't willing to have sex with him...I don't want to go through that pain again, with you, or anyone. Can't you understand?"

He peered at her intently, listening.

She continued, "Look, if I thought this would work, I might consider it, but it won't. It can't. I am the toilet cleaner, and, that wasn't the first time I've been called a skank, just so you know. And I know how rough I look. I'm not like you, all polished and buff. You, you're so...handsome, wealthy and set for life, and could have any woman you want if you snapped your fingers. You don't want me...I appreciate that you want to help me, but it'll never work. I have nothing to offer. I'm not sure I can have kids now after what happened. I've only had four periods in the last two years...and you deserve more than I will ever be, ever have...I can't rub two nickels together. I've watched my life flash before my eyes more times than I care to remember...just to escape him, and what he did to me. I won't go through that with you."

Her words made him change what he'd intended to say. He gently put his finger under her chin, making her look him the eye. "I'm not Prince Charming and I'm pretty sure I won't ever be. I can't promise you anything except that I'll keep you safe. I won't promise you white picket fences or anything else, but I will tell you one thing: I'm not him. I won't ever be him, and I will protect you."

"Look, let me think about this. You'll be changed your mind in a couple of days—"

"No, I won't," he said, interrupting her. "I've thought about it and it's the only way I can truly keep you safe. You'll see. He can't make you do anything, not ever again."

He stood still and stared down at her, dropping his finger from under her chin. "Did you ever stand up to Larry like you did me just now?"

"Many times."

"What happened?"

"He hit me and told me to never raise my voice to him. So I quit...why?"

"For speaking up for yourself?"

"I told you. He fractured my jaw one time, my arm another...what else? Oh, yeah, he beat the hell out of me, many times. So yes, I stood up to him until he beat me so badly I finally gave up..." She dropped her eyes to the floor.

She would not admit to him that Larry had raped her and impregnated her and then later kicked and beaten her so badly the baby had died within her from a crushed skull. She was ashamed to tell him she lived willingly with a man who was capable of such a thing. Fred would think less of her and that thought hurt deeply.

Fred found it odd that through all the verbal arrows, flying hair and blazing eyes, she made him want to take her and kiss her long enough to find the source of that inner fire. In the midst of her rant, a line from Shakespeare's A Midsummer Night's Dream popped into his head. *"Though she be but little, she is fierce."* Yep, she would be a force of nature if pushed. He couldn't understand how a man

130

could hit her when all he wanted to do was find the nearest bed...and that bothered him, too. One day nothing about her appealed to him, now everything she did turned him on. Even her fried-egg bosom. *Maybe Sol was right. Maybe I have been too long without a woman. Yeah, that's it.*

"Look Fred, let's just forget this, okay? I won't mention to anyone that you ever asked me and I know you won't tell anyone. I'll leave and you won't be involved in my mess. I don't want you hurt. And I know what he is capable of doing."

"He won't hurt me, baby doll. Not unless he's got Special Forces training or something. I still go to the gym and work out as you know. And I tote a little pea-shooter myself."

She'd seen his pea-shooter—a .357 Colt Python—with its blue-black finish on his night stand when she dusted. She knew he handled large sums of cash so that was expected. He had no other guns in the house that she had seen—only a collection of guitars. And he was in good shape. She'd never seen him without his shirt in the light of day but she had a vivid imagination and lately it had been working overtime. She'd thought of him many times in his tighty whities.

"So you want him to win? Is that it? Do you want him to keep making you a damn victim? The choice is up to you."

"No! I can't let him win. I won't go back to that. Nor do I want to ever live with anyone like that. I won't. I won't play second fiddle to alcohol—any of that—ever again. When, and if, I ever get married again, I want my husband to respect me. I've never had anyone's respect in my whole life except for Sarah Wentworth's. I won't accept any less from you."

"You don't have to. Let's get married, doll, and you'll have my protection, and my respect, for as long as you want it. How's that?"

"Let me think about this…okay?"

"No thinking. Just doing."

He strode away, out of the house, his end of the conversation over, leaving Joy standing there, with her mind full of things she should have said, needed to say. He just didn't know her situation, not all of it, and she didn't want to go there today.

Joy would never tell anyone but she loved it when Fred called her a pet name—doll, baby doll, babe, and once he'd called her 'sugar babe'. She was sure he didn't mean a word he was saying at the time but those words sounded like words of endearment coming from Fred. There was an inflection that she heard in his magnificent voice. *But surely he didn't mean them. A girl could dream though.* Coming from other men she had been offended. Those words, coming from Fred, were magical and sweet music. It's odd how that happened. She'd blessed him out for doing it once, but he'd continued doing it. Had never stopped, actually. But she loved hearing them…now.

# Chapter Eleven

*"Hoss, if you can't do it with feeling—don't."*
~Patsy Cline (American country music star, 1931-1963)

Less than two days later, they were married in the courthouse, with a passel of county employees craning their necks to see who one of the town's most prominent citizens, and eligible bachelors, was marrying in the middle of the week. Since there were no blood tests, or waiting period, Fred had Joy in and out of the courthouse before she could say a complete sentence.

*Did everyone in this town bow and curtsey to the rich Garrett family?*

The probate judge was a close friend, the witnesses were practically family and the courthouse workers, mostly women, were way more interested than they needed to be.

The pre-nup was never drawn up as his lawyer was conveniently out of town on vacation. Fred said that was all right, though, as he'd trust her to do him right, whatever happened.

The honeymoon night was spent in the cabin, Joy and Fluffy in their usual spot on the sofa bed and Fred in the bedroom.

Nothing had changed except now there was a ring on her finger. She was not into jewelry having had no money for any in her life. Why start now? Maybe it would be valuable enough to pawn later on if she needed money. There was a big sparkly stone in an elaborate setting with many smaller stones circling around it but they were all most likely cubic zirconium. Fred wouldn't spend big money on a ring. In fact, it was so big, it looked fake. Joy thought it was called a dinner ring, but maybe it was an engagement ring. It wasn't a wedding ring. Her idea of a wedding ring was a gold band that meant forever. This thing was as phony as her wedding ceremony had been. Just for show.

She hoped it had not belonged to another of Fred's previous girlfriends. Or his dead wife. That thought had entered her mind and it bothered Joy to no end. It had not been in a box so who knew? Oh, God, please don't let it be Lori's. I don't want it if it belonged to her.

Fred had kissed her right there in front of God and a number of witnesses in the courthouse so everyone would think this whole sham was for real. He'd held on to her and never left her side, so she felt protected but had she gotten herself into more trouble? The idea of marriage to Fred keeping Larry away might work in theory, but at what price?

She'd lied to herself many times in the past days. She liked Fred way more than she'd admit. He appealed to her on many levels. He was kind to her, generous in many ways. And she could get lost in the depths of his blue eyes. *And that kiss. Oh, Lord.*

134

She'd always remember the heat, the toe-curling intensity. She'd held on to him for dear life and somewhere in the background she could hear women sighing. *He'd been in no rush to end it, either.* He was a great actor, too, she'd give him that. That kiss felt like he meant it, but Joy knew better.

She looked at the gorgeous dress Fred had bought her for their simple civil ceremony. It was a champagne-colored two-piece confection of layered sheer fabrics. So feminine, romantic with antique lace, and an uneven hemline. It was the most beautiful thing she had ever worn. He'd not bothered to remove the sale tag on it but that didn't bother her. The dress was just for show, anyway. He'd bought matching heels to wear with it and now they all were in Fred's closet. Like nothing had happened. Fred had worn a navy sports coat, tie and gray pants. He had presented her with a tiny bouquet of pink roses with antique ribbons that matched the dress.

Used for less than thirty minutes the dress was stored in a garment bag and the flowers had started drying. The whole thing seemed so flippant on his part. Like a game or a practical joke. Would she wake up and realize it was all some cruel joke on her?

Joy was a romantic at heart and she'd wondered for years why God brought Larry into her life. How bad he was to her and how she yearned for love! She wanted old-fashioned love: the romantic man who brought flowers and chocolates to his wife and kissed her when he left for work. What she got was a groom who slept in a locked room and went back to work the next morning.

Fred waited for almost a week and called Hart to tell him the news. Hart had sounded pleased and invited the couple down for a meal. Fred accepted on Joy's behalf without consulting her. He could talk her into going. Fred told Hart about Joy's great cooking abilities and Hart told him that if she 'can cook biscuits, she's a keeper', and that Ginger's cooking got him, 'hook, line and sinker and sealed the deal' in their relationship, although Fred knew that Hart loved Ginger before Hart ever admitted it to anyone, including himself. Fred agreed that he loved Joy's biscuits and gravy. Fred knew that home cooking equated to love in Hart's mindset. Symbolically maybe it did.

Then, with more than a little glee, he called his mother. As he anticipated she was not pleased. Elaine Garrett wanted to meet this 'Joy person'.

"Who is her family? Is she from the Smiths up in Mountain Brook?"she asked, her tone less than pleasant.

"Nope. She's related to Mavis Duncan some way. She's been divorced for six years. She's held a lot of different jobs, cleaning motel rooms and such—"

"Fred! Are you crazy? Your father will have a stroke. I hope you signed a pre-nup. Oh, God, she's pregnant! Is she pregnant? Oh, I hope not. You men just can't keep your pants zipped, can you? Fred, you should know better! You need to talk with your father. Wait, let me get him on the phone. Maybe he can talk some sense into you! We'll get this taken

136

care of. We'll get it annulled like it never happened. We can get rid of the baby—"

She went to get John and Fred broke the connection. He hated the words that had come from his mom. *That's what she would do, too, if she had her way— get rid of Joy and a baby if that happened.* The thought sickened Fred. His mother was an awful person. He should have known what to expect from her, but he was hoping she'd mellowed a little. *Oh well, maybe not.*

If Fred had dated any girl more than once his mom had the girl checked out. Was she from the 'right' family? Did she have money? What kind of house did her family have? What sorority was she in? Like Fred had cared what sorority or family a girl was from. When Lori started coming around, his mom pushed her into his life and what a mess that had turned into. Of course, Lori's family was an upper crust family and that's all that mattered to Elaine Garrett. The name. The social status of the family.

The cell phone rang a few minutes later and the caller ID showed that it was Ginger Wakefield. She was all excited over the news of his wedding.

"Freddie, y'all have to come for supper, maybe spend the night. You can stay in my old house if you want to be alone. I want to take Joy over to Headland to have Lynnette do her hair. She'd be a knockout with some highlights, maybe a trim. I'll spring for a facial, manicure and pedicure, too."

"Sounds like a plan. We'll do it. When?"

"Tonight too soon?"

"Nope, just right. We need to get away from here

137

for a while anyway. What time do you want us there?"

"Six work for you?"

That was four hours away. Joy could pack in ten minutes, he had no doubt.

"How many bedrooms are in your old house?"

"One now. There's another but it's full of supplies, no bed. Why?"

"Just wondering. See y'all then."

Fred's phone beeped for an incoming call and he knew it would be his father, and he confirmed that it was. He grinned as he turned off the phone. He'd let his dad stew for a while. This was getting good. His life had been boring and lonely for a long time.

Damn, he wanted to take Joy to his bed and not let her go for long while. She had looked mighty pretty in that little dress he'd bought her. It was on sale, but it looked like it was made for her. It emphasized her tiny waist and the little ruffled flounce made her hips look fuller. The saleslady said it was a peplum style. *Whatever the hell that was, it sure made Joy look good. Maybe clothes did make the person.* That's why he didn't want to stop kissing her. His body still remembered the sizzle that sparked between himself and Joy. It was truly amazing and he wanted to kiss her again and again and see where it took them. He'd not been able to get her off his mind and he'd locked the bedroom door just to remind him of his promise to himself not to let this 'marriage' become more than he planned.

138

Fred was walking around with a Cheshire cat grin, like he'd swallowed a canary. Surely he had made a lot of money at work today or something for him to be in such a good mood Joy decided as she packing for their overnight stay at Hart and Ginger's. Fred's bag was packed already with his usual jeans and denim shirts. Joy had learned how to pack from Mrs. Wentworth who often took cruises and left her to house-sit.

Honestly, she'd been all too happy to get away from this place. These last few days had been so long. Fred had kept his distance and not touched her at all. That worried her, too. He was up to something. He'd just walked in and demanded that she pack clothes for a couple of nights. He told her they were going to Hart and Ginger's for the weekend, and to pack a bag for him, too. He'd walked out leaving her to the task, with lots of questions and no answers. The bossy jackass was at it again. Telling her what to do and just walking out.

Joy knew she shouldn't be calling him names but he made her so furious at times. She wanted to just shake him but as big as he was she knew shaking him wasn't even possible. He'd say things to her and just walk away. Like he was expecting her to meekly obey him. Arrogant rascal.

Fred covered Joy's car with a large blue tarp that he had in the storage room. He locked the barn doors from the inside and exited through the single door and locked that from the outside. He carried the only keys on his key ring.

They set out for Tumbleton, and honestly, Joy was glad to put Eufaula behind her. She secretly wished they could just drive off into the sunset and keep going. Fred had been nice to her and she knew in her heart this was just a temporary marriage, at best. For her protection, he'd said. And she'd almost believed him. It would end, though. No way was he really wanting her for a real wife. He'd made no advances toward her other than the courthouse kiss that he'd done strictly for show.

After a week of not touching her in any way, she knew that she wasn't good enough, pretty enough, whatever enough, for him. He didn't want to be with her. Fred did everything with a passion and she'd felt like a princess in his arms during that wedding kiss, in her pretty dress...just for that moment, but she knew in her heart that it wasn't real. All that passion had been her imagination. Willing it to happen.

Joy held the ring up to the light and squinted at the brilliance. She'd sold her first wedding ring—a diamond chip compared to the rock she was wearing—to pay for gas to leave Larry. She'd held on to it for as long as she could, hoping it was worth more than the thirty-five dollars the pawn shop owner had said. The stone was real but was only a chip, she was told. There was no gold in it. She should have known. The thing kept turning her finger green. This gaudy ring hurt her soul since day by day she was more and more convinced that it was Lori's.

# Chapter Twelve

*"Having a place to go is called home, having someone to love is family. Having both is a blessing."*
~author unknown

Supper at the Wakefields was a splendid affair. Ginger had brought out silver candelabras, good china, linens, silverware, crystal, the works. She'd strayed from her usual country-style cooking and had prepared a gourmet meal of filet mignon steaks with a peppercorn sauce, potatoes gratin, steamed vegetables, homemade yeast rolls and an elegant chocolate and cherry torte. Champagne was brought out to toast the couple.

Hart and Ginger thought that this sham of a marriage was real, Joy realized.

Ginger had taken a good look at Joy's wedding ring and declared it perfect.

"Whoa! Freddie, you did good with that ring! What's that center stone, about three, four carats?" Ginger had quizzed Fred over the meal. "It's a whopper. You dropped some cash on that thing. I love that setting, don't you, Joy?"

Ginger was one of those folks who thought it and said it, pretty much. She was open and sometimes had no filter on her mouth.

Fred just shrugged off the question but Ginger had been close to the mark. The center stone was three carats. The other stones totaled two more.

Joy answered since Fred was silent. "Yes, it's nice.

It's the nicest thing I've ever had. It's too much, though. I told Fred I didn't need one like this. Just a gold band was enough for me."

Hart and Fred later played a few songs, trying out a new piece Hart had composed just the week before. Joy and Ginger played with baby Jimmy and Joy helped put him to bed. She'd held him and given him his bottle.

The evening soon came to an end.

*****

Fred and Joy were given the back door key to the house next door. They brought in their luggage, a duffel bag for each.

Joy explored the house, oohing and aahing over the kitchen and the big old-fashioned bathroom with its claw foot tub and girlie decor.

"This whole place is adorable. I wish I had a house about this size. It's just right. Easy to clean up and I love the old antiques she's left," Joy said as she checked out the small bedroom that was filled with an assortment of old furniture and boxes of cooking supplies.

"Most of those pieces belonged to her great aunt, I think," Fred said from the bedroom door. He'd scoped out the sleeping arrangements. The sofa was a dinky chintz-covered piece that would break under his weight. There was only one bed and it was a standard double. Where would he put his feet?

"I'll sleep on the sofa and you can have the bed," Joy told him, walking back into the kitchen, getting ice and water from one of the refrigerators. She took as much time as she could. Maybe he'd go on to bed and she'd sleep on the loveseat. It was small but she'd slept on worse.

She needed something to drink and time to think about the upcoming night. She didn't think Fred was a mean man but she just couldn't think of doing…that…with him. Maybe he'd change his mind. Maybe she was thinking about something that would never take place. He'd left her alone for days now. Why would he wait? Maybe he had a reason for not wanting to consummate their marriage. Joy knew what she was, who she was, where she came from. Fred knew as well. Besides she wasn't sure if she wanted to do…the deed. She remembered the pain and misery from years back. *Do not think of the past. Do not allow his name in my mind.*


As Joy sipped on her ice water, Fred was doing some thinking of his own.

Joy would not want to share his bed tonight, but he needed her to, wanted her to be there. She appealed to him and he'd never felt such tender feelings toward a woman. She'd looked so pretty in that dress he'd bought her for the wedding. He'd dreamed about her for the last two nights. *Something had to give.*

He cleared his throat a couple of times like he was trying to find words. "Joy, I've done everything backwards with you and you deserve better I know."

143

He sounded so sincere, and looked so handsome in the kitchen light. His blonde hair tended to curl when it was longer and he towered over her like a mighty archangel. Joy's heart wanted to say 'yes', but her mind kept flashing back to the bad times.

"I don't know what I deserve, Fred. I have no expectations. I quit doing that many years ago," she admitted, and put her glass in the sink.

"I may not be the man of your dreams but I want to protect you...take care of you. I promise to be kind... I hope you know that. And you do deserve expectations. You have a right to be happy just as much as anyone. This waiting has been torture to me and if you say 'no', it's all right. I won't force the issue. I won't like it, but I would never hurt you."

Joy wanted to believe him, even though she knew it might lead to more heartbreak, she wanted him, too. Needed him to hold her in his strong arms and whisper sweet words. She had never heard sweet words from a man but she wanted to hear them from Fred. She yearned for the safety of his arms. She knew, somehow, she'd be safe there. She could pretend this was a real marriage, and theirs was a real love, couldn't she? Maybe he'd fall in love with her. *It could happen. Please let him love me, Lord.*

He locked the back door, turned out the kitchen light, and held his hand out to Joy. He kissed her hand, pulled her close, ran his hands through her hair and kissed her gently. He led her to the bedroom.

They discovered that the double bed was plenty

big for the two of them as Fred made sweet love to Joy until almost daylight.

*****

A phone was ringing and neither Fred nor Joy wanted to rouse from their sleep.

Joy opened her eyes and looked at the bedside clock to see the time. 10:30! She'd slept until the middle of the day. She literally jumped up from the bed as Fred told Ginger that Joy would be ready in ten minutes.

On her end of the call Ginger smiled knowingly and told Fred that ten minutes was good and they'd drive over in her car and that the guys could hang out.

Joy ran to the bathroom and started brushing her teeth. She had a beard rash on her chin but didn't have time to worry about it. *Maybe no one would notice it.*

*****

Ginger smiled as Joy got into the car. Joy was sporting a beard rash and she had a look of strange contentment on her face. *Last night must have been a doozy* Ginger thought to herself. Later she'd pull out the cute little dress she'd bought for Joy on sale at Kohl's in Dothan. She had to guess at her size but the bodice was elasticized and she hoped it would fit.

145

Ginger wanted Joy to put it on and wear it back home after their trip to the beauty salon. She wished Joy had put on something besides flip flops but they would do and it was a surprise.

As they passed Ralph Hinson's place, Ginger told Joy how Mr. Ralph had become a match-maker, 'a meddler', as Hart called him, and was more than a little instrumental in Hart's decision to marry her. Ginger went on to tell Joy how Mr. Ralph had married Betty Ruth Johnson a few months earlier and how happy they were.

"Betty Ruth's husband had divorced her years back and left her with a daughter to raise alone. The daughter came back with her kids after a bad divorce and Betty Ruth went to work for Mr. Ralph as his housekeeper. She's a wonderful cook and there's a few years difference in their ages, but he worships the ground she walks on and she dotes on him. He's a sport. They went on a little honeymoon down to my beach house and traveled with a group from their church to the mountains. They are living large and enjoying life. His wife had been dead several years, like Hart's, too. They hold hands like teenagers and she drives everywhere. He bought her a new car. She's happy as a lark, and Mr. Ralph grins from ear to ear every time we see him. She's added years to his life, I told Hart. Of course, he says Mr. Ralph needed Betty Ruth and she needed him."

Joy noted the old unpainted house and saw the new red Toyota sitting in the yard. "It looks like a really old home place."

"It is. We'll have to stop one day and let you meet

them. You'll love both of them. He's given me all kinds of plants from his yard. And Hart got my kitchen sink from him. That was Mr. Ralph's wedding gift to me," she laughed. "Hart installed Mr. Ralph a new one that Betty Ruth says she loves. Hart also added a few cabinets in the kitchen but kept the feel of the place. You'd love the inside. Not a drop of paint—anywhere."

Twenty minutes later Lynnette Palmer was appalled at the woman that Ginger Wakefield brought to her shop. Ginger was all polish and knew volumes about clothing, hair and makeup. This Joy Garrett had never set foot inside a beauty parlor if her hair and nails were any indication. Lynnette and Stacy had their work cut out for them.

Joy was so nervous when she walked inside the nice, but homey beauty shop.

Ginger picked up on Joy's reluctance to talk and continued telling everyone how Mr. Ralph 'meddled' in her and Hart's 'courtship'. Ginger had brought in the dress but no one seemed to notice as she put it across an empty chair.

"Hart was building Mr. Ralph some handrails and a ramp and Mr. Ralph was extolling my virtues to him every time he stopped sawing or nailing. He eventually got aggravated and told Mr. Ralph to give it a rest or the handrails would never get built but the old guy just wouldn't give up," she said, laughing. "Hart said it finally helped him to 'see the light' but when Mr. Ralph married Betty Ruth, Hart had to kid him a little, too. He wrote Mr. Ralph a song about never being too old to fall in love. He sang it at their wedding. It was the sweetest thing. There wasn't a dry eye in that church. Hart was his best man. Mr. Ralph has no family and Betty Ruth is the best thing to happen to him. His health has improved and he's getting around much better. Hart says that Betty Ruth put the 'spry' back in Mr. Ralph," Ginger said.

Joy sat quiet as everyone in the shop laughed at Ginger's story. At least no one was paying attention to her.

Lynnette asked Ginger if she was missing New York and its many shops and restaurants.

"Mostly the Chinese take-out, some of the street vendors and the corner markets. I have to drive all the way to Headland, or Abbeville if I need anything other than what the little store at the intersection keeps in stock. I love being here and having Hart, and Jimmy have made it all worthwhile. I wouldn't go back for any amount of money. I'm so glad I left all that behind."

Ginger called Hart to check on Jimmy and they chatted for a few minutes, their child being the main subject. Hart and Fred were babysitting, enjoying each other's company and 'shooting the bull' Hart told her. Hart and Fred were best friends so there was no telling what Fred would tell Hart by the time Ginger got Joy back home.

## Chapter Thirteen

*"You could stop a clock..."*
~from "Pink Houses" written & sung by John Cougar
Mellencamp

Joy was glad Ginger was talking and dominating the conversation. She'd hoped no one noticed the beard rash, but in the end, it was covered with makeup. Stacy had done a quick facial on Joy as well as the pedicure and manicure. Joy said she felt like royalty from all the pampering, buffing and polishing. Lynette and Stacy wouldn't let her see herself in the mirror until they were done. Ginger's mouth fell open when Stacy turned Joy around to show her the finished look.

"You're beautiful!" Ginger exclaimed, over and over two hours later. She had pulled out the dress very casually and told her that it was part of the 'treat' for Joy and that she'd bought it on sale at Kohl's. Everyone raved over it and Joy felt better after putting it on and finding that, indeed, it was a sale item. Ginger had left the tag on it. Joy put it on and walked out from the restroom.

"Freddie's gonna love it!" Ginger said and hugged Joy, as she pulled the tag from the teal colored dress. It fit her well and everyone agreed that it was a sweet dress and the color suited her.

Ginger had paid for Joy's transformation and she

had tipped both Lynnette and Stacy a very generous amount. They had well earned it. She could not wait for Fred to see the new Mrs. Garrett.

Lynnette had highlighted Joy's dark hair with the faintest tones, waxed her bushy eyebrows (a painful experience Joy vowed would never be repeated without anesthesia) and applied tasteful makeup to cover up the very visible rash on her chin. Joy had picked out a rosy pink polish for her nails. Her fingers and toes looked like they belonged to another person and she kept looking down at them. She'd never had a facial, a manicure or a pedicure. *What a luxury! And to think that some women got to do this every couple of weeks.*

She'd put on flip-flops when she left and even they looked good with her painted toenails. She felt so feminine, lucky and pretty as she ran her hands over the lacey teal fabric.

She had left as a drab brown wren, in Fred's eyes, but now, she stood there in an elegant dress, like a beautiful, royal peacock with shimmering hair and silky, touchable skin. She'd returned as a stunning, desirable woman. He pointed at her not saying a word, and twirled his finger, indicating he wanted her to turn all the way around for him. And she obliged him, her hair swaying and gleaming in the light as she turned.

The look on his face was priceless. It was as

though he was seeing her for the first time.

*"That's her. I chose her for you,"* a quiet still voice said to Fred. Fred looked around for a moment, to see no one close. Ginger and Hart were standing silent a few feet away. And that was not Hart's voice. *Who is talking to me? God, are you telling me something?* He'd heard of folks who said that God talked to them in a quiet voice. Was God directly telling him that Joy was 'for him'? *Why now, God? Why not that day she walked into the marina? Or the day we got married? Why? If I tell anyone they'll think I've lost my mind, or been hitting the booze.*

Fred locked eyes with Joy and he saw the future in her eyes. His future. He shook his head, trying to shake away the warped stretching, expansion of time. It was like being drunk except he was cold, stone sober.

The words to John Cougar Mellencamp's Pink Houses popped into Fred's mind when he saw Joy's Mona Lisa smile—the line about *'you could stop a clock'*. She had stopped his clock— time stood still, again, as he looked at her. She looked amazing. He could imagine her in something that was short, tight, red, and low cut. With her coloring she could wear rich red with matching heels, and gold jewelry. He smiled at her as his mind thought of other things she could wear. This color looked good on her, too, and he knew Ginger had picked the dress out with Joy in mind. She needed some jewelry, maybe ear rings and a diamond pendant to hang in that one perfect place. He knew she had pierced ears but had never seen her wear any earrings.

Ginger was always dressed well but not to any extreme. She was still plump since having had Jimmy and he knew she was no lightweight before she and Hart married. She was also almost six feet tall. She was a knock-out, though, when she dressed and did her hair and makeup. Fred had been Hart's best man and Ginger had been drop-dead gorgeous in her wedding gown specially made for her by a New York designer friend.

Hart had shown Fred the tear sheets from Ginger's modeling days and he had been as blown away with them as the first time Hart had looked and been transfixed. Ginger had graced the cover of Elle, Vanity Fair, and other national fashion magazines.

"Oh, my God, Hart, she looks like a goddess," Fred had said that day, as he'd gazed at the photos of Ginger at her best. She was amazingly beautiful with her amber eyes made up and her long mahogany hair blowing. But most times he'd seen her she was rather plain, but carried herself with a poise that years in front a camera had brought. Ginger wore an air of serene beauty around her. Hart had smiled that day, nodded his head, and patted his own chest, indicating that Ginger was his. Fred could easily see why Hart was so mesmerized by her.

Joy now looked like Ginger, all polished and glamorous. She could have been on those magazine covers.

*Oh man, what have I done?*

Joy's dark hair shone with a lustrous sheen he'd never dreamed possible. Tasteful makeup made the most of her slanted green eyes and she was wearing a kissable shade of lipstick. *She could be a beauty queen.* He'd thought that she was plain and ordinary. He'd made a mistake by underestimating her—even her looks. *God, are you punishing me for my past sins by sending Joy to haunt me night and day? Isn't it enough for me to deal with Lori and Katie?*

Ginger jabbed Hart in the ribs as they watched Fred watching Joy. Hart looked at Ginger, laughed, shook his head and winked. They noticed that something had transpired in that moment between Fred and Joy but they didn't know what was happening.

They'd shared another meal at Hart and Ginger's before retiring to the quaint house that Joy had fallen in love with. She told Fred that it reminded her of her late grandmother's home in Union Springs.

Both women had worked in the kitchen, preparing the meal and enjoyed the other's company. Joy loved to cook and she and Ginger worked as a team, preparing a simple supper of fried breakfast pork chops, grits, eggs and biscuits. It was one of Hart's favorite meals, Ginger said. Joy had once worked in a diner so she knew that many folks loved breakfast for supper. It was comfort food.

Fred and Hart had played a few songs, and Fred had remembered the song he'd recorded on his phone that stormy night a few months back. Hart liked it and offered to write words to it with Fred's permission. No one had heard it before and Fred was slightly embarrassed to let Hart know the depths of his heartaches. Hart owed Fred so much for helping him sell his songs and Hart was now comfortably well off because of it. Fred's music company had bought the songs and several were already recorded by up and coming artists.

Joy and Fred stayed another night in the cottage before returning to Eufaula.

As they entered the cabin, Joy was hesitant to enter the bedroom. Would she sleep with Fred in his king-size bed? The double bed at Ginger's place had been perfect although she had to admit not much sleeping had actually occurred.

Fred brought their bags in and threw them both on the bed. "Yep, in here. With me. Fluffy can sleep on the couch or at the end of the bed." He walked out after making his statement.

*Well, that settled that.* Was he a mind reader? *Dang his hide!* He always seemed to know what she was thinking.

Fred walked down to his pontoon boat to check it out. No one seemed to have bothered it and the security guard said no one had been around when he'd inquired earlier. Boats ran up and down the lake all the time with skiers, fishermen and pleasure boaters.

No one at the marina had reported seeing or hearing from Larry but Fred had a suspicion that the guy was around. Fred wanted to smoke Larry out of hiding but wasn't sure how to do it without endangering Joy. She'd suffered enough at the hands of the bastard.

The water was always calming to Fred. The misty haze from across the wide lake took on an ethereal life of its own, shimmering, sparkling and of late, mesmerizing.

Fred stared for minutes, thinking of Joy, his...happiness...with her. She'd come into his life and he wondered if the Good Lord had seen fit to shine His goodness on him again. For a while, it seemed to Fred that a lasting relationship with a woman was not in the plan. He'd been a playboy before Lori and there after her death, too. But the women in Eufaula were few and far between. None appealed to him. Any that he was interested in was only after his money and he wanted more.

He didn't love Joy he was pretty sure, but she suited his needs. His purpose. He almost wished though that Ginger had not taken Joy to the beauty salon. His plan was set but seeing her like that, all pretty with her highlighted hair, tasteful makeup and painted nails had forced him to see Joy in a new light. One that he had not planned to see. She no longer looked like a maid, or a housekeeper. He realized his thoughts made him sound biased toward folks who couldn't afford some of the small niceties in life. Could he help it if he'd been born into money? Had always been well groomed, well clothed, well fed? The fact that others were not as privileged hit him like a ton of bricks. He needed to give Sol and the others a raise.

Fred stood at the threshold looking out to the lake. Joy was painting on the porch, her favorite place, and he watched with interest. Her hair was messily twisted up with a yellow butterfly clip. He found out that she loved color, loved wearing bright colors and loved painting with them. He'd also found out from Joy that she had painted some in high school and was told she had talent. That was an understatement.

She had on one of his denim shirts that fell almost to her knees. The sleeves were folded at least a half dozen times and it was unbuttoned down to her bosom. He surprised himself by wondering if that was all she had on. She was unaware of him as she bent from her waist, with a brush in her hand, studying the corner of a large canvas on the easel. Her legs were shapely now and her butt had a nice fullness to it, too.

*Nope, not a bra line or panty line in sight. Damn...why does she do that to me?* Lately everything she did seem to turn him on and he'd promised himself that he wasn't going to let that happen.

They settled into a routine. She cleaned the house each morning while he went in to work. At noon, he came home to have lunch with her. Usually it was just sandwiches or tuna salad, but it was always good. Frequently they shared a 'nap' (wink, wink) before Fred went back to the marina.

Later in the afternoons, Joy painted. She tried the acrylics and threatened to throw them away. She couldn't get the hang of them. With the oils, on the other hand, she excelled. She'd sit and sketch for

156

hours, too, making the preliminary drawings work to her satisfaction before she painted on the canvas. She remembered from her high school art class that a good drawing was the basis for a good painting.

She worked on a sketch of Fluffy asleep on the porch sofa, curled up on the old quilt that was a cover-up on cool nights. The play of the quilts faded colors worked well against Fluffy's yellow and white fur.

This was the first of August, and the fall festival was in October. Fred had secretly hoped Joy could produce enough paintings to enter the art festival. She'd come so far within the last few days and he could see what a quick student she was. She needed an art teacher, someone who wouldn't mind coming to the cabin and Fred knew just the lady.

A phone call later and the classes were set. Joy's teacher, a painter from Australia who had settled in Eufaula, was a treasure. Jean Thomason had the most wonderful accent and Joy would ask her questions just to hear her talk.

# Chapter Fourteen

*"Love isn't something you find. It's something that finds you."*
~Loretta Young(American actress, 1913-2000)

After a month, Joy had produced several paintings that were of a quality that Jean showed them to a local gallery and frame shop, who framed them and put them on display for sale. Joy signed her work, 'J. Garrett' and was pleased that Fred liked each piece she painted. Her scenes of the lake and trees were his favorites.

Jean suggested that Joy show her work in the fall festival to get exposure and Fred agreed.

Fred's parents had yet to show and Joy knew that they were mad with Fred. He'd said they were upset but that they'd get over it. Maybe they would. She was nervous about meeting them, knowing they'd look down on her. She was a nobody, a homeless person, unfit for marriage to a member of Eufaula's elite families.

Fred and Joy had gone to Hart and Ginger's for the monthly music fest and Julie had not shown up although Joy looked around at all the folks she didn't know, expecting her to show up any minute.

Hart had written a naughty little song about Fred and Joy's nights at Ginger's house: something about greasing the squeaky bed springs and hot springs at night.

Ginger laughed and told Joy that she'd been the 'subject' of his songs herself. Joy asked Hart where his information came from and he just wiggled his eyebrows and grinned.

Knowing her face was red with embarrassment, she confronted Fred about blabbing to Hart. His vow of innocence seemed almost sincere.

Fred introduced Joy to Jack Turner and told her that Jack's lake house was right next door to his and that Jack's mom lived there. Jack had seen Joy out painting on the deck he told Fred and he'd wondered who the pretty little lady was staying with Fred. Jack slapped Fred on the back and congratulated him on his marriage.

"Jack's been slipping the noose for years," Fred told Joy, turning the table on Jack. "He's got more girlfriends than he can keep up with."

"I am trying to find a woman that can cook, clean, and help around the farm. Ain't none of these young things want any of that. They're all too damned lazy to work."

"Joy can do all of that, but she's spoken for," Fred told him. "You need to get on one of those online sites and post a want ad for a live-in cook and ask if she can drive a John Deere."

"Hell, I can drive the tractor. I just need somebody to help around the place and cook me a decent meal once in a while. Everybody I've hired has been run off by Mama or they can't cut the smells or the time I have to spend working. Anyway, I ain't got nobody. Ms. Joy, you got a sister back home?" he teased.

159

"No, sir. Sorry, I was an only child. That's why I love kids. I was alone way too much as a child. I always wanted someone to play with."

Jack was very attractive, in his early forties or so, and a decent singer. Darn good, in fact, Joy thought. He'd sung a couple of Alan Jackson songs and was well received. He had talent and a singing voice that was a little rough but strangely fascinating. He'd make some woman a great husband. Of course, he wasn't Fred.

*****

Between the sheets there were kisses, caresses and whispered, but guarded, words. Away from the bedroom Joy was a live-in maid and cook. Fred was kind, cordial, respectful. He'd whisper sweet words, touching her tenderly, reverently, but no words of love came from his mouth. He made love to her, but did not love her. Joy had never been treated so kindly, almost worshipfully, and she allowed Fred's gentle touches and kisses. He cared for her, she knew that. He had a sweetness of spirit that Joy found to be a contrast to his rough and rowdy, warrior-like, exterior.

Being with Fred, around him, made Joy happy, and that was something she'd had little of in her life. It felt good, luxuriously good. Warmth flooded her being, and her soul finally felt at peace.

No man had ever touched her as Fred touched her,

and she longed for Fred to whisper those words of love. *Maybe he loves me and just doesn't know it.* Each day found her wanting to say them to Fred, but she held back. *Should I tell him that my feelings for him are growing in leaps, that I thought he was a knight in shining armor, from the very first moment when I opened my eyes in the ER? That I melted in the gleam of those blue eyes?*

Fred had moved a section of his clothes to make room for Joy's expanding wardrobe and shoe collection. He'd given Joy her own credit card but she had yet to use it, and normally she bought cheap things from Wal-Mart when groceries were purchased.

Jean Thomason was fast becoming an influence on Joy's life. She'd traveled to many countries, was well educated, well informed. Joy sometimes felt as if she was in a European finishing school with Jean discussing politics, world and national events, religion, sports, art. Every time Jean came, she brought art books from her own collection.

Joy studied the works of artists from Renoir to Rembrandt, old Flemish masters, and the contemporary artists like Warhol, Wyeth and Edward Hopper. She longed to paint the majestic mountains and scenic vistas of the West, like Albert Bierstadt. Instead, she found the lake, pine and moss-draped oak trees of her surroundings to portray in rich oils. She was from the 'make lemonade with the lemons you are given' school. 'Make do, or do without' was her motto. She knew she'd never go west, to paint or anywhere else.

She was a sponge, soaking in each tidbit of knowledge. If Joy wasn't working in the house, she was painting, or reading about artists, or studying art techniques. Jean could see Joy's work improving daily and she told Fred that Joy was gifted and offered her the use of a pop-up tent to use in the upcoming fall art show.


Fred had been busy with his own project: adding on to the house. His plans were already designed, drawn quickly by a local draftsman and Hart was scheduled to break ground within days. Lori had wanted a large mansion as Fred dubbed it, 'something in keeping with the Garrett name', she'd said. Fred had built it, lived in it with Lori and Katie until they had died and then, he sold it. He'd had Hart build the cabin where he now lived. Fred had previously lived in an apartment and had been quite content there. The mansion had been over the top for him.

Fred knew that he wanted children, at least one or two, and had planned to have more. He'd loved Katie although he knew that she wasn't his. Lori had chased him, running into him at places he frequented, just 'happened to be there', she'd say. Fred knew better. And he knew that his mother had helped put the noose around his neck with that whole affair.

With Joy, there was no expectations on her part. That one fact drew him to her as nothing else did. Joy was not a gold digger. From the short time that Fred had known Joy, he knew that if anything, she was honest. He'd left $349.09 lying around in the bathroom and she'd not touched it, nor the other cash and expensive watches he'd left around, just checking, testing her. And finally had given her a credit card. She could have taken advantage of her newly acquired wealth, instead she seemed oblivious to Fred's unlimited money.

*****

A thick letter arrived at the marina addressed to Joy Smith, in care of Garrett's Marina, Eufaula, AL. There was no return address and as soon as Fred saw it, the hairs on the back of his neck stood up. He wouldn't open it. It was addressed to Joy, but he damned sure was going to be there when she opened it.

That night, he told her a letter had come for her. He wanted to open it, just in case, something other than mail was inside

"It's from him...I know it is," Joy said, her eyes already filling with tears.

Fred ran his hand over it, to make sure nothing alive was inside, then with long scissors, he carefully cut one end and slowly slid out the contents. There were two folded pages, a double-page National Geographic photo of a gigantic hairy spider and a tiny bird, caught in its web. A white sheet of paper had the words 'I know where you are bitch' spelled out in collaged letters, cut from a magazine. Joy turned as white as a sheet and she sat down hard.

"He knows I hate spiders, and that…that ugly thing caught a little bird…that's me…he thinks he has me in his web."

"I'll get the bastard, doll. If I see him, I'll get him, and beat him to a pulp and that's a promise. It's okay….here, take a sip." He handed her some water. He could feel her trembling and he wanted to squeeze the life out of the man who hurt her. Right after he put his fists between the man's eyes and his size 15 boots to the guy's sorry ass.

"I'm scared of him, Fred. He's crazy."

"That's all right, babe, I'm crazy, too. If he shows up here, we'll know about it. Do not go anywhere without me, or someone. Take whoever is at the gate with you if you need to go out. Never go out alone. You understand? Tell me you do."

"I promise, I won't."

*****

When Hart showed up with his construction crew and a set of plans, Joy was asked what she wanted in the new master bathroom. No one had ever asked her opinion of a bath, or what she thought—about anything. Hart would be in for a surprise when he and Ginger found out that her marriage to Fred was a sham, a ruse, to protect her from Larry.

"You just build whatever Fred wants, Hart. I'll like

164

it. As long as it has four walls and the needed fixtures, I'm not picky. The bathroom we have is fine enough for me. I don't see the need for more than one," Joy said, turning the pages of the house plans.

The front elevation of the house was to be changed to include front-facing gabled wings on each side of the existing living and kitchen area. The garage would be attached to the house via a breezeway. Fred's large screened-in porch was to become a glassed-in and air-conditioned studio with windows all around. It faced due north and Jean had pronounced it perfect for a studio. The plans were well designed and the finished look would be stunning with matching glass, cedar and stone on the additions.

Hart shook his head. He'd never worked with any woman who told him to 'build what the husband wanted'. This was a first. But yet, knowing Joy's background, he understood. Fred would want the best, but Hart was mindful of spending others' money, and although Fred had plenty, Hart knew he would not get carried away with the building expenses. Fred wanted the addition to match the existing house, as it should. The existing house was nice, but not over the top as some that Hart had built, so pleasing Fred and Joy would be easy. Fred didn't want to be bothered with the details of how much things cost. If he wanted it, Hart built it, and presented the detailed bill to Fred, who paid it after casually perusing it. Fred had never argued over any amount Hart had asked for. He wanted the best and Hart built it, without question.

# Chapter Fifteen

*"Blessed are they who see beautiful things in
humble places where other people see nothing."*
~Camille Pissarro

Fred had been shopping online and the FedEx
truck had left a number of parcels with the guard at
the gate. Although no other word of Larry's
whereabouts had surfaced, Fred was vigilant,
somehow knowing that the man would not give up his
search for Joy.

"Packages for Mr. Garrett," Ted Grimes, the day
guard told Joy from the intercom.

Joy opened the door and took the packages from
Amazon and other retailers. Fred had been busy
burning the plastic she mused and watched as the
packages were placed on the kitchen counter. She
would never dare open anything that belonged to him.
She respected his privacy and had no desire to snoop
around.

She had learned to relax with the high metal fence
that surrounded Fred's property on three sides. Other
neighbors had fences but none were as nice as Fred's
and none had gates or an armed guard, twenty-four-
seven.

"Why didn't you open the boxes, babe?" Fred admonished her when he got home. "You didn't have to wait for me. Everything in them is for you, anyway."

"Like what? I didn't see my name on them. I won't open anything that isn't mine."

"Well....let's see. This one right here is your camera. It's a good brand. And this one has your computer in it."

"Why do I need a computer? I don't know how to use a computer—I wouldn't know how to turn it on—"

"Photos, my pet, photos. You take photos with that thingy over there and download them on this thingy right here and they'll be where you can look at them and paint them. You can print out the ones you want, if you need to. I'll teach you everything you need to know. It's simple. A child could do it, you'll see." He didn't bother with technical terms. He knew she probably didn't know much about computers or digital cameras and printers. Even children could work computers and printers.

He grinned from ear to ear. He was glad to give her supplies for her art. She'd come so far, so fast that Jean Thomason was hoping for many sales in the October art show for Joy. She'd told Fred that Joy would need a good amount of work to hang on the display stands, to make a good showing. Twenty to thirty pieces, at least.

He made a spot for Joy's laptop and installed the camera program on it. The camera was more than a point and shoot variety, but Fred helped her learn how

167

to turn it on and use it.

After a couple of hours the computer was up and going, and Fred had an idea.

"Come on, we're going riding. Bring your camera and some snacks, cokes, water, whatever you want. We're off to find something for you to paint. Something besides trees and the lake."

Soon they were riding along the same back roads that were in the vicinity of Hart and Ginger's house. He assured her that they weren't going to the Wakefields' house, that this was purely a pleasure ride to gather new material for Joy to paint.

"Stop, stop!" she suddenly told him out of the blue.

He slammed on brakes and Joy was thrown forward, sliding on the leather seats. He glared over at his wife. "What? What's wrong?" Fred asked, glad no one was behind them on the gravel farm to market road. Her sudden outburst had scared him for a few seconds. Was she having a spell? Needed to use the bathroom?

She had a faraway look in her eyes. Was that inspiration he was seeing there?

"Look at the rust on that silo. And the vines running over it. It'll make a great painting with all that bluish gray, burnt sienna and the dark green vines."

It looked like an ordinary rusty farm building to Fred, and he didn't say more until Joy pointed out its artistic appeal as seen through her eyes. He shrugged his shoulders and drove, thinking silence was best. He didn't want to squash her enthusiasm in any way by his off-handed and sometimes bawdy remarks.

In a few minutes she took photos of a herd of cows.

She didn't seem to appreciate his crude remark about them, though, as she got back in the truck. He mentioned that a bull had been responsible for a wreck back in his younger days. He had multiple scars from that night. He'd told her the 'cleaned up' version of the story, too, and laughed about the bull breaking his 'man part' while making amour as Fred and Art waited for the ambulance to arrive. Joy did not want to hear about broken bull parts, but Fred thought it was funny—now, and so she laughed with him.

"I was about to die from the pain and seeing that bull get hurt trying to make babies with about six lady cows made me hurt worse," he said. "Art wasn't badly hurt since we landed on my side of the Jeep. Somehow my seat belt came loose and the flip threw me out before the thing landed, or it would have killed me. Art just had some cuts and abrasions so he popped his seat belt and walked to the nearest house to call for an ambulance. We didn't have cell phones then, and there wasn't anyone at home there except an old widow woman, and we were out in the middle of no-damn-where. She wouldn't let him in—not this huge black guy standing on her porch at midnight, dripping blood. He finally convinced her to call for an ambulance.

"My new Jeep was totaled, my football days were

169

over, and that bull's days as the herd stud were over, too. Art says they probably made hamburger out of that big boy. Poor ol' thing. I guess I could have hit him instead of trying to avoid him, but I was doing about fifty or sixty and he would have landed in the Jeep with us. I laid there, couldn't move at all, with my Jeep almost upside down with the headlights shining on that bull as he crossed the ditch and knocked down that fence. Some of the cows got in the middle of the road, and then that damn bull doing his thing, me in the weeds with broken legs, kneecaps, and a dislocated shoulder, watching the whole scene play out. I can laugh about it now but it wasn't funny then. That poor ol' bull bellowed and bellowed when he broke his...uh...manhood. I didn't hit him, thank goodness. My folks just about stroked out, though. Art had enough sense to throw all the beer cans away before anyone got there. I guess we'd both had a few..."

They stopped a couple of times and when she'd say, "Look," Fred knew he would have to pull off the road. "See that gate, and that sycamore. I love that." She loved it all, Fred thought, but he'd never complain about her taking photos. After seeing her talent grow, he knew he'd do anything to help and encourage her. He slowed his driving so the sudden stops were not so 'sudden' when she decided she needed to take a photo. He was giving his brakes a workout today, although the truck was fairly new and had less than 5,000 miles on it.

She took scene after scene, having Fred stop every mile or so, as he drove through the country side. All the places she'd wanted to photograph just a few weeks earlier, were now captured in her state-of-the-art camera.

Fred would not tell her how much the camera cost since he knew she'd refuse to keep it. She didn't want anyone's charity or pity and he knew that. Had learned it the hard way. The little lady was proud of the smallest gifts, from a pair of five dollar flip-flops to a pair of off-brand blue jeans. She would tell him that anything was better than what she'd had in her previous life and he now knew that was the truth. She'd never had anything nice in her life.


That night, she decided to confide in him.

Fred's heart had been torn when she'd told him of the rape by Larry, the subsequent pregnancy and the beating that ended that pregnancy after just six months. Larry had taken her to the emergency room and left her. Alone. He never came back for her. Joy lied to the ER physician telling him that she'd fallen down a flight of stairs. Larry would, indeed, kill her if she told anyone about him beating her. He told her as much when he'd left her. The doctor had questioned her over and over, but Joy, ever faithful, had kept to her story. Joy could not allow her son to be bagged and disposed of like hospital waste, so she arranged for a cheap casket and burial plot to be paid for by the month.

Joy had not gone back to Larry or her apartment. Instead she called her friend, Bethany, to pick her up at the hospital and to drop her off at an attorney's office. For a day or so Joy stayed with her friend, mending, crying and making decisions that would change her life.

Fred had held her as she cried, slowly revealing her heart-wrenching tale.

Bethany and Joy had waited until Larry had left late one afternoon and they went to gather her few books, purse, wallet, and a garbage bag full of clothes.

Joy worked for that very attorney, Sarah Wentworth, cleaning her office, her home and living in her garage apartment for sixteen months, allowing time for Joy to heal and for the divorce to become final. Mrs. Wentworth had generously paid for the burial of Joy's baby boy and a tiny headstone. The hospital had offered to 'take care' of her precious child, but Joy would not hear of that.

Her legal fees were paid by the work that she did for Mrs. Wentworth, whose own husband had passed away just two years prior. Mrs. Wentworth was childless so Joy was taken in and treated kindly, although she worked hard, even helping in Mrs. Wentworth's fabulous rose garden, caring for her aging cat, and house-sitting.

A pair of private detectives working for Mrs. Wentworth had waited for Larry to sign the divorce papers and he did, under their watchful eyes. He'd refused at first and they said they would not leave until he'd signed it. Making sure he signed his legal name, they finally had what they'd waited for. Joy suspected that they'd had to strong arm Larry to cooperate.

Larry had evaded them for many months, Joy told Fred.

"He probably thought they were cops after his gambling buddies."

"Yeah, that's what they told Mrs. Wentworth, too. She's smart, though. She took pictures of all my bruises and especially my stomach area. It was black from where he'd kicked me, over and over. She also got copies of my records from the hospital, from the other times, too."

"So, she's been collecting evidence against him?"

"Yeah, she's got it all. I told her everything, about every time, all the gambling stuff, too. Mrs. Wentworth told me to leave Bethany's and not contact her any longer because she knew that Larry would finally figure out where I'd stayed. So I know he'll track me down. He finally called Mrs. Wentworth's office, asking for me. He's smart. He knows the questions to ask. He found out where Mrs. Wentworth lived and would sit across the way from her house. She lived where we could see the gate. He'd stay, just sitting in his car for days, watching. Waiting."

"He's not ever going to touch you again, I can promise that," Fred told her, touching her face, running his fingers over her silky skin. "You're mine now and I'll protect you with my dying breath, if I have to."

His sweet, though possessive, words sounded much like words of love to Joy. It was the closest Fred had ever come to saying he loved her. Surely he did.

The days rolled on. Soon, it was September. Hart was coming along nicely with the additions to the cabin. Joy told Fred that they'd have to quit calling it a cabin since it was quickly turning into a really big house. He agreed and laughed as he told her that all he'd wanted was a little space for her to paint and look what had happened.

Fred seemed happy with their marriage arrangements. At least he'd not complained about anything. But he had his secrets she knew.

She'd learned one thing about Fred: he didn't like being pushed and he didn't like being quizzed. So Joy in her wisdom decided to let him tell her about Lori and Katie, in his own time. She'd come to trust Fred and felt at ease with him. He offered no threat to her, even though she'd seen him mad, a time or two, he had not repeated raising his voice to her.

Joy's paintings were being finished right and left. She found several of her photos to be worthy of painting. A field with round bales of hay along a fence row, framed in front by a farm gate and an oak tree with lots of character, made up one big canvas. She discovered she liked painting big and this piece was thirty by forty inches, her biggest to date. Fred loved the piece and quickly claimed it. She would show it, but it would not be for sale. Another painting was of a beaver pond, with dead cypress trees and still, dark water. A log with five turtles was in the foreground with a gray egret perched on one leg in the shallow water, his body reflected in the water.

Fred's parents had still not shown up to check out Joy and Fred knew they were picking their time. He'd called them once to tell them he was happy and that Joy was wonderful. His mother had been cool. His father seemed quite unperturbed by the whole affair, saying that it was Fred's business if he 'wanted to marry some tramp who was just after his money'.

Fred could have lambasted his mother and father, but he chose not to. He'd let things work out on their own. As he saw it nothing he said would change their minds, anyway. As he hung up the phone he realized that he'd always done what they wanted him to do, to make them happy, to make him happy. Well, they didn't count this time. They would not ever be a part of the equation again. He wouldn't call them again.

He had not invited them to his house, nor did he tell them about Joy's art. If they found out, so be it. The art show was the second weekend in October and they normally went to the show, strolling down the boulevard perusing the various arts and crafts on display. Fred's grandmother loved to see all the artists and had favorites that she bought from. He could barely wait until she saw Joy's work.

He was so proud of what she had accomplished since they'd been married. And the changes in her were significant as well. She had a new sense of self-worth and assurance that she never had before. She wasn't cowed down, he noticed and for that, he was most proud. Joy was small but she had fire burning within her heart.

Jean Thomason had mentioned to Joy that she should wear clothing at the art show that reflected her artistic flair. "So you won't disappear in the crowd," Jean said as she suggested a layered peasant skirt and fitted tee-shirt with sandals to match, along with statement jewelry. Joy had tried on several combinations at one of the little shops in town before she found the look she liked and that Jean thought flattered her small frame. A pair of turquoise and brown hand-tooled cowboy boots soon joined the stack of purchases. Joy loved them although they were a luxury as none she'd ever had. She shyly slid her credit card toward the clerk. She'd not used it until this day.

"So, you're the lucky lady," the middle-aged woman said. "Fred's a hunk, isn't he? I imagine his marriage to you broke a lot of hearts around here. There's a string of sweet things that set their hat for him. Not that he was paying that much attention. He's always had a mind of his own. Congratulations," she added as she handed the card back to Joy.

Joy had spent well over five hundred dollars on her purchases and she showed Fred what she had gotten. He was pleased that she bought something that flattered her. Lots of folks would be seeing the new Mrs. John Frederick Garrett, IV. Lori would have spent that amount on one item. Joy told Fred about everything she did, including the amount she put on his credit card.

# Chapter Sixteen

*"Joy had risen like a golden phoenix from the fires and ashes of hell, had been cleansed and polished by the flames of her past life."*
~Fred's observation

The art show was just over a week away. Joy woke up one morning and the minute she moved, her world tilted. She made a mad dash for the bathroom, throwing up just as she reached the toilet. Fred was there by her instantly, bathing her face.

"Are you coming down with something? Is it something you ate? You don't need to get sick. You just started looking better."

He was so kind, it made Joy want to cry and so she did, melting into his arms. He lifted her and took her back to bed where she slept until after lunch.

The next morning the same thing happened as she got up. This time Fred was right behind her again. And holding a small box.

"I think you might be pregnant," he said. "Take this test when you feel like it, okay? I'll go feed Fluffy and give you some privacy."

Had Fred kept a pregnancy test kit hidden someplace, just in case? Did he want her to have his child? Lord, she prayed that was the case. After her periods had stopped she thought she'd never have a child...ever. Now, with her health returning, her periods had started again but were still sporadic.

The test was positive. Fred picked her up and twirled her around when Joy told him. He seemed ecstatic. Joy's happiness was marred by thoughts of Larry's behavior when she'd told him the same news. He'd gotten drunk and told her she couldn't quit work, so she'd have to do something with 'it'.

As if reading her mind, Fred got her attention by kissing her and telling her that he was so happy.

"Put whatever happened in the past back into the past. Let it go. This is today, and I'm here, not Larry. Always remember that."

She nodded and started crying. She was happy. Fred might not love her as much as she loved him, but, it was obvious that he wanted a child with her. He'd love his own child. His heir.

As soon as could be arranged, Joy had an appointment with an OB-GYN, who surprisingly was not friends with Fred. Finally one person in the whole town who was not in his circle of friends. Of course, Dr. Latoya Ferguson was new in Eufaula.

Dr. Ferguson confirmed that Joy was, indeed, pregnant, almost two months by her calculations and exam. Fred was present for most of the examination and told Dr. Ferguson about Joy losing a baby by being kicked by her ex-husband. He also mentioned that she was still underweight and was on supplements.

"That's good. She'll gain weight for sure, now. You'll be wishing she didn't eat so much before long." The doctor's jovial manner set Joy's nervousness to ease. A follow-up appointment was set and the doctor promised to come see Joy's paintings in the art show.

Fred wanted to tell the whole world his good news. And he did consider it good news. He'd longed to have a child and now, it was going to happen. Fred drove back home where Hart was working. He called Hart over so they could talk in private.

"We just got back from the doctor. Joy's expecting. We're gonna have a baby!" Fred could not contain his happiness. His arm stayed around Joy as Hart hugged them in a big group hug. Hart knew Fred had gone to hell and back, losing his wife and baby. Hart, himself, had lost his first wife when their daughter was born, so he'd had his own share of sorrow.

"I'd like to keep this to ourselves for a while, if you don't mind," Fred told Hart, who nodded his understanding. His and Ginger's baby, Jimmy, had made him feel ten feet tall and bulletproof, the best feeling in the world. "You can tell Ginger but we want to savor the moment for a while."

Fred's idea of savoring the moment was to go to their master bedroom, lock the door and make sweet love to his wife, touching her more reverently than ever, kissing her tummy, over and over.


Joy was gorgeous in her new outfit, the first thing

180

she'd ever owned from a boutique. She wore her hair down, lightly highlighted and cut in layers that tried to curl. She'd decided to wear the cowboy boots since they added height that made her feel so good about herself. Fred watchfully stared at her from the closed street, where he'd taken a seat on a lawn chair. How she'd blossomed in the past few weeks. Now she was pregnant with his child. And she was excited about the baby, and her art.

The judges had passed her booth and had written in their notebooks. He hoped that was a good omen as they'd bypassed some of the artists not bothering to slow down.

There were some really outstanding nationally-known artists here. Fred knew Eddie Leroy, Eufaula's own nationally known wildlife artist, and also Matt Kennedy from Birmingham, Alabama. Fred had bought several pieces from them. Leroy would take best in show and Kennedy would take first or second place, Fred figured from what he'd seen. Joy didn't stand a chance against those masters, but she was good, even to Fred's eye.

Jean Thomason had helped Joy and Fred set up the tent the night before and at seven this morning, Jean had helped Fred hang all the paintings. Joy had been sick all week and he could help with this. This morning, they'd headed off the nausea with dry crackers and a soft drink. They had to ask the doc about something to stem the nausea. Fred had missed the first part of Lori's pregnancy but she'd told him how sick she was for months. He wished his mind wouldn't keep dredging up Lori.

At 11:00 a.m. the head of the art show stopped by Joy's booth, with a ribbon and an envelope. She'd won one of the Merit Awards, and fifty dollars. The newspaper had taken photos of the winning painting, not Fred's hay bale piece, but instead, the beaver pond painting.

Fred returned to his seat and watched the folks stroll by, commenting on the various artists and their offerings. He hoped Joy got to hear only the good comments as everyone was an art critic. He also hoped Joy would be hungry soon and that Jean would take over the booth while they left to grab a quick bite. Fred was starving and his stomach growled noisily.

The crowds swelled and Fred was frequently talking to folks, a few who congratulated him on his marriage. Others just knew him from either the marina, the country club or through his folks.


"Well, well...you certainly fell into the big time, didn't you, *little girl*?

Joy's heart almost stopped as a dreaded voice came from behind her. The blood in her body turn to ice as she turned to see him. Larry was standing not two feet behind her.

He reached toward her and before he could touch her, Joy by pure instinct, drew back her fist and hit Larry right in the nose, hard as she could. As he held his nose with both hands, to stem the spurt of blood, she kicked him between the legs with her pretty little turquoise and brown cowboy boot, as she yelled for

182

Fred at the top of her lungs.

Within seconds Fred was on top of Larry, practically sitting on the smaller man and punching in 9-1-1 for the police. He was furious that Larry had slipped by his security men. Larry had colored his hair and now sported a full beard. He was huddled on the ground, one hand on his bloody nose, the other between his legs.

As soon as Fred hung up from calling the police, he called the two men he'd hired specifically for today to keep an eye on Joy. One reported he was in the public restroom and the other was at the opposite end of the street. Had it not been for Joy's quick thinking, she might have been kidnapped, or even hurt by her ex-husband. It was over before she or Fred realized what had happened.

Fred kept asking Joy if she was okay.

"I'm fine, the hand's fine, my foot's fine. Calm down, Fred. I'm good."

"Are you sure?"

"I am fine, but I'm about to starve. I wish the police would hurry."

By that time, one of hired security guys had found his way back and was red-faced from being caught with his pants down, so to speak. The other guy had gotten tangled up with some folks who thought they knew him, as southerners do.

She felt fine. She'd done something she'd always wanted to do but was afraid of doing. She'd acted on her own, her survival instincts kicked in, literally and figuratively. Other than being a little tired, she felt great, as a matter of fact.

Fred was furious with himself that he didn't get to beat Larry to a pulp. Yeah, he was glad that she took control of her life, for once, but he so wanted to bury his fists into Larry's face or gut. A few times.

Larry was hauled off to jail with all the tourists and fellow artists craning their necks to see what was going on.

Joy stayed with her booth, with Jean Thomason and Fred right by her, for the rest of the day. Joy not only won an award, she sold three paintings. One went to a local business, a bank, who had committed to buying a painting, a 'purchase award'. She'd had won an award, made money, kicked Larry where it hurts most, and bloodied his nose. What a day!

"I didn't know I married Jackie Chan. She kicked his ass, Jean! I think she broke his nose with just one hit and then she lit into him with those killer boots! Got him right where it hurts." He hit his knee and laughed, deep down. It was funny, now, that it was over. She'd been so scared of Larry before, yet she'd jumped on him like a guinea wasp.

"My little doll took him down in two licks. She'd done it before I could get to her, too!"

Fred was so proud of how she reacted, almost as proud as Joy. She'd stood up to Larry, for the very first time and had brought him to the ground.

Fred had told this story at least ten times since the incident and it got funnier and funnier to him. He weighed some two hundred thirty-five pounds and stood six foot four and Joy weighed maybe ninety pounds, soaking wet, at five feet three.

"It's a good thing I got there as soon as she hollered for me or we'd been picking ol' Larry up with a scoop. And he's gonna sing soprano for the rest of his life, too. I hope you don't get mad with me, honey. The bigger they are, the harder they fall, you know," he grinned at her.

And it then dawned on him that Joy had risen like a golden phoenix from the fires and ashes of hell, had been cleansed and polished by the flames of her past life. Now he watched her with her styled hair, nice clothes, and cowboy boots. Her skin was flawless, as though she glowed from within. He'd always heard pregnant women glowed, and now he saw it for himself. She was radiant. Or was that love she radiated right toward him. Her eyes lit up when she looked toward him. Only him.

It hit him in the gut. She loved him. Really, truly, deeply loved him. And now he had fallen for her. Hard. He swallowed back the lump that suddenly formed in his throat. He'd told himself he wouldn't fall for her, that he'd use her to get what he wanted, then he'd dump her. All he wanted was a mama for a couple of kids. Joy was just convenient. Available. The fun had come in standing up to his folks, contradicting their wishes for him and getting Joy pregnant. He'd loved every minute of doing what he wanted, not what his folks expected of him. For years he'd thought he was a grown man, strong and capable of anything. He was wrong. He'd followed right in his father's footsteps, doing almost everything his parents had wanted. For him. What. They. Wanted.

For. Him.

He saw it all so clearly now. His mother had prodded the glamorous Lori Chapman into pursuing Fred, relentlessly. Eventually, he gave in. Made love to her. Look how that turned out. It was a train wreck waiting to happen and in his heart, Fred knew it going into the marriage. He'd started drinking heavily just to tolerate being around Lori. Katie had made his life fun, really fun and it almost killed him when she died. He cared, in his own way, for Lori, but he loved Katie. Her smiles, giggles and the way she called him, "Dad-dee" melted his heart. He could still hear the word and it echoed through his mind. Haunting him. Fred thought he should have been the one killed. *Why Katie, God? Why her? She was innocent. Only three years old.*

Sunday afternoon passed quietly, uneventfully, save for the sale to Fred's neighbor, Jack Turner. He'd stopped by and stayed a good while, admiring the art and finally selected a large painting for his home.

The time came to take down the tent and take the remaining paintings home. Jean Thomason had returned to help man Joy's booth and to support Joy after her encounter. And Joy was exhausted, wrung out, ready to go home and take a nap. She was so tired that she fell asleep on the way to a restaurant for supper. Fred woke her up, insisting that they eat and then they'd go home so she could rest. She managed to eat her barbecue sandwich and some of the French

186

fries. Fred finished off the remainder and practically poured her into his truck.

At home, he knew the two day's events would hit her. And it did. She'd bathed in the shower and made it almost to the bed when she started crying. She didn't have to tell Fred what was happening. He knew. She'd faced the devil and won. What she'd feared for over eight years had happened. The adrenalin was now gone, all that was left was the relief. She sobbed for a while before Fred gently dressed her in one of his tee shirts and put her in bed, and wrapped his arms around her. They both fell asleep.

# Chapter Seventeen

*"Seven things that money can't buy: a happy family, true love, passion, time, wisdom, respect, and inner peace."*
~author unknown

Joy's ex-husband demanded that Joy come to see him in the Eufaula jail. The chief had called Fred telling him that the man was driving the jailer nuts with his continuous noise. Larry was making a fuss about seeing his ex-wife. He needed to talk with her about money he was entitled to from some old lady.

Joy, and Fred, had finally consented to visit Larry, to confront him, even though Joy had already given her statement to the police.

"The old lady, Ms. Wentworth, left you a pile of money. I want my share of it. I want alimony, Joyce, or whatever you're calling yourself these days. I see you've already fell into the money so I want my share. You're in this with me. You owe me. Without me, you'd still be waiting tables and cleaning toilets at the motel. I want what's mine. I don't care nothing about you no more...just get me that damn money. Or—".

"Or what, you pile of crap?" Fred took over the talking. "Like you're ever going to get out of jail?" he laughed. "Mrs. Wentworth kept a real thick file on

188

you, buddy boy, and if Joy has anything to do with it, you'll never see this side of the bars again. Spousal rape, beatings, killing your own child! Man, do you think you'll ever be anywhere but jail?"

"Joyce ain't got no proof of—"

"Mrs. Wentworth has photos of bruises, hospital records, x-rays, all the visits to the ER. All of it," Fred said as coldly as he could. If he lost it in here, they'd arrest him. He wanted to pound this lowlife into the concrete floor with his bare hands.

"Even the hospital security tape showing you taking Joy in, blood running down her legs, on her face and arms. It showed you leaving her, too, not ten seconds after you put her into a wheelchair. You walked out. On your wife, who could have hemorrhaged to death. But you didn't care. You just wanted to kill the baby because Joy couldn't work with a baby, could she?" Fred stopped. His fists were clinched and Joy reached for his left hand, to calm him down.

"What does he have I don't, Joyce? Tell me that. More money? She's just after your money, I know," Larry said looking toward Fred.

"He has my heart," Joy said softly, not sure that Larry nor Fred heard her.

She pulled Fred away from the jail cell where Larry sat, his face in his hands. She never looked back. What a sick, pathetic man Larry Blackstone was. How in God's name had she ever managed to think she had loved him at one time? Had she been that desperate to get away from her 'father'? Right into the hands of someone who was just like him?

How embarrassed and ashamed that Fred had seen how low she'd been. How terribly, misguided and stupid she was. How foolish.


Sarah Wentworth was dead. Almost five weeks earlier, she'd died peacefully in her sleep at her home and was found by her law partner, Jim Andersen. Jim was Sarah's executor and had been relieved when he'd gotten a call from one Joy Smith Garrett, currently residing in Eufaula, Alabama.

"Mrs. Garrett, you need to come to Talladega. I can't give you all the details over the phone since the estate is substantial," Jim Andersen told Joy on the phone a couple of days later.

Joy needed to find out for herself about Mrs. Wentworth. She and Fred had done a search on the Internet and found that Mrs. Wentworth had died, but the obit gave no details nor listed any relatives. Joy knew that there were none. Sarah Wentworth, regal and every inch a grand old dame, died childless with no kin. She was the last of her family line. The lady had been so kind to Joy, giving her refuge, time to mend, advice and more than a few meals. Without Mrs. Wentworth, Joy would have probably gone back to her previous life, ignorant, broke and broken. Larry would have talked his way back into her miserable life and without Mrs. Wentworth, Joy would have relented after the first few months of being alone. Mrs. Wentworth had gotten Joy a restraining order against Larry, given her a place to stay to hide from him, in relative safety. Her home was gated, secured by high fences and a security guard was on duty twenty-four hours a day at the exclusive subdivision. Joy had left her when Larry found the Wentworth home. He'd sat for hours in front of the gates, and Joy knew he'd end up hurting Mrs. Wentworth if she stayed around.

Sarah Wentworth had left half of her estate to Joy Smith, formerly known as Barbie Joyce Burns Blackstone. Her share came to some sixteen million dollars plus the huge house. Jim Andersen had not been left out, either. He'd been left Mrs. Wentworth's business, an equal amount of money, and other holdings. He was quite happy with the arrangement as Mrs. Wentworth's clients were many and most were wealthy. Joy knew that the elderly lawyer had been part of a group that had won a class action law suit against one of the largest drug companies in the world. Her holdings amounted to a king's ransom. Mrs. Wentworth had been kind to him, as well, he said, helping him financially, since he'd struggled as a new lawyer with no clients and a baby on the way.

Fred had gone with Joy to Talladega to visit the attorney's office. He wanted to make sure that Joy's interests were taken care of, in fact, had his own attorney call Jim Andersen, just to be on the safe side. A tax attorney would be called in to help deal with the amounts of money and properties involved.

Joy wanted to sell the house. It was huge and Joy had already established another life, in another more comfortable home, with Fred. She had no desire to own such a place as the Wentworth home. It was probably worth a million or more given its prestigious location and excellent condition. It was only a few years old.

Fred was astounded at the large and elegant two-story Tudor home in a gated subdivision. Joy was pleased that the rose garden was still being cared for. She took many photos of the roses in the garden, recalling how she had tended the roses, pruning them and caring for them, and making gigantic bouquets for the parties that Sarah Wentworth loved to host. Joy had learned so much from her employer, who treated her more like a daughter than a housekeeper and companion.

Jim had Joy's files safe, locked in Mrs. Wentworth's fireproof vault, as well as digital copies in another location. Fred had asked about that right away, before Joy had time to think of it. Fred knew that those files would keep Larry behind bars and Joy safe.

Fred asked to see the grave and he held her as they grieved for the loss of the infant. He said he'd pay for the tiny casket to be moved to Eufaula if Joy wanted to do so. "You can visit Danny whenever you want if we do that, doll," he said, as he looked down at the small granite stone that read: "Daniel Lee Smith, Precious Angel, September 9, 2009". She nodded, with tears on her cheeks. He said he'd take care of it. Mrs. Wentworth had been buried in a church cemetery and Joy's baby was buried in an outlying section of the old city cemetery. And even though Larry was Danny's father, Joy had loved her baby from the moment she knew she was pregnant. This gesture from Fred was unbearably sweet.

*****

The first thing Joy bought was a used car. Never having had a new car, she was just as happy with one that worked, had tires that weren't bald and the windows operated. Fred wanted to get her to buy something nice, like a Mercedes or a Lexus, but none of the expensive cars held an appeal for her. Instead, she chose a used compact station wagon, one large enough to haul kids or her paintings.

Fred received a call at work a few days later. It was the sheriff of Barbour County. Larry Blackstone had been killed in a scuffle with another incarcerated person in the county jail. He'd bled to death before anyone had noticed him slumped over in his cell.

Joy was finally free.

Now that Joy was financially secure, forever, and her ex-husband was no longer a threat, Fred wondered if Joy cared enough for him to stay married to him. After all, he'd taken her in, given her what she needed: a home, food, clothes and security. Now, she could buy anything she wanted. She was in many ways his equal, her financial footing was as solid as his. She had confidence, had art to make money from and more importantly, she carried his child.

Women do not realize the power they have over men. Fred had seen it, time and time again. A man would do most anything to protect his sex partner, or wife, his children. Wars had been fought, battles had been won and lost over women. Fred knew that first hand, when Lori had called him up one night, stating that she was pregnant with his child and that he had to marry her, right away, within a few weeks, she'd insisted. She'd already called his mother and told her 'the good news'. She'd turned his life upside down. Now, the same thing was happening. The saving grace was that Fred knew this child was his...there was no doubt of that. The battle plan now was for Fred to keep Joy with him. Now that she could leave, he'd come to realize what'd he'd lose if she did.

She had power over Fred and how Joy chose to use that power was an unknown that worried Fred. She cared for him, she had to. He'd heard her remark at the jail. 'He has my heart', she had said. Maybe, he prayed, maybe she loves me. *I think that's love in her eyes when she looks at me. I love her. Why can't I find the words to just say it?* If she ever found out how devious he had been with her, pushing her into getting married, it would be over.

Fred knew he must come clean with Joy but the time never seemed right. She was on top of the world at the moment. Inheriting a humongous amount of money, Larry's death, the success of her art. All of it had made Joy a better person, expanded her horizons, giving her ideas of what she was truly capable of doing. Fred had seen it all along. She was quick. Jean Thomason had attested to that, saying that Joy was the best student she'd ever had and that Joy was 'already a better artist' than Jean herself was, with her classical art training.

Joy had just come from her OB visit. She'd gained more weight, quickly. Fred had gone with her and the sonogram had shown not one baby, but two.

Fred was ecstatic. There were no other words for it. He was over the moon, higher than a kite, drunk on good news. His babies, twin babies. Two babies, a boy and a girl it seemed.

John and Elaine Garrett showed up out of blue almost a month after the art show. John had honked his horn until Fred had opened the gate. No security guard was needed now that Larry was dead. However Fred was enjoying the gated entrance to his house, knowing it afforded some privacy for them, as well as a measure of security that he knew Joy needed.

The couple came to Fred's new front doors and into the new and impressive foyer with its vaulted ceiling and slate flooring.

Joy had been painting, a new piece for a group show art show she'd been invited to participate in at the Wiregrass Museum of Art in Dothan. Paint smeared her fingers and she wore Fred's old shirt that hung past her knees. Her hair was in a messy ponytail and all she could think of was that at least the house was clean. Spotless. She and Fred had cleaned it thoroughly just the day before. Fred was good about doing the sweeping and mopping, helping Joy out now that she was getting bigger and fatigue set in right after lunch.

"Mom, Dad...this is my wife, Joy. And as you can see, she's an artist."

Joy stood there with a paint rag in her hand, not knowing what to do. She put it down after wiping the acrylics from her fingers. The smell of oil paints now made her nauseous and she'd switched mediums.

They didn't offer their hands to shake nor did Joy. She followed their lead.

John Garrett was as handsome as his son, although not as tall. Joy could see where Fred got his ram-rod stance. Elaine Garrett was also tall, but had graying dark hair that she had cut in a stark blunt cut that hardened her classic features. They made a striking couple.

Elaine was the first to speak.

"Well, it's about time we meet. I've heard a lot about you, Joy." Elaine threw an inflection on Joy's name that wasn't attractive. "I wasn't sure what to think when our son called and said he was married to a virtual stranger, a former maid, at that."

"I'm sorry Fred has kept me to himself, Mrs. Garrett. He's been busy and I've been painting a lot, and we're adding on to the house, so that's taken a lot of time. Won't you and Mr. Garrett sit down? Fred, entertain your folks for a minute and let me change. I wear old clothes when I paint", she said in apology. "I know I must look a mess."

Joy left as quickly as she could, almost running to the master bedroom and closing the door. She opened the closet and picked out a pair of dark stretchy leggings and a flowing top with a flattering neckline.

196

She'd bought some outfits that fit her changing body. She slid her feet into matching flats and brushed her hair down from its perilous perch. After looking in the mirror, she decided that she was looking as good as she would. Forward into battle.

She walked in just as Mrs. Garrett was commenting about Fred's choices in furniture. Elaine clearly had her opinions and Fred was not one to care if his sofa wasn't new or in style. Fred's face was red and he was obviously flustered with his parents.

Joy stepped into the room and said without missing a beat," Well, we can get newer stuff after the kids get on up in age. This lodge look is very 'in' now, you know. It's in all the magazines." She knew the furniture was nice. She'd seen enough high end catalogs to know that western lodge furniture was very in style, and expensive.

*In for a penny, in a pound.* She'd beard that lion right here and now. *Just get it out and air all the laundry at one fell swoop.*

"Has Fred told you our good news? We're having babies...twins! Isn't that wonderful? Fred is over the moon."

"Fred? Is that right? I thought you'd wait a while before starting a family. You know, after the other."

Fred spoke up, at last. Joy felt like he'd left her to hold the bag, for a moment.

"Yes, I decided that I was getting too old to wait much longer and Joy loves kids. So, why wait? Joy's got a lot of love to give. I'm glad...We're glad," he stumbled out. What in hell was wrong with him? His parents were just his parents. They weren't going to

197

disown him, would they? Well, what if they did? He didn't need their money.

"Look, Joy," John Garrett said, "what will it cost us for you to get out of Fred's life? I'm talking money, right now, today. Just name your price and you can pack up and move on. Twenty-five thousand? Fifty thousand? Seventy-five thousand? We can't allow our son to stay married a person who comes from…..from…nothing. Isn't that right? You come from nothing? Am I right? Come on, tell the truth. I'll bet Fred has never heard the whole truth. We've had you investigated. Joy Smith's not even your real name. How can you stay married to this…woman…Fred?"

Fred had heard enough. He'd allowed his father to talk, get it all out in the open. He knew this was coming and he'd hoped that his and Joy's relationship was sturdy because his parents were out to get Joy out of his life.

"Just a damn minute, Dad." Fred's voice was calm. "Maybe she didn't have the best upbringing. I don't know, and I don't really care. I haven't met her father. Her mother is dead, she told me. But, none of that matters. Joy is my wife. I married her, for better or for worse. I know she loves me and I love her and I love these babies she's carrying and I can't wait to be a dad to them. I've been miserable since I lost Katie… Notice I didn't say Lori. I never loved her. And while we're on the subject, Mom, Katie wasn't my daughter.

"And for your information," he continued, "the only reason I married Lori was because she

198

threatened to tell you, and everyone else, that I had raped her, if I didn't marry her. I told her 'no', several times, to begin with. Yes, she asked me to marry her. When I told her that I didn't love her and had no plans to marry her, then she hit me with the rape threat. That's how conniving she was. What could I do? I didn't want to go to jail, and everyone in Eufaula knew I'd dated her, had seen me with her. I took the easy and high road. At least that's what I thought at the time. I married Lori, in part, so it would make you happy, Mom. I hated that I allowed you to push her into my life. It was a train wreck from day one."

"But, she was so beautiful and from a good family—"

Fred held up his hand to stop her.

"Nothing I did was good enough, cost enough or was anything she wanted. She always wanted more: a maid, a housekeeper, a nanny, more drinking, more partying, more clothes. I couldn't spend it fast enough to suit her. I wasn't happy that she died, but the marriage was doomed, and I had started divorce proceedings weeks before, with poor Katie caught in the middle. I loved Katie, but I let that drunk bitch—Lori— leave with Katie that night. It was storming like crazy and she took that baby out and killed her. I was on the phone with Sol and Lori sneaked her out. It was maybe thirty minutes before there was a knock on the door and a state trooper stood there telling me that Lori had hit that railing at a high rate of speed in all that rain. I didn't know she had even left the house."

He didn't mention that their house was so large, with two stories and six bedrooms and he thought Lori was with Katie in her bedroom. They knew some of the story except for the part about the divorce proceedings, and Lori's rape threat to Fred. He'd kept that nugget to himself probably too long it seemed now.

Joy stood next to Fred, her arm around his waist. He turned and pulled Joy closer. He put his hand on Joy's stomach, pulling the fabric taut, revealing her baby bump.

"Do you see that? Those are my babies in there. We made them. I want them. With her. Nobody else. Do y'all get the picture? Get it or get out. And keep your money. Write me out of the will. Ask me if I give a damn. I don't need your money...I have enough money of my own to last two lifetimes. We don't need your money. Now...if y'all decide you want to be a part of these babies' lives, I'll be happy. If not, get out and don't look back. Right now I don't care if I ever see either of you again. You are an embarrassment to me, and my wife."

Joy could see the black coming in from the sides of her vision. *No...oh, Lord, don't let me pass out in front of these folks.*

Fred felt Joy's legs give way. She slumped. Fred caught her and placed her on the sofa. He called the doctor's office and told the nurse what happened. The nurse told Fred to take Joy to the ER that Dr. Ferguson would meet them there. Joy didn't wake as Fred put her into his truck and left his home, leaving his mother holding the door open.

200

# Chapter Eighteen

*"I didn't plan on falling in love with you."*
~Fred

"She'll be fine, Fred," Dr. Ferguson told him. "Sounds like she had too much excitement. Her blood pressure shot up but it's coming back down. We'll go ahead and check her out since she's here, though. See how those little ones are doing." She laughed and walked away, leaving Fred alone with Joy for a moment. He looked up to see an aid who asked if it was all right if his parents came back into the ER. They'd followed him to the hospital.

"Tell them they can wait for a while. I'll come out in a few minutes. They're going to do some tests just to make sure everything's okay."

Twenty minutes later, Fred kept his word. The exam again showed two babies, a boy and a girl. They were sure this time. The new technology was amazing and Fred had proof in his hand—the print-out showed detailed tiny faces, ears, fingers. He'd shed a tear when the technician had handed the photo to him. The baby boy had a thumb in his mouth. They were okay. Everything was good with the babies. Joy had cried, overcome with emotions from the day. She was feeling better but the doctor was keeping her overnight to monitor her blood pressure.

Joy asked Fred to go home later and bring some things for her overnight stay.

He walked out to the waiting room where his parents were still sitting. He was surprised that they had waited.

"I'm going home to get some things. You can stay here with her, if you want. But if I hear that either of you have said one word out the way to her, it'll be the last time you'll ever see her, or me. You can take that to the bank. I won't stand for either of you trying to manipulate me, ever again. She's in exam room three but they're taking her to a room now," he said as he jogged out the doors.


Fred returned with Joy's toothbrush, hairbrush, makeup and toiletry items, as well as a night gown and robe since she still wore his tee shirts to bed. He'd also picked up two dozen red roses in a blue and white vase that he knew Joy would love.

The hospital room was quiet—too quiet—when Fred walked in with his arms full. Now, he realized he should have stayed a while and went for the stuff Joy needed later. His mistake. Joy had asked him to wait.

His dad was standing by the window looking outside. His mom was sitting in the visitor's chair. Joy looked miserable, white as a sheet. He prayed to God that she would be okay and that he would be given the opportunity to tell her how much he loved her, without an audience.

"Hey, doll. How you feeling?" he asked, as he leaned over her and kissed her on her temple.

He set the flowers and things he'd brought from

home on a table and waited for someone to say something. Joy wouldn't move her head or look up. She was fidgeting with the covers. Her fingers trembled and he knew he'd walked into the middle of a conversation.

"I need to change," Joy finally said, her voice sharper than normal.

He gazed down at her, noticing the way the over-size gown revealed the baby bump and her breasts, which seemed to have expanded overnight. She went from being flat as fried eggs to being really nicely endowed. She had not answered his question about how she was feeling. She was mad, and hurt, he could tell from the tone of her words.

"We'll step outside, son," John Garrett told Fred.

Fred nodded that he'd heard his father but said nothing else to him. He reached for the call button for a nurse to help Joy with the machinery attached so she could change and go to the bathroom.

Fred and the nurse helped her change. The nurse left the two alone after re-attaching the blood pressure cuff and oxygen sensor. He sat down on the bed next to her, holding her hand. He kissed her on the cheek and made her look into his eyes since she wouldn't return his gaze.

"I love you, Joy. I know I've not told you before. I didn't mean to blurt it out today. You deserved to know before now. I just couldn't find the words. I wanted to say them…they just wouldn't come. And I owe you apology. I'm sorry for pushing you into getting married. I knew my folks wouldn't approve of you. They always tried run my life. And I've let them to a point, I suppose. Until you came along and I wanted you for myself. To have my babies, to be with me."

"So you didn't really care for me...love me at all... when we got married?... I had hoped..."

"No, doll. Love no. Desired, yes. I didn't plan on falling in love with you. I tried not to, but you stirred something inside me that I never knew existed. I felt emotions. I don't know if it was love... I'm not sure I know how to love, or what love is. I knew I had to have you in my life, no matter what it took....so I took matters into hand and rushed you off to the courthouse."

"So....all of this....this has all been a game? A huge elaborate scheme? A giant lie? The art supplies, the kind words, encouragement, art lessons? It was all done so I'd stay with you? So I'd fall in love with you? Couldn't you see I was falling for you? You just wanted to marry me, get me pregnant and have children for you? And you didn't have the guts to tell me that you might love me, but you're not sure that you know what love is?"

Fred nodded his head. He'd been too honest, and he knew this was not going to work out well for him, but more importantly, he could sense Joy drawing away from him.

"So, how was this going to work? After I have the babies am I supposed to hand them over to you and just walk away? Abandon them? The love-making— the sex, the sweet words? Those meant nothing to you....at all? They were just words coming from your lips, but not your heart?"

"Not until today. I realized that I do love you but I have used you, for my own purposes and that's what I apologize for. I admit it. For not being truthful with you. I pretended it didn't matter how I felt about you. But it did. I saw you falling in love with me and I couldn't say the words you needed to hear."

He watched her face as his words inflicted wound after wound. He was cruel but she needed to know the truth.

"Bring my car up here tomorrow. I'm leaving you, Fred. I won't stay where I'm not wanted. I told you that from the beginning. Looks like I was right after all. I prayed you'd grow to love me. I hoped those kind words and the sweet lovemaking would turn into love. It didn't, at least, not for you. These babies are all you love. All you're interested in. I was fooling myself...hoping, wishing. I prayed God would put love in your heart for me. You tried to play me for a fool, but I won't stand for it. And then your mom telling me about Lori's ring in great detail. I'll pay you back every dime you've spent on me. I've been stepped on enough for one lifetime already. Your parents tried to buy me off...like I was some disposable vessel... Your mom left a check over there," she said, pointing to the bedside table. "Get it and give it back to her...I guess they wanted me to have these babies and leave them with you. That's not going to happen. My babies don't have a price tag on them...for them...or for you! I'm leaving and you don't have to love me. You won't see me again— ever.

*God, I sound like a parrot, repeating myself over*

205

*and over. He doesn't care. It's not going to change his heart. Only God can do that. Nothing I can do will change him. It's over.*

"Joy...you don't mean it. You can't just leave. You're not well. You've got to think about the babies. I'll look after you. I promise. Just don't leave me. I can't stand it if you leave. It's not just the babies. I love you, too. I do. Trust me, baby, please."

Joy's mention of the ring went over Fred's head. It was just one of the things that Elaine Garrett had taken great pleasure in telling Joy. Lori was beautiful, and a beauty queen. Lori was in the best sorority, and her parents were in the correct social set. Lori was perfect. The hateful words still swirled around in her mind. Elaine had spared Joy nothing.

"I trusted you, Fred. With my life. You said you'd protect me! Was that a lie, too? You've lied, by omission. You've never told me about Lori or Katie, other than that they died. All I wanted was your love and trust, Fred. You denied me both. You knew I was falling for you and you let me. You never tried to stop me. You let that Julie kiss you right in front of me to make me jealous...Well, it worked. Do you know you've never explained about her? I know there's more to the story, but, I don't deserve the truth from you, right? Your parents said you married me just to make them mad. Is that the truth? I can raise my babies...alone...I can do it...I have money...I..I don't....don't need....you." Joy stopped, the last words coming out between sobs.

A nurse came running into the room.

"Mr. Garrett, get off the bed. Your wife's blood

206

pressure is off the chart. She's got to calm down. If you can't let her rest, we can make you leave the room, or the hospital."

The old biddy was talking to Fred like he was six years old.

Joy was visibly trembling from emotion and Fred was at fault. He'd started all this by trying to assuage his own guilt.

"I'll be back in a little while. After we've had time to cool off and calm down."

He left. His parents obviously had left already since she didn't see them again.

\*\*\*\*\*

Dr. Ferguson came in later and talked for a long while. Joy told Dr. Ferguson everything, word for word that had happened. She had to talk with someone. Dr. Ferguson left and Joy cried herself to sleep. She'd wanted Fred. As mad as she was with him, she wanted him near. She still didn't feel safe without him. Even though Larry was now dead and gone.

Hormones had her emotions going off the chart. Fred wasn't coming back tonight. It was after ten and he had not come back. He was drunk. She knew that in her heart. His parents hated her and they had been awful to her. Comparing her to Lori and telling her about Fred buying that dinner ring for Lori as a birthday present. It was real but, 'someone like you, a maid who cleans toilets, didn't deserve to wear it', Mrs. Garrett had told her. Those hateful, awful words swirled around her mind. *'Fred doesn't love you. He just wants the babies.'* She was a handy, and willing, vessel, a brood mare he picked up by the roadside. He'd take the babies away—the Garretts would see to it. They told her so, just before Fred had walked in. Elaine had thrown a check for fifty thousand dollars on the table.

He found a bottle of bourbon, and half a bottle of vodka. All the beer in the house was gone, too. He drank it first. For the first time in several months, Fred drank himself into a stupor.

His parents had followed him home from the hospital, blasting him to his face, once again. How dare he denigrate their name marrying that street woman. Was he sure those babies were even his? So on and so on. He'd finally had enough and told them to get the hell out, to go back to Florida and not come back.

His mind was fuzzy.

He'd done a bad thing and didn't know how to make it right. He knew he was drunker than a skunk when he started making up words to a song. Joy was right—he couldn't handle his beer any longer.

The words flowed from his mind and he picked Maybelle up and strummed a chord.

*You found me when I was lost.*

*I didn't know which way to go,*
*You knocked me to my knees...*
*You are the joy in my life....*
*Don't you know I love you in my life?*

God, he couldn't make anything rhyme, so he drank some more, waiting for the right words to come. Around midnight, he passed out. There was something he was supposed to do but he couldn't remember what it was.

# Chapter Nineteen

*"Life is so ironic. It takes sadness to know happiness, noise to appreciate silence, and absence to value presence."*
~unknown author

Dr. Ferguson was waiting at the nurses' station, just down from Joy's room when Fred arrived to take Joy home. He had not brought Joy's car, nor did he intend for her to leave him.

The doctor jumped up and stopped him before he got to Joy's room.

"Your wife needs medication to control her blood pressure. She's small and these babies are growing fast and overwhelming her body. I'm starting her on a mild sedative, too, just for a few days. If she doesn't improve, those babies could be in danger. Are you hearing what I'm saying, Mr. Garrett? And with twins, complete bed rest may be necessary in the third trimester, if she can make it that long before having other issues. Her blood pressure fluctuating violently is a problem."

Yesterday she'd called him Fred. Today, it was Mr. Garrett.

Fred nodded. "What should I do?"

"Whatever is bothering Joy isn't going away. So I ask you, do you care enough for her to help her live and carry these babies until term? You and Joy have

210

to make up your minds to put your differences behind you. I don't care what the problem is. Most couples have spats. This goes deeper and I suspect that you know what the answer is. Make it right or you stand to lose all three of them. Am I clear?"

"I lied to her, Dr. Ferguson. It's all my fault. She thinks I don't love her. And I do."

"You don't need to be telling me that—tell her. She's the one whose health depends on you. And she spent the night alone, too. She needed you here. She said you were at home, probably drinking, or drunk."

"She's right. I should have been here. And I was drunk."

He'd had to take a long hot shower to remove the stench from his body. And four aspirin for his throbbing head. *How did Joy know?* He'd never been as drunk in his life he realized just then.

"That's a problem for you and for her, don't you see? You'll have to open up to her and let her do the same for you. She needs you. She needs to know you care, not for just the babies, but care for her. You might want to quit the drinking, too. She doesn't need that to worry about, too. I called your cell phone myself several times but you didn't answer it. She wanted you here. I stayed with her about two hours and hoped you'd come back. I shouldn't tell you this but your parents were awful to her. Joy told me the things they said. I saw the check your mother left on the table. Your wife does not deserve being treated like they treated her. They need to stay away from her. She doesn't need that on top of everything else."

He had not even checked his phone. He knew he

had messages but had not bothered to check them.

"I'm sorry. I've screwed up royally, I know. I left my phone in the truck when I got home. I will stop drinking. I can. And I had a talk with my parents. Hell, I ran them off. They said some bad things when this happened. I'll talk with her about it. Will she be okay?

"You'll have to show her that you love her. Sometimes words just aren't enough. Especially for someone like Joy, who's been hurt before. And *you* need to deal with your parents, *not Joy*. She can't handle the stress on her body now. Her health is at stake. Do you understand what I'm saying? She could lose these babies. Or you could lose her."

Obviously Joy had shared her past and her thoughts on his parents with Dr. Ferguson. Joy made friends easily and Dr. Ferguson was squarely on her side. At the moment he hated his parents. And he was worried sick about Joy but he knew he'd done wrong. Hell, he'd been awful…

Fred nodded his understanding. Dr. Ferguson's words hit him hard. He couldn't answer her for the giant lump in his throat.

*Sometimes words aren't enough. You'll have to show her that you love her. She's been hurt before.*

\*\*\*\*\*

"Did you bring my car?"Joy asked the minute he

212

stuck his head in the door. Her eyes were red-rimmed. She'd been crying and it was all his fault. And his parents'.

"No, I didn't. We need to talk but not here. I saw Dr. Ferguson out in the hall. She said she'd given you your walking papers. We just have to wait for the wheelchair lady she said."

"Where were you?"

"Home. I got a beer after the folks came back again…and I started thinking—I got plastered— Look, I'm sorry. I should have come back. I told you I would. I won't do it again, I promise."

"Fred, listen to yourself. Making more promises that we both know you won't keep. It's okay for you to drink one along. But these babies won't be raised by an alcoholic father." She wouldn't mention the things his parents had said to her, not again. She stopped before her inner fury took over.

He nodded in acknowledgment. They would not get into it here. Not in public. He'd need hours, or days, to make this right. If he could.

They drove home in silence. Fred watched Joy stare out the truck window. Her bottom lip trembled and he knew she was about to crash. She needed to be alone for a while. He needed to plan his course of action—if only he knew what that was.

Hart was there supervising the landscapers working around the new areas of the house, adding decorative stone and low maintenance shrubs. Fred watched Joy go into the house so he walked around to where Hart was overseeing the crew. While Hart was

213

here Fred needed to run to the marina. He wouldn't be gone long he told Hart. Joy needed some alone time.

*****

She left the ring, the American Express card that he'd given her, the cell phone he'd given her, all the new clothes and shoes that he'd bought her. The check from his parents was on top of it all. All that was missing were her old clothes and books, or what little she had bought with her money. Everything he'd bought her was still there: the little red heels, the underwear. She'd even left her much loved art supplies, as well as the coloring books and crayons.

Fred had gotten tied up at the marina longer than he'd planned. He was gone a little over an hour but she'd packed and driven off with Hart there in the yard, not even aware that she had left. When Fred saw Joy's car gone, his heart sank. He knew she'd left him.

Fred had jumped back into his truck and looked for her. She didn't know much about the area, so he headed north—the direction she'd come into town from—as fast as he could with the traffic. He got all the way to Lake Point Resort and knew he'd missed her. She was long gone. She could have turned and gone across the causeway to Georgetown, Georgia, and on to Lumpkin . Or made another turn and gone to Clayton, or Ozark, or God knows where.

\*\*\*\*\*

Joy got on the four-lane highway and drove. Mindlessly she had turned left and stayed on U.S. 431 south. She knew she had come to Eufaula on 431. She couldn't remember much more than that. She was so upset she had no business driving anyway, but she had to leave. She'd watched Fred drive away and knew immediately what she was going to do. She knew how to pack in a hurry and this was not the first time she'd done it, so in less than thirty minutes she had put her few belongings into her car.

Almost an hour later she arrived in Dothan, and turned onto Ross Clark Circle. She was exhausted, so she pulled into a Holiday Inn Express, got a room and fell into the bed. She slept for hours waking just before midnight. She knew Fred would be furious with her but she was past caring what Fred thought or what Fred wanted.

She turned the TV on and dozed until it was time for breakfast. She was starving and knew she needed to eat. And not just for her own sake. There was more at risk now.

She wanted these babies and knew she loved them already but didn't know how Fred would fit in the picture that was forming in her head. She could do this alone. If she had to.

She ate, slept, watched TV, took a long shower, washed her hair and air dried it. A K-Mart was close by the motel so she had bought a cheap phone, charged it, and activated it. She'd left everything that made her think of Fred at his house. Tiredness made her sleep more than she had before and it was a blessed oblivion.

She decided to call Ginger Wakefield and let her talk to Fred. *Thank you, God and Sarah Wentworth,* for the debit card she now had in her own name. She had her own money to pay for the motel room and food. Money enough to last a lifetime. And enough for her babies. Fred would want to split those sheets he mentioned. She had trouble seeing a future for the two of them. She felt defeated, unloved, unwanted and more than a little sorry for herself. She was now glad that Ginger had insisted on giving Joy her cell phone number.

"Oh, my God, girl! I am so glad to hear from you! Fred is turning the country upside down looking for you. He's called me like twenty times wanting to know if you'd shown up here. Where are you? Are you okay?"

"I'm at a motel. I just drove until I had to stop. I've cried so much my eyes are swollen and I can barely see. So I stopped here and I slept for long time." She'd put ice in a wash cloth and that had helped her swollen eyes. She knew she looked awful, but who cared?

"Well, you need to call Fred, Joy. He's been up all night, riding the roads looking for you, calling everyone he knows who may have seen you. He's going crazy worrying."

"I don't want to talk with him right now, Ginger. He got drunk, and disappointed me so…and I don't know what I'm going to do. But I don't want to go home. Not back to him. My ring belonged to Lori, Ginger. It was a used dinner ring. His mom told me…I don't even rate a wedding ring—even a cheap one? I just felt like it was hers the whole time. And I was right."

"Oh, no, Joy. That's bad. I'll ream him a new one for that. I didn't know, Joy….really, I wasn't here then and I didn't know…I just thought it was a big, gaudy diamond ring."

"It's okay, Ginger. You had no way of knowing and he doesn't love me. He just loves these babies and I am just the 'lucky brood mare he picked up by the side of the road' one day. And I came from the wrong side of the tracks. His parents said that, too. He thinks I'm trailer trash….and I am. I know what I came from. No one has to tell me that. And he wouldn't know love if it bit him on the ass. His parents hate me, too, and they're awful. His mom left a check trying to pay me off. She told me to get out of their lives."

"Oh, Joy…I know he didn't think that. Don't say things like that. I know he loves you. Hart says he does, too. He's never seen Fred happier than he is now. He loves you, sweetie…."

"Well, he loves these babies and wants them but he already told me we'd say adios and split the sheets if we weren't happy. I know that's what he wants to do. I'll have these babies and later on, he'll decide he doesn't want me in the picture and file for custody and I won't have my...my... babies..."Joy choked on the last words, her voice tearful. No matter how much money she had now, she had a background, reputation, of being trailer trash, a maid...no judge would grant her custody of her babies. *Not against the influential Garrett family.*

"No, no, Joy. I know that's not what he wants. He may not know what he wants right now. He's been so unhappy, Joy. You're the best thing to ever come into his life. I know that. Hart sees it, too. Don't give up on him....listen I have an idea. Why don't you come stay at my cottage for a few days and think things over? It'll give y'all some cooling off time and no one will have to know..."

"I don't know...if I can find your place. It's in the... middle of... nowhere."

Ginger laughed. "Yes, it is that. I tell you what. Stay where you are and I'll come get you. Hart will be home in a little while and he can take me down then I'll drive you back here. You can rest for a few days and get your bearings. I'll even call Fred for you and tell him the plans. You don't even have to talk to him..."

Joy was crying now at Ginger's thoughtfulness. "You'd...do that for me? You...you barely know me.....o...o...okay...but I don't want...to see Fred...or talk to him. Not now...not for a while maybe.... I have to think about what I want to do....but, yes, come get me. I'm at the Holiday Inn...Express...."

After giving Ginger the location and her room

number, Ginger promised to be there within a few hours.

*****

"Freddie...she's at a Holiday Inn Express. She called me but she doesn't want to talk to you just yet. She's very upset and I don't want to upset her more."

"Thank God, she called you. I'm about to pull my hair out. I ain't even been to bed. I've been to every motel in Barbour County and I've called around everywhere. I figured she went back north."

"I know, sweetie. She's in a bad place right now and that mother of yours telling her about Lori's ring was just the final straw. I can't believe you did that myself, Fred. That was a low blow--a used ring...really? And your mom trying to buy her off? Anyway, she's feeling sorry for herself, too. She thinks she's just a 'brood mare you picked up by the side of the road'...she said that...She's coming to my cottage to stay for a while. I told her I'd go get her and bring her here in an hour or so. Do not go to Dothan."

"So, she's in Dothan? I'm going down—"

"No! She doesn't want to see you or talk to you. Y'all both need some time to calm down. She'll come around but you need to be doing some soul searching and get your act together. I love you like Hart does and we want to see this work. And Joy loves you and those babies. Look, I'll call you back after I get her here and fill you in. I know you want to see her but leave her alone for another day or two and she'll start missing you. I hate the thoughts of staying away from Hart overnight and Joy will miss you, too."

"I'll do as you say, Ginger, but I damn sure don't want to. I'm just glad she called you. I was just talking with the sheriff about putting out a missing person bulletin. I can't tell you what all has gone through my mind. She could have had a wreck or someone could have kidnapped her, and hurt her...or she could have gotten sick by the road someplace..."

Ginger could hear the fear and frustration in his voice, and the break in it, too. The tears he was holding back.

"I know, Freddie. We were up and down all night, too, worrying about her. Jimmy's had an ear ache and he cried most of the night. We've all had a miserable night. I'm going to go get her. She's safe. Go get some sleep. I'll call you this afternoon and talk with you....Bye."

"Thanks, Ginger. Tell her I love her....bye," Fred hung up, and allowed his tears to fall.

Thank God she was safe and not lying hurt someplace. Lord God, what thoughts he had since she left. He'd even gone to Mavis's apartment. But Mavis was alone, having been finally released from re-hab. Mavis told him that Nora and her kids were the ones that had been helping Larry. Fred told her that they'd figured that and it was something to worry about another day, now that Larry was dead. Now Fred's wife was his priority.

Mavis had scolded him over Joy leaving him. He'd

filled her in on the happenings of the past few weeks. He felt bad enough without her crawling his case, lambasting him. God knows he'd blown it with Joy. He deserved every word Mavis had said.

He fell into his bed but not before thanking God for Joy being safe and sound. He'd made some promises to God as he'd driven around all night. He intended to keep them.

# Chapter Twenty

*"Everything happens for a reason. Sometimes the reason is you're stupid and make bad decisions."*
~seen on a sign by the road

Hart drove Ginger to Dothan. Baby Jimmy was finally asleep in the back seat and they spoke softly to keep from waking him. Between Jimmy's ear ache and the worrying and phone calls over Joy, they'd neither one slept over an hour or so all night. Hart had told Ginger that riding had always put Pam to sleep. It worked with Jimmy, too.

Hart drove back home with Jimmy still asleep while Ginger drove Joy's car.

Joy talked on the way to Ginger's house but mostly Ginger listened. Joy made sense and everything she said had hurt her to hear. Fred had used Joy, at least in Joy's viewpoint. He'd lied by omission and everyone who was around her more than five minutes knew that she loved Fred. She hung on his every word and visibly lit up when he was around.

Ginger chose not to say anything but Joy did look terrible. Her eyes were still swollen and red-rimmed, and her nose was red. She was miserable and it showed.

Ginger settled Joy into her cottage and showed her where everything was in case she wanted a snack. Ginger told her she was cooking supper and that she'd bring her a plate or she could come eat with them around six. Joy was glad to be around Ginger and told her she'd go down to their house if it was okay at supper time.

Ginger's cottage was sometimes used for out-of-town guests, like Ginger's mom and step-dad. Pam used it for her small catering business since the kitchen was large. The house was private and Joy could sort out her feelings without having anyone around, while Ginger and Hart were just a few hundred feet away.

Joy sat on Ginger's floral chintz loveseat, stretched out, and soon was asleep.


Hart had taken a nap the minute he'd gotten Jimmy into his bed. Ginger joined him. They were both exhausted from having been up worrying over both Jimmy and Joy.


At six, Ginger came to tell her that supper was ready.

"I called Fred to tell him you were okay," Ginger told Joy as they drove to the old house.

Joy just nodded, not sure what she was supposed to say. She was embarrassed that she'd left without her new prescriptions being filled and didn't want to tell Ginger in front of Hart. He'd think she was a terrible mom-to-be. She had to leave Fred's house and she just threw her stuff in bags and left. She'd forgotten her pre-natal vitamins, too.

Ginger solved her problem later by asking her if there was anything she needed. Hart was going back the next day to meet with the painters who were to return for touchups. Hart always followed up after all his sub-contractors Joy learned from Ginger, running through his punch list to insure all the work was done to his standards.

"Hart, if you will, give these to Fred to fill for me. I'm already supposed to be taking them. I was so upset when I left yesterday I forgot to swing by and get them."

"Sure, Joy. No problem. I'll give them to him and he can bring them back to me," he said. Ginger had obviously filled Hart in on her demand that Fred not come, call, or talk with her.

Ginger had prepared a simple meal of fried chicken, potato salad and white peas. It was one of Hart's favorites and Joy told her that she loved everything Ginger cooked. Joy's nausea was not as bad as it had been in the those first months and she ate a good supper, not having to smell it being prepared. Ginger had made an egg custard for dessert. She and Hart had theirs with coffee and Joy had tea with hers.

"Thanks for letting me stay in your cottage, Ginger. Will Pam need it tomorrow? I know she's in and out now that she has her business going."

"She may come in for supplies from the front bedroom but she won't stay. I told you she had an apartment now with another girl. They are enjoying catering and dating, but you stay there as long as you want, or need. I told Freddie to take it easy and give you some space. He fussed about it but said he would. He said to tell you that he misses you and that he loves you."

"*Show*, don't tell, Ginger. You can't *tell* folks you love them. You have to show them, you know, for it to be real. Actions speak louder than words." Anger and hurt tinged her words.

Ginger missed what Joy was saying for a minute then it hit her. Joy was wanting Fred to make some gesture toward her, showing that he loved her. Telling her was not enough. She'd tell him when she called him but she hoped it was something he'd figure out on his own.


Ginger had learned to respect Joy in the time that she had known her. She had a sweet spirit, was kind and loving. She was street-smart and wiser than most. She loved babies, and dogs. Ginger had told Fred all this in one of her many phone conversations with him.

"She has class, and a certain style about her. You know that's something that money can't buy. You either have it or you don't. Maybe that's the artist in her. She doesn't complain but always is content with her situation—except for this with you. She's very humble. We've talked for hours and hours. She's had it rough all her life. No money, a daddy and a husband that were no count, abusive. That Larry, man, what a louse he was! She's embarrassed he was ever in her life. But we all make mistakes. Freddie, she's just now finding herself.

"Until now she's never had nice clothes or a nice car, or any of the things most folks take for granted. She's always been dirt poor, so she's proud of every little thing. You know that. She'll learn to appreciate the finer things as she goes. She's just happy to be safe. She feels safe with you—only you. I know one thing—she loves the ground you walk on. You don't ever have to doubt that. She told me she fell in love with you the moment she saw you but didn't admit it to herself until later. She calls you her 'knight in shining armor', her 'guardian angel'. Do not mess this up, Freddie. You hear me?"

"Yeah, thanks, Ginger. I knew she was falling for me...I didn't stop her, either. I probably encouraged her, I know. I just wanted her around. I wasn't sure why but she appealed to me on some....inner level. I guess it was love...protectiveness, lust, whatever....I don't know if I've ever loved anyone before other than my granny, my parents...and Katie. I'm....not sure I know how. And every thing I ever said wrong is coming back to hit me square between the eyes. God, I've done and said some stupid things to her. Terrible things."

"You're doing good, Freddie. Just give her a little room to find herself...and love her, and these babies...it's not about money with her, you know that. We all say stupid things, and do stupid things. Lord knows I have. I made plenty of mistakes with Hart. He has made his share, too. We can't let

226

ourselves stay lost in the past, though. You can't punish her for being from the background she came from. Nor is it your fault that you've always had money. You have to move on. Time is getting away from us all. Every day is a gift. Those babies are a gift. You can't waste time on fighting and quarreling. She wants your heart and love. That's all."

"I don't know what to do next. I feel lost without her."

"You have to show her you care. Joy's a beautiful person and if you mess up, some man will come along and sweep her, and those babies right out from under you. And be honest with her. Man up. Now. If you don't love her, tell her now…before you break her heart more than you already have…Don't make her any promises you can't, or won't, back up. You better do her right. You can't just tell her…that's not enough. I don't know what you'll want to do, but not some great, grand gesture. For her, it'll have to be something small, but meaningful…and I'm not talking about a Lexus or big gaudy diamond. It's got to be something personal that comes from your heart. Remember, it's the little things that mean the most, Fred. Every girl wants just a little romance…"

*****

*Damn I miss her! I miss hearing her talk and laugh, watching her move around the kitchen with such ease…I miss her being around…holding her in*

227

*the night.*

He missed her good cooking, and the house was a mess now, with dishes in the sink, socks under the sofa. He realized how much she did around the house. The bathroom sink had toothpaste in it and Fluffy was miserable, meowing all the time like he'd lost his best friend. Well, hell, they had lost Joy. All the old home truths were hitting him hard. Yes, Joy was his best friend and it took her leaving for him to realize that. How he enjoyed coming home to home-cooked meals and conversation with an intelligent woman who hung on his every word. She listened to him talk and didn't interrupt him constantly with prattle. She had respect for his words, his opinions, even though she didn't always agree with him. He realized how unique she was. How much she meant to him.

Fred started the dishwasher and wiped the countertops. Everywhere he looked he found Joy's touches. A tiny painting of Fluffy was on an easel in the corner of the cabinets. Herbs now grew in little pots over the kitchen sink. She kept their home running so well that he never gave much thought to it since she'd come into his life. She did everything well and without complaint—cooking, cleaning, ironing. Most things he'd never asked, nor expected her to do. He needed to explain to her that it was okay to take his clothes to the laundry. She didn't have to do it.

Her paints were still there in her studio, just like she left them, waiting. Fred could see her in his mind, her hair up and messy and sexy as hell, and she had this way of biting her lower lip that made him want to bite it, too. He missed seeing her painted toenails in those cheap neon green flip flops. She moved in a way that made Fred want to kiss her until they neither could breathe and all their clothes were on the floor.

How it hurt him to know of how she'd gone without food, the basic necessities, in times past. Her hips and breasts now had curves and he yearned to touch them, and her silken skin. And to hear her say his name just so in that slow way that made him melt just thinking of it. Her sweet voice as she talked to the cat. He missed the sweet love making and holding her, having her near him. She was nothing like Lori. And he realized how unfair it was of him to keep comparing Joy to Lori. Joy came out the winner no matter what. Her background be damned!

He got in his truck, drove the back roads for hours, and yes, he'd prayed along the way for Divine help.

Fred talked with Hart and was honest with him. Hart now knew all that had happened. Including the drinking. Hart's advice had been pretty much the same as Ginger's: "Tell her you love her when you get the first chance and don't ever let her go," Hart said. "Don't make the mistake of losing her and your babies. You'll never get over it. Do whatever it is to make y'all happy again. Get help for your drinking problem if you have to. Do whatever it takes. You know I was drunk when Connie had Pam and Connie died. You know how that affected me. Don't wait to get help. It took me years to get past that. I know that Joy loves you, I can tell you that. Ginger and I will do whatever we can to make this work. The first step will be up to you, Hoss. Joy is a great person, but you know that. Ginger and I have been talking with her quite a lot and I'm more impressed with her every day. She's not pretentious, she's honest, and a genuine person. She and Ginger are becoming best friends and I'm happy about it."

"I screwed up royally, Hart. I hope I can fix it."

"Do you love her? Really and truly love her? If you do, do what God leads you to do. We've prayed with Joy about it, Ginger's prayed with her every day. Just pray about it, and ask God for guidance. I admit that I ran from the thoughts of loving Ginger for months. I haven't told anyone this, but I drove up to where Connie is buried at Banks and I sat down by her grave. I heard her tell me, 'Let me go, let me go.' Just that plain. I could have sworn she was standing right there. I looked around to find her. She told me she didn't blame me for her death. Do you know I still blamed myself after all those years? It was useless to do it, but I still did. I stopped my truck on the way back and prayed for God to help me put my past with Connie behind me and for guidance with Ginger. Fred, don't let Joy go. Hold on to her, your marriage, those babies, no matter what. Don't waste any time. Don't be a fool like I was for twenty years. Life's too short."

"I appreciate you telling me, Hart. I don't know what to do, but I have been praying. I can't lose her. Losing Katie didn't leave much of my heart intact, and Lori's conniving just about killed the rest. I felt like a Mack truck ran through me and tore away my heart, all but a few strands, leaving me dragging, living half a life. Getting drunk to numb the pain. Sometimes it worked, but this is a bigger hole. I didn't love Lori. I never did. But I did love Katie even though she wasn't my child. Only one other person knows this, but my lawyer, John Lee Harrison, told me that Jack Turner was Katie's daddy. I won't ever tell Jack—I can't. I don't believe he knows it and I don't want to hurt him now. John Lee said that Lori had admitted it to his wife, Anna, one day at lunch. Lori sort of blurted it out but Anna caught her slipup. They were eating at the Mexican place, and Lori had a few too many margaritas, Anna said. Anna told John Lee what Lori said. She could not believe Lori was still drinking and talking about being pregnant by Jack Turner but going to marry me. Yes, Lori drank while she was pregnant. I had several arguments with her over it. She wouldn't quit. She loved booze and partying more than anything else, except for spending money, as you already know. I had told Lori that I had information that would insure me getting a divorce from her but I never told her what it was. When I look at that portrait in my office of Katie, I see Jack. She was his child. There's no doubt in my mind. I don't want anyone else raising my kids, Hart. I'll do whatever it takes to make sure of that."

"Put it in God's Hands," Hart told him, patted Fred's shoulder, got in his truck and drove away, leaving Fred alone with his thoughts.

As long as Hart had known Fred, and as many times as they'd been alone, playing and talking, Fred had never confided about Katie being Jack's child. He knew that had to have been eating at Fred. And was the reason Fred drank. "Lord, You know what Fred

231

needs. I pray he'll call on You for help."

Fred parked just at the edge of Hart's drive, where he could see the cottage. He wanted to go in but knew she'd asked not to see him. He understood why. He'd treated her badly, and his folks owed her a huge apology but he knew that might not ever happen. He had to think about taking a stand if he was forced in that direction. He knew already what he would do. He sat and stared at the cottage for a long time, knowing his future was there. Hart had called him the night before just to verify that it was indeed Fred in his driveway. Hart didn't question the why. He knew and understood.

The lights went off at the cottage, and for the second night in a row Fred drove home.

# Chapter Twenty-one

*"In all thy ways acknowledge Him, and He shall direct thy paths."*
~ Proverbs 3:6

Fred's grandmother, Frances Grace Graves Garrett, had been on an extended cruise and world tour. She had gotten home to news that Fred had married and that John, her son, was livid. Elaine was beside herself and complained loudly to Mimi, as she was called, about Fred's 'latest travesty'.

Mimi Grace picked up the phone and called Fred. He answered on the second ring.

"Hey, Mimi. I'm glad you're back from your trip. I've been wanting to talk with you. I got married and I guess you know by now the folks ain't too happy. But I love her, Mimi. Her name is Joy and we're having twin babies. A boy and a girl."

"Yes, darling, I heard. Boy, did I hear! John is about to blow a gasket and Elaine is her...usual self. One question, love. Does Joy love you?"

"Yes, she does....Yes. I know she loves me. Mom and Dad thinks she's from the wrong side of the tracks and her ex-husband beat hell out of her several times, raped her, killed their unborn son, and she left his ass. He was after her until just recently and we got him here in Eufaula. He walked up to Joy at the art show and she punched him in the nose, and broke it, and then she kicked him in the crotch as hard as she could. She brought him down anyway. He's dead

233

now. Someone killed him in the jail. She's had a rough life, Mimi, and she's a good person, although the folks don't want me to associate with her since she's beneath them."

"Well, Elaine thinks everyone is beneath her. Always has. John...just overlook him. He's as pompous as your grandfather was. I had to bring J. F. to his knees a time or two myself, God rest his soul. I loved him, but he was trying at times. I'm so glad you're not like either of them."

"Anyway, Mom and Dad showed up here and upset Joy so badly she fainted and ended up in the hospital. She's got blood pressure problems. She's a tiny little thing. They said terrible things to her."

"I heard all about her from John and Elaine, but I wanted to hear what you had to say. So....you love her, do you?"

"Yes, ma'am, but it took this to happen for me to realize it. At first I just wanted her around me for company—companionship—and she's a great cook. And I thought we'd get married and have some kids, and if it didn't work out, we'd divorce. There wasn't much love in it on my end...I admit it. Now. She was convenient and I sort of pushed her into getting married. And I made the mistake of giving her one of Lori's dinner rings when we got married. She didn't like that too much. Mom had to tell her. And now Joy has left me. Partly thanks to Mom....and me being stupid, I got drunk...I lied to her...and giving her that ring was the straw that broke it all—that and a check Mom threw at her, trying to get her to leave me."

"Well, son, you messed up big time doing that, and

so did Elaine. We all make mistakes. She must have cared for you or she wouldn't have married you, would she? And why didn't you buy her a wedding ring? Just a simple gold band wouldn't have broken you, would it?"

"No, no ma'am. I know. Ginger Wakefield's already nailed me on that one."

"I'm sure you'll do the right thing, son. Just tell me again—you do love her? This is not one of those lust-sex things, is it? I know how you young folks are. I was young once."

"Well, I have to admit that there's that, too, but I do love her. It took all this happening for me to realize it. I rode around all night praying that she'd be all right. She's an artist, Mimi. She's awesome. You have to see her work. She won an award in the first show she entered."

"Elaine or John didn't mention that. They were too busy putting her down. I'll be up in a few days to see y'all. I'd like to see her work, too."

"Thanks, Mimi. I wanted to call you earlier but you've been out of town for months! That world tour must have been mighty grand."

"It was. I visited all the places I ever thought about going to see. My friend, Allen, and I, really enjoyed it."

"I thought you were going with a lady friend, Mimi. Miss Happy, you said."

"I did. She went along. Happy was our chaperone," she laughed. "We needed someone to throw cold water on us when things got too hot! Happy had herself a fling, too. In fact, I think she may be getting married in a few weeks. I asked her if she was pregnant. Of course, she's too old, but it's fun to kid her. She said they'd fallen in love and didn't want to waste time. Don't tell anyone but I don't think she's ever had a boyfriend before. Allen asked me to marry him, too, but I keep putting him off. He's a little younger than me by a couple of years. His kids think I'm after his money," she laughed. She was pulling his leg and he knew it but he loved her fun spirit. He was more like her than he realized.

"You'll love Joy, Mimi. I know you will."

"Don't let her get away, son. If you love her, you do everything in your power to keep her by your side. Our time on earth is limited enough like it is. Live with someone you love and who loves you. And I'm excited about those babies. Make sure you name the baby girl after me. I'll leave her my money."

"She won't need yours, Mimi. Joy and I have enough of our own. Joy inherited some big money from a lawyer that she worked for a while back. It left her well taken care of. She's got more liquid cash than Mom and Dad, I think." Fred was wealthier than his parents but had never revealed that fact to them, nor his grandmother.

"Well, you will get mine, too, one of these days. I've already made out my will. You'll get it all. Of course, I plan on spending as much of it as I can before I slow down. J. F. thought every dime had to be saved, put aside for a rainy day. Those rainy days come and go. Family is forever. Be happy. Enjoy your life, Fred. Time goes by so quickly. I remember so well the day you were born. It seems like it was just yesterday and now you and your wife are having babies. And I can't wait to meet Joy and see her paintings. I love you, honey. If you need to, go talk with Brother Bob Stanley. He can help you. Turn it over to God, son. Take care of yourself and take care of your wife, too. Talk with you soon."

Fred hung up, relieved that his grandmother was on his side. His other grandmother and granddaddy had died in a car wreck a few years back. They had always been stiff and reserved, like his mom. Too proud to bend. Cold. Unloving.

He walked down to the pier and studied the water as he often did. Boaters were out having fun although the season was over. Fishing was always popular and some enjoyed the speed of the powerful boat engines, and at one time, Fred would have been out there with them. Now he wished his wife was here and they were eating supper in their kitchen. He longed to hear her soft southern voice, the tinkle of her laughter. He missed Joy's being in his bed and in his arms. He wanted to see himself reflected in her green eyes.

Something bright caught his eye and he walked over to the post on the very end and there hung a yellow string bikini. He picked it up with intentions of throwing it in the garbage. He didn't know whose it was but he was always picking up folks' trash. This was not trash. Someone deliberately hung it there since the post's top was a good four feet from the water level. He took it and went to check the cameras pointed toward the water and pier.

After pulling the card from the hidden camera on the pontoon boat, Fred took it to work where he'd have a witness. He hoped there was something on it since the security company had not reported anything out of the ordinary.

Sol looked over Fred's shoulder as the motion-activated camera card showed a boat easing toward the pier. Julie and some of her friends stopped for a few seconds. Julie had put the bikini on the post herself. The women in the boat had laughed and sped away.

Fred called Jack Turner and asked him if he'd seen anything or anyone messing around his dock. Jack said he'd not been up to the lake house but he did reveal that Julie had called him a couple of times, and had been real chatty like, inquiring about Fred and his 'live-in housekeeper'.

"Julie sounded like she didn't believe you and Joy were really married when she called me. I told her it was true, though. Julie's been to the lake house, too, talking to Mama. Mama mentioned it like it was something I already knew. I'm sure she's been around our place. And yours."

"I guess Julie's talked to Mom, then," Fred said. "Mom can't stand Joy and now Julie's out to stir up trouble. I wish you'd take Julie off the market, old man," Fred told Jack, who was a couple of years older than himself.

"Ha! You're crazy! I want somebody who knows how to do something. I don't want to babysit some ditzy bitch who's out for a free ride in life. Been

238

there, done that, had to put a second mortgage on the tee shirt. You know that story."

"So, you don't want to be her sugar daddy, huh?"

"Hell, no! I bought some tobacco and tried to kiss her with a big ol' chaw in my mouth. She didn't want no part of that, although I did it on purpose to run her off. It made me sick to chew it but it got rid of her. And I'm glad it worked! Man, I'm looking for a real woman, not some gold digger that needs a millionaire to keep her up. I don't have the kind of money you do, Hoss. Vivian about wiped me out. I won't be out of debt until I'm 75…"

Jack was not exactly poor. He owned several hundred acres of land in Dale County and an old home. He had strong work ethics and had high standards when it came to the fairer sex, probably too old fashioned for most. Jack's marriage had ended in a bitter divorce. His bride could not adjust to the 'rigors of farm life' as she called it and wanted out— with a considerable sum for alimony after being married to Jack for a few childless years. Years later Jack was still struggling to recover, mentally and financially.

Fred and Jack chatted a few more minutes and they ended their conversation with Fred warning Jack about Julie's conniving ways.

"She's after you, Hoss. She ain't after me, thank God. If she messes around here I'd put her ass to work in the chicken houses picking up dead chickens."

"If that's your idea of a first date, no damn wonder you can't keep a woman around. But, I'd pay to see it,

239

old man," Fred laughed and disconnected.

He thought about what he'd said to Jack, calling Jack 'an old man'. He was getting older himself. The last couple of days had aged him. He could feel it in his aching bones. He'd give every cent he had this second to have Joy back in his arms, in his life. Fred had not told Jack about Joy leaving. He hated to confess how stupid he was. Except for Mimi, and she loved him not matter how much he screwed up.

*Damn it, life is hard. Harder if you're stupid as I've been.*


\*\*\*\*\*


Joy walked down to Hart and Ginger's house. She was miserable, heartbroken, lost. Ginger greeted her at the door and offered her tea and cookies. She was hungry for food but nothing tasted the same. Everything seemed flat, like cardboard.

Ginger made a pot of Earl Grey tea and they talked as it steeped.

"What would you do, Ginger? I thought I'd found the man of my dreams—"

"He is, Joy. Men, and women, too, can do some mighty stupid things when it comes to relationships. And I know that from personal experience. Mine was heartache with a capital "H", and that stands for 'Hart', there at one time. Hart wrote me a note, and I quote: 'to go back where I came from'. He didn't want to get involved with me and he just couldn't say the words to me he needed to say. He'd been so hurt when his wife, Connie, died just minutes after giving birth to Pam. He'd blamed himself for her death. He was out drinking at a 'beer joint', as he calls them, and he didn't know she was in labor. By the time he got there, she was already almost gone. He never got over that. He did quit drinking and he raised Pam as best he could while he worked, but he's been through hell—mentally—because of all what he thought he'd caused."

"That could have happened no matter what. Childbirth is still questionable. I know one of my high school friends died in childbirth not long after we got out of school. It happens."

"Yes, that's what I told Hart, and so did everyone else. Anyway, Fred has made his own mistakes, and has been terribly hurt by his marriage to Lori. I didn't know her but Hart said she was a number one bitch. Excuse my French."

"She must have been for Hart to have said that."

"He said she was terrible to him when he was building their house on the Point. He told me about her stomping her foot and putting her hands on her hips one day and demanding that he build something a particular way and Hart told her that what she wanted wouldn't work within the space that the plans allowed. He tried to show her what would work, and tried to offer a compromise, but he said she called him 'incompetent' and was in the middle of firing him when Fred walked up and caught what she was saying. Needless to say, Hart was not fired and Lori left mad and didn't speak to Hart for weeks and weeks. Hart told Fred he would quit if she showed back up on the job site, too. You can only push Hart so far and then he gets even quieter and madder. I know all about that."

"I find that hard to believe. He's so sweet and gentle."

"*Huh!* I dated this guy, Tom—just one date—and he came here, to my cottage, and tried to get rough, and *more*, with me. I screamed instinctively for Hart to come to my rescue and he came running. He put his pistol to the guy's head and forced Tom to turn me loose. Hart marched him outside and when Hart came back in he had blood on the toes of his boots. Doug, my step-dad, and Mr. Ralph, told me that Hart had broken the guy's nose and kicked him in the crotch with his steel-toed work boots. Hart has *never* said a word to me about it. *Never*. Tom, the guy, lives just down from my mother at the beach."

"Whoa! I bet that guy wished he'd never encountered Hart. Was Hart in Special Forces or something?"

"Nope. Hart is the *jealous* redneck carpenter who loved me but didn't want to admit it then."

"I bet that was a sight."

"Well, it's sort of funny now but Doug told me that Tom apologized to him for what happened but he's never called me to tell me. I know Tom's probably scared Hart would beat the bejeezus out of him again. Men are jealous of their women. I know that Freddie has already figured out that some man could come along and sweep you off your feet and take those babies right there with him." Ginger knew that because she had put that gentle reminder in his ear just to shake him up herself. Of course, she wasn't about to tell Joy that.

"One man's 'trailer trash' is another man's treasure."

"Don't say that, Joy. You are not trash. Do not ever put yourself down like that, again. You may not have had the best circumstances early on but you are a good person. You have to believe in yourself. You have to love yourself first, Joy. You are a gifted artist and a beautiful and intelligent woman. Freddie sees that in you. We are not our parents. You could not help the circumstances of your birth. If Freddie hasn't figured that out yet, I'll be happy to tell him. I got only good vibes from you the very first time he brought you here. And you do know that he's never brought a woman to any of the sings before...ever. Now, Jack Turner has brought a few of his girlfriends over and I do mean girls. One of them was so young Hart jokingly asked him if she was his daughter. In front of her, Fred and me, too," Ginger said, laughing. "Jack's face turned so red. It was funny. You know Hart has a way of getting to the point with just a few words. Jack's a good guy, though."

"He's a good looking man."

"He's gorgeous, but he's not Hart."

"And he's not Fred, either. Hart is a great man, Ginger."

"Yes, he is. Even a redneck carpenter can be a wonderful, loving man. He's the best. He's my heart."

Joy nodded. Fred was her heart, too, and she'd loved him from the minute she saw him in the ER, standing tall with those gorgeous blue eyes.

They looked at each other and smiled. They both knew that both of their men were highly intelligent, hard working, talented and loving.

"What would you do, Ginger? Knowing now what all Fred has done? I'm not perfect but I am willing to make a go of it—only, and only—if he can change his ways, stop the drinking. I'm willing to give him a chance. What else can I do? I'm having his babies…I love him, despite what has happened. I will probably always love him, and somehow I think part of him wants to love me. I'm not sure he knows how to love. He's lived such a privileged life, with no thought of others."

"You can bet your sweet life he's going to change. These babies will snatch him right into the real world. If he doesn't know how to love, it won't take him long. Just one look at those babies will make him fall in love. Instantly. But honestly, Joy, I'm pretty sure he does love you. I'd give him a chance. Give yourself a chance to be happy. You'll never be happy without him. Having those babies alone will be so hard without him there. Hart was my rock through my whole pregnancy. And you know how foolish he is about Jimmy. Hart helps me with him every day. Freddie's gonna fall like a rock for these two. Trust me on that. And he's going to realize how much he loves you…if he hasn't already."

Joy was silent and thinking. Ginger could see the wheels inside her head moving.

"So, you want me to call Freddie to tell him he can come talk with you at the cottage?"

"I'm not sure, Ginger. I'm still so mad with him.

And his folks…oh, I'm so confused. I love him but if his folks are going to hate me, I don't expect him to want me much longer."

"We'll keep praying over it, Joy. God wants families to stay together so I know He'll help you, and Freddie, through this storm. All marriages have their share of these storms, too. It just takes deep roots, and deep love, to weather them. I do know Fred is as miserable as you are."

"You think so?"

Ginger nodded and said, "Hart told me that Freddie has been parking in our driveway until you turn out your lights at night. Do not tell Freddie I told you, but he has. Hart took Joey out and saw Freddie turn in and turn off his truck lights at the end of our drive. Joey barked a few times and Hart had to bring him back in. Hart told me about Freddie doing it. Hart called him just to check that it was him. You have to know how protective Hart is. Anyway, I think it's the sweetest thing, Joy. Freddie's done it for the past two nights. He's wanting to be near you, but scared you won't see him and he knows you've said you didn't want to talk to him. And I wouldn't worry about his folks. They'll come around to liking you, or they won't. It's their loss if they don't."

"I didn't see his truck. I didn't know…" Her voice became croaky with tears. "I don't know what to say—*It was sweet. I didn't know he had it in him— to bend so much, care enough to sit there for hours in the dark—to be near me.*

"Don't say anything, Joy. He wants to be near you. Let him. He's coming to grips with what he's done, sweetie. You know his guilt is eating him alive. Give him time to find his way."

Joy nodded but Ginger noticed the fat tears that rolled down her cheeks. She handed Joy a tissue, and poured their tea. She'd made tea cakes, another of Hart's favorites. They were just the thing to divert Joy's attention.

They discussed the tea cakes and Ginger told her that the recipe was in the cookbook and that it was a passed-down family recipe, but that most families had their own variation of it. Joy told Ginger that she wished she had just one of her family's recipes but that she didn't. She had no family photos. Her father had burned them all. She envied Ginger's having family to pass recipes on to the other, and even Ginger's abilities to write a cookbook. Joy didn't dwell on the past. Today was here, Fred, and the babies were in the here and now. The past was gone and best left alone.

"Will you be doing another cookbook?" Joy asked when her thoughts returned to the moment.

"Yes, I am already working on one. I wanted to ask you about it, too. Would you paint something for my cover? I got Helen Taylor Andrews, from Ozark—she's a friend of Hart's—to paint the first one. I'd love for you to do this one, if you will. Hart is crazy for your work and he said Jack Turner is, too. But no one is as crazy over it as Freddie is. Hart says that Freddie thinks you're up there with the great masters when it comes to your painting. Hart's always telling me about them as he sees a new one. I'd like to buy some from you, too. We have a few

246

places in the front part of the house that needs some artwork. When we finish our tea let me show you what I am thinking and you can tell me if you have anything that would fit the spaces. I know I want one for over our bed. Maybe a large landscape…like a field with a large oak tree, that one out there," she said, pointing toward the tree in her back yard. "Hart and I got married under that tree, so it's special. And in the living room, I'd like one over the mantel. We have an old thing that Hart dug out of the barn over it now, but I'd like something else."

They walked around the house. It was an old farmhouse—a vernacular style (common to the area)— built in the 1880's with a twelve feet wide dog trot/hall down the middle which had been made into a foyer, a bathroom, and closets. A living room, three bedrooms and two bathrooms made up the rest of the house. Of course, Hart and Ginger both practically lived in the over-sized kitchen and dining area which was in a wing attached to the rear of the main house. That part of the old house had never been painted. The rest of the house was now painted in soft earth tones trimmed in white. The exterior of the one level frame house was rather plain with its white siding, steep metal roof, long windows and large square columns on the generous porches.

Joy was glad to be thinking of things other than her personal life. She hated being so confused. Perhaps Ginger was right. Maybe Fred was finding his way. She certainly was trying to find her way. She had no idea what would happen with her art now that she'd left Fred. Being around Ginger helped and Joy was thankful for Ginger's friendship. Ginger was easy to talk to and Joy instantly liked her the moment she met her.

Joy loved the idea of being asked to do the cover of Ginger's cookbook. What a dream come true! What would she paint? Ginger had not said what she wanted. Maybe Joy could present Ginger with sketches for the proposed cover. This meant she was thinking about staying In the area.

Ginger's baby woke from his nap and Ginger changed his diaper and fed him a snack. He played on the floor for a while with some wooden blocks that Hart had made from scrap lumber. Ginger's pots were his favorite toys but they were too noisy and Ginger wouldn't let him play with them at the moment. Of course, Jimmy was the subject of all conversation.

They took Jimmy and walked out to Ginger's back yard where chickens roamed freely. A large garden was to the side of the house. Some vegetables were ready for picking while others were finished for the season. Ginger told Joy how she and Hart enjoyed garden tomatoes, summer squash, okra, peas and corn. She discussed how they froze the vegetables and had put up jams and jellies from wild blackberries and plums from the fence row that ran all the way down to the creek at the bottom of the hill behind the house. The chickens were a fairly new addition and Ginger said Hart was fearful that hawks, foxes or coyotes would get the chickens since Hart and Ginger lived in the country where the wild animals lived and roamed freely. Hart had built a large pen and coop but the door stood open. Ginger went on to say that she let the chickens out during the day to roam freely but they returned to the pen in the late afternoon.

Sheets hung on a clothes line and Ginger laughed. "That's what I missed most about the south, other than the food—sheets smelling like sweet sunshine. I guess Hart thinks it's silly but I love that smell and he's all about saving energy. Mama thinks it's too much work, but it's worth it to me. Hart hung them out for me when I had Jimmy. Bless his heart, he talks a gruff talk, but he's just a softie underneath. He loves good cooking, and me enough to go along with whatever I want. Of course, most of the garden, and the fruit trees were his ideas. And the martin bird house."

She pointed at the apartment-style bird house high on a pole out in the open behind Ginger's house. "The martins eat mosquitoes, he says. He built those bird houses to go in my Victorian garden at the cottage, too. And he didn't fuss about building them. Sometimes I ask for him to build things for me and he'll give me that look, like 'are you crazy?', but he'll do it. Sometimes it helps if he thinks it's his idea, though."

"Yes, I looked at those yesterday. I just love that house….the flower beds, the brick paths, the way it's decorated inside. It reminds me so much of my grandmother's house. All it needs is a white picket fence with pink roses growing on it and it would be my dream home. Ginger, your life with Hart is as perfect as it can be. I only wish my life could be as beautiful as the life that y'all have built for yourselves here."

"We are blessed, but Hart had a plan in his mind years earlier, and he told me what he wanted to do with the place, his vision. I could see it and embraced it with him, and added a few of my own dreams: a garden that produces food for us, chickens for eggs, heirloom flowers. Maybe later on we'll have a few cows. He likes to wind down in the afternoon walking through the garden looking for anything ready to pick, and then early before he goes to work, he'll bring in what's ready. Okra has to be cut almost every day once it starts producing," she said and laughed. "So we've had it about three times this week, and I'm freezing it, too. I never run out of anything to do, but we both love it and nothing beats home-grown veggies."

They walked further around the yard and Ginger pointed out various plants that Mr. Ralph, her elderly neighbor, had given her. The more Ginger talked and showed her, the sadder it made Joy.

Hart had planted blueberry bushes, fig, peach, and pear trees and as Ginger showed them to Joy, Joy's heart sank as she thought of how it would be to have a garden with Fred or make jams. That was not likely to happen…now.

Jimmy was enthralled with the chickens. It was fun to watch him reach to touch them and make 'chuck, chuck' sounds. Ginger had told Joy already that Jimmy could say 'Da-da' but not 'Mama' yet, and he knew how to say 'no' and 'go', and other words really well. Of course Hart was thrilled with that. Ginger not so much. "He just grunts a long

250

'mmm' sound for me. Maybe he can say 'Mama' soon. You know they develop at their own speed. We were worried since he wasn't talking as early as some but the doctor says he's perfect for his age."

Ginger seemed so content with her home, husband, and child and she said so.

"I waited years and years to find the right man, to find my way home, and to have a family. I am blessed beyond measure. I only wish I had quit modeling years ago and followed my heart. I am trying to talk Hart into having another baby—I'd love a little girl— but he's not interested at the moment. He loves Jimmy so much and he thinks he's getting too old for another child, but he's not. I can't keep waiting because my biological clock is running down."

Joy thought about her little ones and wondered what they would look like and wondered if they would be living with her, or if Fred would force her into giving him joint custody. She couldn't think of that. She was weary from thinking and worrying.

Before she walked back to the cottage, she and Ginger held hands and prayed again over the situation. Ginger had prayed that the *'fire of love between Fred and Joy would catch and burn bright, hot and new, and forever'*.

"How do I fan the fire? They're just cold gray embers, not burning. I don't know how…"

"Use what the Lord *gave* you to work with, girl. That's what women have been doing since Adam and Eve."

# Chapter Twenty-two

*"What wings are to a bird and sails to a ship, so is prayer to the soul."*
~Corrie Ten Boom

Time crawled for Fred. He did some serious soul-searching and a lot of praying during those long hours. Joy had brought him to his knees by simply driving away—no shouting, no screaming, no cursing, no doors slammed, no plates thrown against the wall. She couldn't have hurt him more if she'd driven a stake through his heart.

She'd proved that she could and would leave him and she was savvy enough, and had money enough, to evade him for a long time—forever—if she chose to do so. She'd made her point and he'd gotten the message: straighten up or she'd ship out. Her, their babies and what was left of his heart. God, he couldn't stand the thoughts of losing her or them. She had the money to travel to any place in the world. What would he do if she stayed mad and refused to come home? She didn't need him...not now.

He prayed that she loved him. She had to. Her love for him would be the only bond that could bring her home. And his love for her. Yes, he now realized that it was a two-way street.

He sat for hours staring out to the lake, not seeing anything, lost in memories of their times together. How he wished he'd told her of his love for her while she was shaving him in the shower that night...those nights. Her small hands touching his face, shaving him with exquisite care as he sat on the tiled shower seat. She had lathered his skin, skillfully shaving his cheeks, and neck, lovingly kissing him here and there as she'd finish a spot. Or how she made sure his food was always hot, waiting for the exact minute to call him to eat. Ironing his favorite shirts without him mentioning it. The little things, intimate things. It was so obvious to him now. She loved him with her every action. She did more than he ever expected of her. Whatever she did, she did with him in mind. His comfort, easing his life. He'd been cruel and had held his tongue, knowing she craved his love and attention. She was giving, caring, loving. Everything that he had not been in return. Could she forgive him for the wrongs he'd piled upon her? Would she?

He turned into the parking lot of the little church where his grandmother once worshipped and carried him to Sunday School when he was a little boy. The pastors had changed many times over the years but he knew the current one, Bob Stanley. Bob loved to fish and Fred had taken him fishing a few times.

It had come down to this. Hart and Mimi had told him to take it to God, so here he was. All the money in the world could not fix what was going on his life and he knew he must make this step. He needed guidance and help. He'd gone to the bottle for the last time. It offered nothing, solved nothing and Fred was at his wit's end. Joy said she didn't want her babies around someone who was an alcoholic. Joy had been through hell with Larry's drinking and abuse. Fred understood that, and respected Joy for having a moral compass. And no, he wasn't an alcoholic but he abused it and realized it.

What next? He felt lower than he'd ever felt in his life. Something had to give and he realized that it had to be him. Joy had done nothing wrong. Fred knew he could not, nor would not, let her walk out of his life. All this was on him. Maybe God could take away this hurt, this agony of loss.

*I don't even know how to pray. How do I talk to you, God? How do I make this right?*

Brother Bob, as everyone in town called him, met Fred at his office door. "Come in Fred, and tell me what's on your mind."

\*\*\*\*\*

Two days later, Joy agreed to talk with him and he drove down to the cottage with a jeweler's box, a small bouquet of flowers, a bag of cheap chocolate truffles, and hope. Bro. Bob's last words to Fred still rang in his mind. *"You've won her heart already, Fred. You just have to learn to treasure it, and keep it, and her, safe forever."* Fred had told Bro. Bob about God speaking to him about Joy. Fred had not told anyone else and Bro. Bob told him that not everyone heard from God.

The old glass door rattled from the impact of his

hand as he knocked on the back door.

Joy opened the door to let him in, immediately turned away and walked into the living room at the front of the house. She couldn't look him in the eye and he noticed that. She looked sad and he hated he'd done that to her.

She didn't know what to say to him, now that he was here. He would have to talk first. She and Ginger had prayed about it a number of times over the past couple of days and she'd put it all in God's hands. *'Hear him out',* were the words that she had heard late in the night.

Fred had to make the first move. He followed her to the sofa.

*Oh, Lord, he looks so good.* She watched him from the corner of her eye, not wanting him to see her staring. He had not shaved in the past days and his beard was considerably darker than his blonde hair which now curled around his ears. Now that she'd seen it longer, she loved the scruffy look on him. He looked like a rogue standing in front of her in his faded Levis and tight black tee shirt. She liked it and longed to touch his face, and feel that roughness on her skin. Joy could not take her eyes off him. Hormones!

He watched her until she finally decided to sit down. Her skin seemed to glow from within and her breasts looked as though they'd expanded in the past four days. The top she wore was low cut and if she'd worn it to entice him with her cleavage, it was working. She had a touch of glossy lipstick on her full lips, making him want to kiss her. Her hair was raven shiny and fell down her back. He yearned to run his hands through it.

Joy was surprised by what Fred did next.

Without a word he got down on his knees in front of her as she sat on the chintz sofa, and handed her the jeweler's box, as he put the chocolates and flowers on the floor.

The floor had no carpet and it was hard. She knew his knees bothered him so this was a desperation move on his part.

She took the box from him, and at his nod opened it slowly. There were two rings inside, one large, one smaller.

"Yours is the little one with the flowers," Fred teased, his voice rough.

Joy could tell he was on the verge of tears.

"Look inside it."

His blue eyes lasered hers with their intensity and Joy didn't want to pull her gaze from their pained depths. He had changed. *Something was different about him. He looked older. His demeanor was subdued. What had happened to him?* Had her leaving affected him so much? Had he suffered as much as she?

Joy read the engraved words and tears rushed into her eyes. *'Fred loves Joy.'* The ring was a circle of flowers, artfully designed with diamonds and gems in the centers of the flowers. He'd looked at everything in the store before picking it out. It was not that expensive, but it looked like Joy, and everything on it was real: rubies, diamonds and emeralds. The annoying salesgirl had been disappointed when the wealthy Fred Garrett had spent less than six thousand dollars on both rings. She'd kept trying to push a large and expensive diamond solitaire on Fred but he knew Joy would never have it.

"Now, look inside mine," he prompted. His was of heavy gold with a simple roped edging.

"Joy… loves… Fred," she croaked, sobbing.

He nodded. He handed her the small bouquet of mixed flowers tied in lacy ribbons and the chocolate truffles.

"I'm sorry for everything, doll."

Tears streamed down his face, his voice was rough, and he didn't care if she saw him crying. She had to know how he felt. How lost, how miserable, how desperate. He had to tell her. Everything.

"Forgive me, please—for being stupid, for doing everything wrong. I admit I married you for my own selfish reasons. You are not what I thought I was looking for—you are more. I never intended to fall in love with you, but I did. Head over heels, blind as a mad dog, in love with you, and I thank God I did, but don't ever…ever leave me again. You don't know the hell I've been through since I came back from the marina and you were gone. I wanted to hit Hart for letting you drive away, but it wasn't his fault, it was mine. He didn't know you'd left. I should have stayed with you. I can't sleep, I can't eat, I can't work. I was lost, and miserable without knowing where you were or if you were hurt, or in a wreck…I was worried sick, baby. Don't do that to me again. Promise? I couldn't bear it if you did. I love you, Joy…I love you so much. I want you. I want you in my life. Can we start over? Will you marry me? We can do it right this time…in a church if you want. You can get a dress—a real wedding dress. One that you choose."

He'd given considerable thought to getting married in a church. He thought that would make her happy. The words came out in a rush and he wasn't sure what he'd said, but he hoped they were the right words. He'd prayed for God to give him wisdom and the words to bring her home, back to him. Brother Bob and Fred had prayed for not only Fred's salvation but for the saving of his marriage.

"Can I trust you? Your parents hate me. They want to take my babies away from me, or me to leave you and have the babies and never see you again. They told me so. They think you just want the babies, and not me. They said I had choices. You saw that check. Your truck probably cost more than that. I wanted to laugh in their faces. Do they think they can buy my babies? Or pay me to leave you? Those are *not* choices."

"My parents don't have a say in this—any of this. These babies are yours and mine—I know that even if they don't. My folks will have to stay away and let it go. I'm sorry for what they said and did, but we don't need them. It's up to you, baby doll…I give you my word, my promise. I won't ever let you down again. You tell me to leave now and I'll go. I love you enough to let you go if you have to, if that will make you happy. Tell me right now that you don't love me and I'll walk out that door. But I want to spend the rest of my life with you, with our babies. And I hope that's what you want, too. We can have a church wedding...we can start to church...whatever you want to do. God knows I've prayed enough in the past few days...I'm becoming a changed man," he said.

He felt like a changed man but didn't know how to tell Joy what had happened in Brother Bob's small office—how he'd cried like a baby and told Bro. Bob everything—all his bad deeds, his underhanded treatment of Joy, his love of Joy, what his parents said and did, his drinking. All of it—including Lori's manipulation of him and how he'd hated her, and how that hate still festered within him. Bro. Bob encouraged Fred to release that hatred and to forgive Lori. *'We all make mistakes. God forgives our sins if we ask Him. We're human and as such are not perfect, and we make bad choices. Let the past go,'* Bro. Bob had told him, too.

"We're...already...married. That was real...in the courthouse...and legal...wasn't it?"

"Yes, it was all legal, but don't you want another ceremony? I'd do it again if you wanted one," he said, knowing he'd do anything to keep her with him. "I don't want ten groomsmen and ten attendants, though. Just you and me, a witness or two and a preacher."

"This can be our wedding....right here. You just asked me to marry you. You even brought me flowers, and the rings, which I love...We don't have to have another ceremony. It won't make us any more married—if you love me—"

"Doll, I do love you with all my heart, my being.

259

Will you stay with me forever and bring the color back into my life?" he said with such sincerity she wanted to believe him. Tears pooled in his eyes.

"How do I know you won't start back drinking or whatever? How can I trust you, Fred? Tell me how? I want to believe you. But I'm scared that I've made another mistake. One that's as bad as Larry was. I couldn't bear it if you took my babies away from me. Or if you said you loved me and you really didn't. How do I know?"

"You brought me to my knees, Joy. I'll give up everything I own to keep you with me, and our babies. You have my word, my heart, my promise. I don't have anything else to give you. You have it all...I'll follow you to the ends of the earth and love you forever. I watched you bloom like a flower bud changing into a brilliant, exquisite rose...your skin, your hair, your body. It was torture to watch you and not touch you. That's why I locked my door...I had to keep my hands off you. I wanted you so. I still do. You are so beautiful, and I love everything about you. I believe in you, in your talent. I want to see how far you can go with your art and I'll do anything I can to see that you succeed...I have been through hell since you left...I can't get you off my mind...and I'll do whatever I can to make this right. You have to understand that. I went to see Mimi's preacher, Bob Stanley. I had a long talk with him yesterday morning, we prayed, and I cried like a baby. I gave my heart to God, Joy. I needed to get myself right—to ask God into my heart. Bro. Bob said that was my first step. I had to make myself better for you, for our

260

babies, for me. I want to be the man you want me to be, the man you deserve. He told me that we can't change the past, but we *can* change the future. You are my future."

"I want to believe you, Fred."

"Please, please, forgive me. I can't make it any plainer. I was wrong. I used you, and it came back to bite me...not just on my ass. When you left, it tore out the rest of my heart. I don't know what else to say to make you believe me. We belong together. God sent you to me...to teach me the lessons that I need, and to be mine. You need me, too, baby. We made these babies together, and I'm not walking away from my kids, no matter what my folks say or do. Let's raise them together. You don't want to raise them alone. You need me as much as I need you."

She continued to look at him but was silent.

"I can't bear to not be with you....I want to be a father to them and I want you to be their mother. I want to help you with them...I want to hold them and rock them...I want to watch them nurse. I want us to have more babies. As many as you want. Bring Joy back into my life," he said, pointing at her. "Doll, only you have that power. You are my all. Be my love, my best friend, my princess...my queen. You will never have to settle for anything again. I'll spend the rest of my life making you the happiest woman on earth. That's a promise. My heart to your heart."

His last words were said with his fingers over his heart before touching her chest. God had put words in his mouth because he had no clue coming in what he was going to say or that he would say so much—only

261

that he'd prayed for God to give him the words to bring her home.

*Did I say too much? Or not enough?*

"Yes," she said. It was as simple as that.

Fred's heart soared. His words had opened her heart's door. *Thank you, dear God!*

She nodded and he slid the ring on her finger. It felt perfect. She put his ring on his finger. When they'd married at the courthouse, he had not brought a ring for himself and Joy hadn't thought anything about it at the time. Some men didn't wear rings, or want to, for whatever reason. It pleased her that Fred had bought one for himself, although she would have rather bought it for him. It was not important now. He was here. That was important. And in her mind's eye she could see his blond head bowed as he held their baby and rocked it. That visual hit home with her and grabbed her heartstrings.

Joy said, "I love you, too, and I forgive you...Can we go home now?"

She could not stand it. She reached out and ran her fingers over his beard.

He put his hand over hers as she caressed his face. He turned his lips toward her hand and kissed her palm, her fingers. He wiped her tears as she wiped the wetness from his rough cheeks.

She wanted to weep from the sheer beauty of his words. It was almost too much to take in. Joy was sure that in heaven legions of angels wept joyfully hearing those humble words from the arrogant and proud John Frederick Garrett, the Fourth. *How did he know that was what I wanted, yearned, to hear?*

She'd always dreamed of being the princess, instead of being the chambermaid—the hired help. *My prince got on his knees and begged me to come home, to love him.* For the first time in her life, Joy felt like a princess, a queen. How humbling it was to see him on his knees. And to hear his words about believing in her and her art. That made her heart, and soul, soar. God had opened the floodgate and poured wondrous blessings upon Joy in these moments.

"Maybe later. We're going to see if Hart fixed those bed springs first. I don't know about you but I'm not spending another night alone." He wouldn't tell her he'd parked just a few feet from where she was staying and watched until she had turned out the lights. Nor to what depths his sorrows had taken him—so low that only God could bring him back. And how he'd wanted to bang on the door and make her listen to him apologize. For everything. Beg her if he had to.

"Are we staying here?" she asked. She missed their house, but wouldn't admit it and Lord, how she missed sleeping next to Fred. Just the sound of his breathing in the night was a comfort, as was the feel of his body next to hers, the safety of his arms.

"Yes, this is the first night of our honeymoon, my darling. Then we're going home, but we're not staying. Just long enough to pack a few things. We're going away for at least two weeks. We should have gone on one before. I'm sorry I didn't realize it at the time. Forgive me for that, too? Please?...Where do you want to go? Be deciding...okay? You'll want to pack your watercolors and camera, too. I have Sol ready to come look after Fluffy, unless you want him to go along. He can but I don't know how well he travels. He might throw up."

"I might throw up."

"Yeah, but his are hair balls and they're nasty."

"I need to put these in a vase," she said as she held the sweet bouquet that she knew Fred had chosen with great care. "I love them."

He got up from the floor slowly. His knees were hurting him, but he held his hands out to help her up from the sofa. He held on to her and kissed her with great passion but let her go after a few moments— before they got carried away.

"Hold that thought," he said, and winked at her. They had time for loving—the rest of their lives.

She didn't see a vase so she got a blue mason jar from a display, added water and put the bouquet on the kitchen island. She headed toward the bedroom.

"Bring the chocolates," she said looking back toward him over her shoulder. "I'm hungry."

"Me, too."

A few minutes later Fred grumbled low in Joy's ear, "Hart didn't fix these springs."

"Don't tell him. He'll write a song about it."

"He already did. Remember?"

# Chapter Twenty-three

*"The Lord is my strength and my shield; my heart trusts in Him, and He helps me. My heart leaps for joy, and with my song I praise Him.*
~Psalms 28:7 NIV

They got into his pickup and he looked over at her. He had not shaved. Joy had practically begged him not to, and though his beard itched for the time being, he'd let it grow until she said otherwise. He'd told her to pack light and she had.

"Where to, doll? Pick the place you've always wanted to go. Somewhere romantic? Scenic? Your wish is my command. We'll pick up whatever we need along the way. The cat's taken care of. Say the word and I'll drive until dark. I don't like driving after dark in strange places. My night vision ain't what it used to be."

"We'll go anywhere I want? You're serious? What if it's to Texas or Arizona? Or to the mountains? Tennessee or Virginia?"

"Name it."

"Okaaay....well, let's see. I've never been any place much, but I've always wanted to spend the night on top of a mountain in a log cabin....or by the ocean. That would be fun. And we could walk on the beach and pick up sea shells. And I'd like to see the desert. I've read that the light in the desert is different…"

"So….we do…them all?"

"Yeah," she said, looking at him as though he'd hung the moon.

"Where do you want to start?"

"North. The mountains," she said. Fred had mentioned romance. Did he mean it? And he seemed different. Maybe a little quieter? Calmer? Less arrogant? Less confident than ever? No, somehow he seemed humble, yet even more confident.

Six hours later, they stopped north of Atlanta. Joy had fallen asleep two times and Fred hoped he was doing the right thing by taking her away from home. They needed time alone, away from distractions, away from work, away from his folks.

They were in no hurry and Fred stopped a number of times, for bathroom breaks and to take photos. Joy saw beauty, potential paintings, in the most mundane things: fields, cows, fence rows, old trees with Spanish moss, or tractors plowing the red Georgia clay. He knew how much each thing meant to her and didn't complain. He was glad to do something that made her feel good. He wanted her creativity to flow. He knew she was truly gifted. The discovery of her artistic side had been a fluke on his part. He recognized her talent with crayons. He could not have guessed the depths of her talent until he heard the comments from those who walked by her exhibit, bought her paintings or the praise that Jean heaped upon Joy. Even Jack Turner had bought her most expensive painting. Everyone could see that she was destined to become an accomplished artist.

The next day they arrived in Townsend, Tennessee, and rented a cabin on a tiny gravel road high on the side of a mountain. Joy walked around like a little kid, taking pictures of rocks, fir trees and the log cabin.

Fred had started a fire and Joy enjoyed the ambient lighting from the blaze. She moved around taking shot after shot of Fred sitting on the floor in front of the rock fireplace, the light reflecting off his golden skin. Her love for him showed in every one.

He took the camera from her and took several photos of Joy. Eventually they moved to the sofa where they fell asleep in each other's arms.

Joy woke first and wiggled to give herself a little room. Fred had his arm around her and she was sure it had to be hurting him. Her tiny movements woke him.

Something, maybe it was a dream, made her think of Fred's words to her in the cottage when they had been talking and Fred had told her about going to see Brother Bob.

"What did you mean when you said you'd given your heart to God? Did you really?"

"Yes, I did. I prayed and asked God to come into my heart, into my life and to change me and make me a better man. I asked Him to forgive me of my sins and Brother Bob talked with me about forgiving Lori and to let go of the hatred I've felt for her."

"Oh, love, how wonderful! I'm sorry but I wanted

to ask you about it but I was so glad to see you and then we talked about other things. And then I sort of forgot about it."

"Yeah, and those things included moving to the bedroom. What say we move there now? My arm is hurting since someone slept on it, and I need to make a trip to the bathroom."

"Me, too. Are we sleeping in?"

"Oh , yeah. Did I tell you I love you, Mrs. Garrett?"

"Not today."

"I love you," he said.


The honeymoon continued as Fred treated Joy to Cade's Cove, where deer played just feet away from tourists' cameras and bears kept their distance. Joy took photo after photo, after photo. The trip was far from over.

They shared long spells of companionable silence and he loved her ability to observe without chatting constantly. She laughed at his jokes. His wicked sense of humor was once again at play. They often held hands as they drove and Fred loved having her near. He'd missed her so, the closeness of their relationship—the long talks in the night, or quiet times around the table eating breakfast or a leisurely supper. He knew his life would not complete without her. He realized in that moment that she was his other half. His heart felt whole for the first time.

Joy would look at him and he'd wink at her, a twinkle in his eyes. He thanked God daily that she had agreed to come back into his life, and it was more than the babies. They were a given, but she brought him happiness, being next to him. Back in his arms, his life.

He felt better mentally as well. Lighter, like a weight had been lifted from his shoulders. Guilt over Lori and Katie no longer ate at him. What a blessing to have God in his life and love shining in the eyes of the woman sitting beside him.

Eight days later, they'd been to Kentucky, Virginia and were now in Kitty Hawk, North Carolina. Joy loved the sand dunes but thought that the place was the most desolate she'd ever seen. She loved it, though, and did a few small watercolors that Fred instantly claimed as his.

Fred made sure to show Joy all the lighthouses in the coastal areas. He personally loved those, but chose not to try to climb the many steps to the top because of his knees. Joy could not push herself that hard, either. He wouldn't let her, if she'd wanted. They decided to wait on the trip out west as Joy was having such a good time seeing the coastal sights. There would be time for other trips, and later, cruises. This trip turned into a leisurely affair, with no planning. They drove until they wanted to stop, would look at a map and decide on their next destination.

Long walks on the beach and sweet nights in a seaside cottage, picnics and candlelit suppers at a quaint bed and breakfast were the stuff that made honeymoons special, wonderful. Fred had turned into quite a romantic person, although she knew he'd never admit it. He was too macho for such an admission. He was showing her, though. He bought her some clothes along the way—a loose white dress, elegant little sandals with silver starfish on them, and a pearl necklace that struck his fancy. She wore them together for him and they slow danced on the deck of the cottage, the surf the only music other than the soft song he sang low in her ear. That small gesture made her all tingly and feel truly special. She knew he was trying and the words, and actions, were more endearing than Joy could imagine coming from Fred, who enjoyed playing hard and living harder.

They'd found bucketfuls of sea shells, sand dollars and sea glass. Joy had projects for all those and Fred found delight in hearing her laughter as she found a special one. He bought her little trinkets: a bracelet with seashells made of silver and sea glass and a necklace of turquoise, and earrings as mementoes of these precious moments. She found antique fishing lures at a quaint shop that Fred loved and blue and white china in others. They visited art galleries but bought nothing because Fred told Joy that none of the work was equal to hers.

It had never occurred to him when he'd hurriedly married her to take time off for such a thing as a honeymoon—a silly notion that meant so much to one tiny pregnant woman.

She noticed, too, that he had not had any beer, nor a sip of wine which she knew he also liked. It was sweet tea or Dr. Pepper strictly for him, even with raw oysters and the seafood that he enjoyed. She told him it was fine if he wanted to drink wine or a beer, but he said he was trying to get away from using booze of any kind as a crutch and although he liked wine and beer with his food, he wanted to turn over new leaf. She agreed to let him deal with it on his own.

She knew in her heart that Fred was sorry. He'd shown her in a thousand ways, begged her forgiveness, in his every action. She loved seeing the tender, loving side of Fred because it gave her inner peace.

*****

Joy felt better than she had in weeks. The nausea that had hit her hard was now a thing of that past. She craved dill pickles and peanut butter, French fries with mayonnaise—sometimes all at the same time. Fred was amazed at her eating habits. How was she able was to eat all that food? Where did it go? And how could she stand those combinations?(Except for the fries and they were good with the mayo. Who knew?) These babies were going to be giants before they were born.

The honeymoon was over, after two weeks away from home. Fred was rested and Joy was painting again. She had hundreds of photos to paint from and she worked a few hours each day painting and reviewing photographs for future pieces.

The Wakefields' music fest was coming up in a

week's time and they was looking forward to it. Joy had painted a landscape as a Christmas present for Hart and Ginger. Fred had bought a nice frame for it and they were anxious for Hart and Ginger to see their gift.


Fred's grandmother showed up while Fred was still at the marina one Tuesday. She'd driven her red Ford Focus right through the gate which was now kept open.

She rang the doorbell.

Joy jumped when she heard the buzzer at the door. The gate had been closed for so long she forgot that they could have a normal life now. She looked down at her dirty top and shrugged. Whoever was there would see her like she was.

A trim older woman stood at the door. This had to be Fred's grandmother. She was dressed demurely in denim pants, matching jacket and a faded denim blouse, with a multi-strand pearl necklace. She was about Joy's height with reddish hair.

"Hello, Joy, I'm Fred's grandmother. He calls me 'Mimi'. May I come in?"

"Oh…of course. Come on in. Excuse me, I look a mess. I've been painting and baking. I'm so glad to meet you. Fred talks about you all the time." She briefly hugged Mimi and led her into the kitchen where she'd been cleaning paint brushes as bread baked in the oven. At least the house smelled good.

Fred's grandmother took in the tiny, but hugely pregnant woman standing eye to eye with her. Her dark hair was pulled into a messy ponytail and her olive skin was clear, with a glow. She was wearing leggings with one of Fred's giant tee shirts which pulled on her bulging stomach.

Grace Garrett thought Joy was beautiful with her green almond-shaped eyes. She loved Fred and that was all that really mattered in the scheme of things to Grace. Joy's voice was soft, slow in cadence, sounding southern as corn bread. She exuded serenity.

"I get too many things going at one time...painting and trying to bake bread..."

"It smells wonderful. Is it about ready? I could eat a slice or two with some butter and tea if it is." It was late in the afternoon and Joy was ready for a snack herself. Of course, she was always ready for a snack lately.

"Oh, yes, ma'am. It's almost time---about five more minutes. I hear you just came back from a world tour. How wonderful! I'd like to do that in the future. Of course Fred doesn't like being away from the marina for too long. Those two weeks we were away, I bet he called them a hundred times. He said he was just 'checking in'. Shoot, he missed it," she said. "He loves that place. Please sit down. The bar stools are comfy."

Grace sat down and watched Joy as she talked. Joy finished washing her brushes, dried them carefully, and put them aside.

"Yes, Fred always liked fishing, boating and the outside...sports. I had a great time on my trip. We stayed about three months. I traveled to every country that I thought I'd ever want to see. I took my friend, Happy Hanson, with me. And my friend, Allen Reese. He's a retired attorney who lives in Panama City, where I live. Although I'm thinking about moving back up here, at least for part of the year. I want to be near these babies."

"Oh, Fred would love that. He's getting excited about them now, too. You should see all the stuff he bought them for Christmas and they're not even here yet. My Lord, their room is stacked to the ceiling." Joy laughed and Mimi chuckled.

"No one has given you a shower, Joy? I thought surely some of Fred's friends would do that."

"No, ma'am...I don't think many of his friends come around since he married me, except for his poker buddies. I don't want to go to any place where I'm not welcome, or don't know anyone, anyway. It's okay. Fred and I can buy what we need. I inherited money from a lady I used to work for—Mrs. Wentworth."

"I heard that. Who was she?"

"She was a lawyer I met when I divorced my first husband, Larry—the one who beat me, and raped me. I'm sure you've been told the story by now. I don't think Fred's parents believe it, but it's all true. Larry's dead now. He got stabbed in jail here awaiting transfer to another facility."

Mimi didn't say a word but she knew that John and Elaine had Joy investigated. She wanted to meet Joy and see for herself before she formed any opinions.

The oven timer chimed and Joy removed the two

loaves of bread from the lowest of the double ovens.

"We'll let this cool just for a couple of minutes and I'll brew up some tea. Would you like Earl Grey or something else? I think I have a few other brands."Earl Grey had been Mrs. Wentworth's favorite tea and Joy had learned to enjoy it while in her employ.

"Earl Grey is fine. Do you have some jam or jelly and butter?"

"Yes, I do. Ginger gave me a whole case of blackberry jam she and Hart put up this year. It's so good. Fred loves it, too. They made wild plum jelly, too, but I've already eaten all of it with toast. I stay so hungry I could eat the paint off the walls when I get up. I hit the floor and start eating."

Joy put on a pot of water to boil, and found unmatched cups and saucers, sugar and sliced a lemon. She and Fred had picked up a few pieces of blue and white china on their honeymoon. Joy had admired Hart and Ginger's large assortment of old china and decided she wanted to start a collection. They'd bought cups and saucers in a country junk shop near Pall Mall, Tennessee. The back of Fred's truck had been full of boxes from their two week honeymoon. They had brought back many treasures as mementos.

"May I see some of your paintings while the tea brews a minute? Fred told me your work is awesome. That was the exact word he used. I want to see for myself."

Joy led her to the glassed-in porch that now was her studio. Stacks of canvases were in a cabinet that

275

Hart had built against the house wall, along with drawers for art supplies. Joy had a painting sitting on the aluminum easel that she'd stopped on earlier. It was of a large urn filled with flowers. It was gorgeous and Mimi said so.

"Joy, this is beautiful! Do you have others like this? I'd like to see them."

Joy walked to the cabinet and started pulling out canvas after canvas. Some were of flowers, but most were of rural landscapes—typical scenes from south Alabama—fields with cows, farm ponds and cloudscapes, grain silos, hay bales and rusty tin buildings. Mimi took time to study each one carefully.

Mrs. Garrett picked up a couple of them, studied them, nodded and picked up another. She didn't comment on the individual pieces.

"Let's go get that tea, Joy. I want to talk with you about something."

Joy poured the Earl Grey and they both took sugar and lemon, no cream. The warm, fragrant bread was buttered and blackberry jam was spread liberally.

"Oh, my. This is delicious! I haven't had home baked bread in years. I used to make it myself. Everyone has stopped baking at home now. I'm glad to see you enjoy doing it."

"I love it, but I know I won't have much time when these two come. I may have to give up the painting, too. I'll see how it goes." She sat down carefully, always uncomfortable now.

"I want to come help you and Fred, Joy, when the babies come. It would be a true gift if you'd allow me

276

to do that. I'd love spending time with them and you'll need the help. I don't want you to quit painting, Joy. Ever. In fact, I want to contact some of my friends who are in the interior design business and see if I can help you sell them. They're wonderful, Joy. I know you know that."

"Fred tells me they are. I was so shocked that I won an award at the art show this time. It was my first show. And I did sell a few. Our next door neighbor, Jack, bought one, too. I made several hundred dollars. I couldn't believe it."

"I think you can sell them for thousands to the right folks. And I am serious about helping with the babies. I can rent an apartment here in Eufaula or find a house to rent someplace. I sold my house several years back. Living at the beach is great and I have my circle of friends there but I miss home."

"You could stay with us. Fred added on...as you can see. We have three more bedrooms, and two more bathrooms, and a foyer. We don't have furniture in them, yet, though. We have room enough for you with no problem. I'd be happy for the help, too. I've already been talking with Ginger Wakefield about what to do when these two get here. Two of everything and double the work, too, I know."

"Yes, but double the love, too, Joy. I miss seeing Fred, so I'd love to be around him more, too. Talk with him about this. And the paintings. I'd like to carry some of them with me back to the beach when I go. If I could select from them....would that be all right? Do you have a show coming up?"

"No. I just put a piece in a group show, but that's

it. I can't do much now. It's only a few weeks before the babies come and I'm doing all I can right now. My energy level goes up and down. I fall asleep if I sit down. Just take the paintings you want and I'll take photos so I'll know which ones you have."

"That's a good idea, honey. And may I ask what your prices are on them? I wouldn't want to sell them for less than you have them priced."

"I have it on the back of each one. I did that for the show, and I can put it on the newer ones. But sell them for what you can. I'm not trained like some of the top name artists."

"I think your work is great. Let's finish our bread and tea and we'll look at them again."

Joy and Mimi drank tea, chatted and seemed to enjoy the other's company. Joy had painted a small still life that she had placed on a short wall near the kitchen. Mimi commented on it.

"Tell me about that piece, Joy. It's not like your others. I see some family heirlooms, and antiques. I love that, and it's a good size. Just right for a small space."

"Hmm…let's see. The oil lamp is one I found while we were on our honeymoon and the little blue dish is one I found under a pot of flowers someone gave Fred, and the embroidered handkerchief belonged to my grandmother, Asia Willoughby."

"Asia Wilcox Willoughby? From Union Springs?"

"Yes, she lived there growing up. They moved later on to Ramer and that's where she died. She didn't die until just after my mom passed away two years ago."

278

"Honey, I knew your grandmother. We were friends and went to the same high school. We were close. She came from a great family, too. They owned land and had a farm…"

"They lost it all over the years. And Mama marrying Daddy broke their heart. They never wanted my daddy around. Of course, he was mean to Mama. He didn't want her seeing them or going to their house. She'd take me to stay with her. When Daddy hurt Mama once, they had him arrested. Of course, he got out of it. And that made it worse. Anyway, it's a long story. That little handkerchief is all I have left of Grammy. Daddy got mad and sold almost all that Mama got of Gram's. Some of it, he burned. That little hanky was tucked in Mama's Bible. She gave it to me right before she died. I don't even know where Daddy is." Larry had thrown away the Bible later but Joy had tucked the little hanky into her purse and saved it from being thrown away, too. Mimi didn't need to know all that, not now.

"Asia was the salt of the earth, Joy. I know--"

In the middle of their conversation, Fred came in. He hugged his grandmother, kissed her first out of respect and then took Joy in his arms. He kissed her with unabashed affection and held her close. Public displays of affection were not his usual thing until God came into his life, but he'd learned not to ignore his wife nor to ignore their hello and goodbye kisses. He'd seen his grandmother and J.F. kiss at every parting. He did not recall seeing his mother and father ever touch each other during his childhood and that always bothered him. Mimi was a loving person and

279

wasn't embarrassed to lavish kisses on her only grandchild, Fred.

"I want to help when your babies come, Fred. Joy invited me to stay here, with y'all. I'm game if you are. I won't have to rent an apartment and I'll always be around…."

Fred had trouble swallowing the lump in his throat. He was touched beyond words. How he'd wished his mother had received Joy, and the babies, like his loving Mimi.

"We'd be honored, Mimi. And I'm already looking into hiring someone to help Joy, too. If you're up to the task, we'd love to have you. Joy can decorate a room, a suite for you. One of the bedrooms is private and has its own bathroom and walk-in closet. Hart planned it like another master bedroom. It can be yours. Let's go look and see if it'll fit your needs. You won't have to move any furniture or rent or anything. Just come when you want. Or leave when you want."

"I'd love that, Fred. I told Joy I'd love to spend time with you and now these babies. Now, I have my own room. Joy, I'm used to a queen -sized bed, but other than that, anything you do will be fine with me."

Fred turned toward Joy and said, "Go change clothes in a little while, doll. Let's take Mimi out to supper. I know for a fact that she loves fried catfish and hush puppies."


Mimi Grace had bestowed her approval upon Joy

and both Fred and Joy were grateful for it. At supper they discussed the babies' needs, the paintings that Mimi was taking home with her and plans for Mimi to come up soon for an extended stay. Fred asked Joy to find some bedroom furniture for her room either locally or order something online. Joy liked antiques and knew just the place in town to look.

"Fred, I knew Joy's grandmother, Asia Willoughby, from Union Springs. They were fine folks. I was in the grade above Asia in school, but we knew each other well. Asia's father owned a grocery store and was quite well-to-do for the time. Everyone in town had an account with him. They delivered groceries for years, even after the self-serve chain groceries came and closed down most mom-and-pop stores."

Joy and Fred were fascinated by Mimi's stories from Union Springs and Mimi entertained them well into the night. Joy had heard the stories but remembered little of the good life that her grandparents lived. Her mom seldom talked about them and she yearned to ask Mimi more, but knew that time would come for that. Mimi left to spend the night with a friend.

Fred was thankful that Joy had taken Mimi to her heart and that she was amenable to having Mimi come in to help with the twins. He held Joy into the night and fell asleep, happier than he'd been in years.

## Chapter Twenty-four

*"Weeping may endure for a night, but joy cometh
in the morning."*
~Psalms 30:5

Ginger and Hart had invited Fred and Joy to spend the night in Ginger's cottage. Joy was thrilled to spend some time with Ginger and offered to help with the massive amounts of food that Ginger prepared each month for the music gathering.

The painting was boxed and wrapped, along with other presents for baby Jimmy, Pam, Ginger and Hart.

"Wow! Look at you," Ginger said, delighted that Joy was glowing with good health. Joy still had ten weeks to go in her pregnancy, but she looked further along than that, due to the two babies and her small stature.

"Are y'all sure there are only two babies in there? I think there's four or five. I'd have that doctor do another sonogram," she laughed. "Of course, I have no room to say anything about size. I gained so much weight that Hart said I'd have to go to the hospital in a dump truck. After he jokingly made another comment behind my back about me being a 'wide load', I threatened to make him spend the night on the couch and I'd quit cooking. He decided it wasn't so

282

funny after all. You have to keep these men in line, making all those smart remarks. They'll all come back to bite them on the butt, won't they, Joy?"

"Well, Fred's been really good about keeping the 'fat jokes' to himself," Joy said in her soft, slow voice. Fred was so good to her that she wouldn't say anything negative about him to anyone.

Fred was quiet. He'd gained weight right along with Joy. There was no explanation. She gained. He gained. Of course, he was so tall, no one had noticed. Joy was discreet and didn't mention Fred's weight gain to anyone. He'd popped buttons off two shirts and had to go up a size in shirts and pants. He'd ordered them online but Joy noticed when he opened the packages but didn't comment to him.

"Joy's gift to y'all is in that big box right there, Ginger. I want Hart to open it, if you don't mind. He's going to love it," Fred said.

The large painting was truly one of Joy's best and Hart did love it. Joy had used her artistic license to paint Hart's old home as it would have been in years past, with clean- swept yards, chickens scratching in the sand, flowers in bloom, clothes flying in the spring breeze. She'd even included a black and white dog that she'd heard Hart describe as one of his childhood pets. The detail she'd put into the piece made Hart admire Joy's work more than ever. As he'd worked on their house construction, he'd observed her painting many times. He was taken with her use of color and architectural details.

The folks arrived and the food was ready. Ginger had not allowed Joy to help other than setting out dinnerware, flatware and linens. Ginger still used real china, real flatware and cloth napkins. 'The food deserves better than plastic,' she had been quoted in a local magazine. Most of the food was prepped the day before, and slow cookers simmered with chicken and dumplings, vegetable soup and barbecued pork.

Musicians from around the Wiregrass area played their favorite country, bluegrass and a scattering of contemporary songs. Joy and Ginger sat side by side admiring the way their husbands looked, and sounded, on the stage that Hart had made from a low trailer.

"Fred's gained a few pounds, hasn't he? Sympathy weight," Ginger laughed and continued, "Some men do that when their wives are expecting."

"Yeah, but don't say anything. He doesn't know anyone's noticed it."

At the intermission, folks lined up to eat their fill of Ginger's country cooking. Plates were piled high with a sampling of all the dishes as couples sat side by side on the long screened porch. Sometimes Ginger called everyone to eat prior to the music starting, but if folks were slow to arrive for the sing, she'd wait until the intermission to call everyone around and Hart to say the blessing.

A few couples, and handful of single folks ate outside where bonfires were burning to take the slight chill off the night air.

Joy had not noticed Julie's presence until she was sitting down next to Fred and discovered that the woman had perched her narrow butt on his other side. Julie's plate had almost nothing on it.

"Julie, do you remember Joy, my wife?" Fred asked, as Joy sat on his other side after making her third trip to the bathroom. "Joy, you met Julie already. That night we were going home."

Joy sat down with Fred, as Julie stared at her the whole time. Joy knew who she was and displeasure shot through her, but she quelled the desire to hit the woman. Julie was made up and dressed to the nines with her high-heeled boots, skin-tight leggings and low-cut sweater that displayed a good portion of her perky plastic breasts.

"So how far along are you? You look ready to pop any minute. I hope you don't have to deliver that baby on the way home tonight, Fred!" Julie said, with a smirk on her face that just wasn't attractive.

Joy wanted to tell her that, but decided to be sweet, after all she was wearing Fred's wedding ring. And Joy looked good. She had learned to apply discreet makeup with Ginger's gentle instructions, her hair shone with good health and her clothes were from a boutique in Eufaula.

"No, you don't have to worry about that. We've got about ten weeks to go yet. We're having twins, Julie. Didn't anyone tell you? A boy for Fred, a girl for me…like the song. We're debating on names. I'm just not into John Frederick Garrett, the Fifth. He'll come up with something good before time, though. And I'm nowhere as big as I'll get before these two are born, I'm sure."

"It must be terrible carrying around that much

weight! You're as big as a cow! I can't imagine doing that. How much do you weigh? Like two hundred pounds?"

Joy decided not to answer the weight question, not that she weighed anywhere near two hundred, but instead decided to hit Julie with some home truths.

"It's just part of what a woman does for the man she loves and their babies, Julie. The weight is just a part of it. Mother Nature helps women get into the hang of it all, though. After the nausea and vomiting for weeks on end, then the swelling, gas, heartburn and indigestion starts, the peeing every fifteen minutes, the boobs expanding daily and the hips get wider, the tummy stretching until there's enough room for two to play kick ball inside, and then the fun starts—the itching and stretch marks. And—", she stopped and looked across the table at Hart and winked before continuing, "we're up at 2:30 in the morning eating butter pecan ice cream because *we*," she cocked her head toward Fred," can't wait for breakfast. I could eat everything in sight the minute my feet hit the floor. Before that I couldn't smell bacon or eggs without throwing up. Fred had to buy biscuits and gravy from Hardee's, because I couldn't stand to cook them. Now we're eating—"

Ginger sat down and interrupted, "Everything that's not nailed down? That sounds like me. Then the leaking boobs start. Every time I would bend over, mine started leaking, no matter where I was—even in the grocery store—and the drug store. It was so embarrassing. No one had warned me about that."

Fred put in, "Joy's not to that part yet, I think I'll

like that part."

"You like it all," Joy said, "especially the size of my bosom. One day I didn't have any at all. Fred said I was 'flat as fried eggs', and the next day, almost, I had these—things—the size of grapefruits—"

"Cantaloupes," Fred said, jumping in, gesturing with his hands to indicate a size, and grinning.

Joy swatted lightly at Fred's hands, and whispered loudly to him, "They are not that big!"

He grinned directly at her and just nodded.

"I've changed bra sizes three times and I'm sure I will again before the babies come," Joy said, shaking her head. "I think they'll be giants like Fred."

"You love me, doll, even if I am a giant."

"Yes, I do and you know it," Joy told him. "These 'cantaloupes', as you call them, won't stay this size long, though. I'll be back to fried- egg- size and they'll probably hang to my knees."

"I like fried-egg-size, too," Fred told her.

"See, I told y'all, he likes it all," Joy said, laughing. "Anyway, I haven't seen my toes in weeks and I can't paint my toenails. That's where Fred comes in handy. He's good at it. I was going to the nail place, but it's hard to get out of their chair now. And I have to buy tents to wear since I've blossomed, as Fred calls it. I went from a junior one or two to a maternity large and now I'll be going into a extra-large soon. It's too hot most of the time for me to wear those clingy maternity tops, so the tents work. And I can't wear my cute cowboy boots because my feet are so swollen. That's why I'm wearing these flats tonight. I can't wear any of my pretty shoes or my wedding ring," she said and held it up on a necklace. "And my doctor knows my bottom better than she knows my face. I'm sure she could identify me even if my head was covered."

Fred and Hart winked at each other. Jack grinned at Fred and Fred grinned back. Hart slowly shook his head, seeing and enjoying the exchange. He knew Fred's position. He'd been there with Ginger.

Fred leaned over and kissed Joy lightly on the lips.

"I love it all, doll. I think you're the most beautiful woman in the world," Fred said.

Everyone within hearing distance said, "Aww....", except Julie.


The mighty Fred, *the Hoss*, has fallen hard, Jack thought. Joy was a gorgeous and sweet woman. Jack was a little envious, and he was learning plenty about the birth process that he'd been clueless about. Well, except for cows and cows didn't discuss lady parts, or expanding and leaking boobs.

Jack Turner had turned around in his seat to watch the action going on at the table behind him. It was all fascinating, and more than a little funny, to him.

"This is better than any TV show," Ralph Hinson loudly told his wife, Betty Ruth, and those sitting at their table, who all nodded in agreement. They were sitting with Jack. The show was beside them so they had all turned to listen and participate.


"Eew!" Julie said, scrunching up her face, ignoring

what Mr. Ralph had said. Her mind was still on Joy's pregnancy and Fred's infatuation with his wife. "I just couldn't wear those giant maternity clothes. They're just so—so gross. And I can't get that big. I'll just have to adopt. Of course, I'm not all that into changing diapers and wiping snotty noses. Can't you just get them when they're about two and just so adorable with those little smocked jumpers?"

"Eew!" Hart, Fred and Jack said, simultaneously, and all three perfectly mocking Julie's whiney voice.

"Not my son. No smocking. Ever," Hart said to Ginger.

Jack just rolled his eyes. Julie Adams was trouble everywhere she went and tonight was no different. Julie chased him until he tried to kiss her with a big 'chaw' of tobacco in his mouth one night. He normally didn't chew tobacco but he knew she'd run like a scalded dog if she knew he was chewing it. And she did and that had been the end of that. He kept it handy just to scare her off. A plug of 'Taylor's Pride' had come to his rescue.

"Mine, either," Fred echoed. He looked at Joy pointedly. She got the message. No smocking. That was okay, as she wasn't into all those cutesy clothes for kids, who outgrew them before they could be worn a second time. And the clothes she was wearing were not giant. They were somewhat fitted and not tent-sized at all—yet.

Hart could not resist adding his two cents worth, picking up on the direction of this conversation. "It doesn't work that way, Julie. You can't just adopt a child because it's cute. Ginger, you need to enlighten her about the birthing process. Man, I almost lost it."

"Almost, my hiney! You were two seconds from being 'daddy down'. That's what the nurses say when the daddies pass out from the blood and gore. It's not real pretty, that's for sure. And it hurts like heck, too. And Hart cried like a baby when he held Jimmy that first time, just like I did, *no matter what* he says. It is worth it all," Ginger admitted, grabbing Hart's hand, "and I want to do it again. Even though I felt like a walking milk factory until I wasn't producing enough milk for Jimmy, if you can believe that. I found out the hard way that you cannot make milk on a low-fat diet. Joy, eat all the rich, high-fat foods you want. It's important for milk production…no one told me about that. Still, it's a wonderful experience. Babies are miracles."

Fred didn't open his mouth. He was with Lori when Katie was born and he was one of those daddies that woke up, on a gurney, after the birth was over. It was the grossest, yet most wondrous, thing he'd ever witnessed. And he'd missed part of it. Joy was right. The bigger they are, the harder they fall. He was praying that Joy would have an easy time, since Lori had let everyone within a mile radius know that she was in pain, needed drugs, and wanted that 'blankety-blankety-blank thing out'. He could not imagine Joy saying the vile words that had spewed from Lori's mouth.

"You didn't tell her about the pineapple and peanut butter sandwiches, doll," Fred told Joy, in an aside. "I don't know where she puts all of it," he told everyone within hearing. "She can't have salt because it makes her feet and hands swell and shoots her blood pressure up too much. She was all about dill pickles smeared with peanut butter, homemade French fries and mayonnaise, but had to give up the pickles and salty fries."

"Ginger ate sauerkraut and Vienna sausages. That grossed me out totally," Hart added.

"Yeah, I stole his Vienna sausage stash. That grossed him out. That's what he takes for lunch—Vienna sausages and pork and beans. He buys those by the case," Ginger threw in for good measure. "I fussed at him for eating all that nasty stuff before we got married and then when I was expecting Jimmy, that's all I wanted. Those canned sausages! I looked the pantry and refrigerator over for days trying to find what it was that I wanted to eat. Hart told me to close my eyes, and the rascal put one of those Vienna sausages in my mouth and bingo! Who would have thought that was the taste I was craving? It's like he knew. It was the pregnancy hormones, I swear, y'all. It was. Now he won't let me live it down."

Mr. Ralph piped up, "And Hart grins like a mule eatin' briars every time he tells anybody about it, too, honey…sneakin' his 'Vi-ennie' sausages."

Everyone in hearing range laughed at, and with, Ginger and Mr. Ralph. Ginger still had just a touch of Yankee in her voice and to hear her say 'y'all' was funny.

"You're like the queen of cooking and your husband takes Vienna sausages and pork and beans for lunch? I'd thought you'd send him off with gourmet roast beef sandwiches on homemade focaccia bread or vichyssoise soup," Julie said.

Hart took over. "Hell, no. She hasn't had a good night's sleep in over a year, before or after, Jimmy was born. Or me. The little stinker isn't going to sleep all night. Up every two hours to begin with, now it's about every three or four. Always needing a bottle or a clean diaper. Now he wants to sleep with his mama and me at the most inconvenient time, if you catch my drift. There is no alone time, or locked doors any more. Just 'Jimmy time', and Lord, I'll be glad when he will sleep through the night," he said. "I take something canned for lunch so Ginger won't have to cook for me. She's got enough to do running after that little scamp. That's a full time job since he's started walking. God knows what he'll be doing by the time he's two. They're good when they're little and you can keep them contained in a baby bed or a play pen. Behind bars!"

Everyone laughed at Hart's description of life with a toddler.

"But he's so-oo cute," Julie said in her whiny voice.

"Cute is, as cute does," Ginger told Julie. "See how cute he is when he's thrown up all over your new sixty dollar navy blue blouse just as you start to leave the house, or he throws spaghetti-o's—his favorite— all over the place and his face is covered, his hair, his clothes, the high chair, the wall, the window. At least the sauce matches his hair, though. Hart puts a drop cloth under his high chair to hold down on the mess. We took it up for tonight. I'm exhausted at night just following behind him, trying to keep the place half-way clean. We've had to put locks on the toilets. He's flushed bath toys, twice, and one of Hart's watches. You cannot leave him alone, or turn your back, even for a second. And when he takes a nap, I take one with him because I'm exhausted and he's been up since 5:00 in the morning, wide open. Which means one of us has to be up with him. You can forget sleeping in ever again. Oh, and those diapers. Whew! Talk about grossing you out! It's either green slime or mustard—and little boys will pee right in your face if you're not paying close attention."

Hart pointed at himself and said, "He got me, yesterday, and grinned while doing it. I think he did it on purpose."

Laughter came from all but Hart.

"Mamas are experts on poopie…and pee pee. And spit up," Hart added, solemnly nodding, as though they were discussing the meaning of life.

"What about a nanny?" Julie asked. "You both could afford one of those…an *au pair*? Folks with money hire those. You know, like a foreign exchange student who baby sits?"

Joy and Ginger just looked at each other, like either one would actually allow a young female in their home. Ginger was already a little jealous of the women swooning over Hart's singing and his Sam-Elliott- like, rugged looks, like it was. And Joy, no way.

"Yeah, right," Ginger said. "There's lots of those floating around in south Alabama, honey. Just try finding yourself one. I'll stick to looking after my baby love right by myself. That's what real mamas do, you know." It was a statement. Not a question.

"You know when Joy starts 'nesting', you can hang it up, " Hart said to Fred. "She'll be sweet as an angel one minute, demanding, and about as mean as the devil the next...trying to get everything just so, fixing this, cleaning from one end of the house to the other, moving that, depending on her mood swings. I finally told Ginger that 'whatever Mama wants, Mama gets'. And it worked just fine. It was easier that way."

"Amen," Fred said. "Whatever my 'little mama' wants, she'll get it, too."

Joy thought it was sweet that Fred was so willing to do whatever she wanted, not that she had any doubts.

"What's nesting?" a younger guy asked from another table.

Everyone close by laughed at his question.

Julie got up from her seat and stomped off. She slammed the screened door, her boots loud on the wooden steps. Several folks had laughed as she had hastily exited the porch.

Joy and Ginger high-fived each other over the table and burst out laughing. Fred winked at Hart and Jack and they all started laughing, too.

After Julie left, Hart entertained everyone who had missed the 'having a baby' story. They all laughed, wiping tears as Hart put his spin on the telling, with helpful interjections and hand gestures from Fred.

Betty Ruth got into the conversation and told of child birth in her day and how miserable she'd been with no air conditioning in the south in August, with

100 plus degree temperatures, and gaining so much weight with her daughter that she never 'got all the weight off' and how she still needed to go on a diet forty-five years after the birth.

Mr. Ralph stole the show when he patted Betty Ruth's hand and told her, "I love every pound of it, Betty Ruth. Don't you go and start losing weight now, honey pie. I wouldn't want to hurt any of these fellers if they started giving you the eye."

Ralph's hearing aids had improved his hearing but he still talked too loud. "What was that TV show we were watching the other night, shug? The one with all them duck-lipped women on it?"

"I was changing channels, honey. You wanted to watch it, not me. I'm not going to let you watch those trashy women."

"They looked like they had little animals sewed to their hinnies. All sticking out. You could set a plate on that one girl's butt, and her lips looked like a mallard's," Mr. Ralph said and everyone laughed again.

Betty Ruth was an excellent country cook. He loved that she put up vegetables in their freezer and shared with those In the community. He was happy and it showed.

Ginger told everyone that she wanted another baby but Hart wanted to wait. She wanted a little girl she said but Hart was too traumatized by Jimmy for him to even talk about it. Everyone commiserated with Ginger…and Hart.

"Ralph and I will keep Jimmy for you, honey…any time. Y'all hurry up and have another one. We ain't getting any younger and neither are y'all," Betty Ruth said to Ginger.

Hart shook his head. "Don't encourage her, Mrs. Betty Ruth. She's already been sweet talking me about it. She's made all my favorite dishes lately. I know what she's up to, though," he said, his deep voice full of humor.

Hart was in love and happy. Ginger was as perfect a partner, wife and mother as any man could ask for. Jimmy was the joy in their life. Hart knew he was a blessed man—blessed beyond measure. No money worries, and Ginger was not one to complain nor nag him. Actually she'd only asked a time or two about borrowing his tools and he thought it was so cute, and out of character for her, that he wrote a song about it.

She was right beside him, step for step, as they planted fifty blueberry bushes and she worked side by side with him as they plowed, planted, hoed and harvested the bounty from their large garden. She was planting roses and heirloom plants to replace the ones that once bloomed around the house. The garden, the flowers—all of it was something he'd dreamed of doing for years while living and working, being miserable in those foreign lands. Finally he had his dream: the wife, the family, the house, the family farm. Hart's only regret was that Ginger had not come into his life earlier so he'd have more years with her. Yes, she aggravated the tee-mortal hell out of him just as much as she ever did, but he realized now that they were like magnets—drawn to each other. She appealed to him on every level and she obviously was madly in love with him since she wanted another child with him. God was good.

Joy scanned the folks to see if Julie was still around. She didn't see her but Joy wanted to know where she was...keep an eye on her. Julie bothered her on every level. She just didn't trust her. At all. And tonight especially Joy felt like something was going to happen. Maybe it was her woman's intuition, or perhaps she was perceptive, or it could be an overload of hormones. But she waited and listened to the conversations and the music. She sipped on lemonade and nibbled on veggies that Ginger had put on their table. Ginger always put roasted pecans or peanuts, or veggies at each table for those who wanted to munch before or after the meal.

When the music started back Hart stepped up to the mike.

"My woman's crazy about my tool belt,
She says it's not just my tape and nail set,
She loves my level and my speed square, and needs my hammer to hang something way up 'there'.
She's been watching those TV shows
What she'll want next, heaven knows.

She says she needs another shelf to fill,
but I say, 'I have a new house to build.
I can't take the time to spend on that.'
And she tells me *where* I can put my speed
square
I say that ain't on my tool belt—anywhere.
I see her eying my tool belt,
And I know that she ain't done yet.
We'll have more shelves, you can bet on that.
I'll build another room, 'cause she says she
'needs her space'.
I'll build it since she puts good food on my plate.
She'll end up with her space and
That 'addition' she's been talking about,
Because I'm crazy about her and
She says I'm a *stud* in my tool belt.

Hart finished and everyone laughed and applauded except Ginger, who wiggled her finger at him indicating that they'd talk later. The space she wanted was a sitting room off their bedroom. It would also serve as a possible nursery and a place where Ginger could do craft projects, have a space for reading by the fireplace she wanted in it, and it wasn't like they couldn't afford it. She'd hire someone else to build it but Hart would pitch a fit if she even mentioned that. She did not know he'd written a song about it, though. Everything that happened was fodder for his 'songs'.

*I wonder if that 'addition' he's talking about is a baby? Yes, they would talk. Hart is softening up to the idea. And I only called him 'stud' one time. Darn man, doesn't forget anything!*

Fred stepped up to the mike and Hart moved away and sat on a nearby hay bale.

"Hart, I believe you might be in trouble after that song. Maybe you and your lovely wife will get it all sorted out soon."

Hart shook his head. "Nah, I'm not worried. We'll work something out," he said and waved at his red-headed wife. He had not intended to sing that last verse the way it came out and had actually changed the words on the spot. *Was it a Freudian slip? Lord, help me! Another baby!*

"I wrote this for my beautiful wife, Joy. We're expecting twins in a few weeks. This one's for you, baby doll," Fred told the audience which numbered around forty folks. He played the song alone on Maybelle.

I love you, Joy. Did I tell you today?
This song is for you, and your sweet, loving ways,
How much I need you and want you to stay
With me forever, and a day
I can't find the words, I don't know what to say,
But know that I love you , more every day,

You're the joy of my heart, joy of my soul,
I couldn't tell you, how could you know?
How much I need you and want you to stay
With me forever, and a day.

I love you, my Joy, I'll tell you today
How much I love you and I hope and pray
That we stay together through eternity
We'll grow old together, with our family
That God gave us, so happy we'll be.

I gave up the bad things that I used to do,
the drinking and cursing. You wanted me to.
You knew what I needed, when I was so wrong,
Come stand by my side, right where you belong.

For you are my Joy, the song in my heart,
I'll love you forever, and never we'll part,
For you are my Joy, the song in my heart.
I'm thankful to God for the Joy in my heart.


Fred got a standing ovation and he held his hand
out to Joy, for her to come forward to him and she
did, practically running to the stage where she and
Fred shared a sweet kiss and hug. The song had not
embarrassed her. It had endeared Fred to her more
than ever. She knew in that moment that he did love
her. She wiped the tears as did everyone else in the
audience.


*****

Later that night Fred and Joy lay close in the double bed.

"I didn't want Julie to kiss me that night, doll. She just walked up and I didn't know she'd stoop that low. She saw you with me and was jealous, that's all it was. I've dated her two times over the past three years. That's it. Nothing serious. She was after my money. Her folks ain't got a pot to piss in. Of course, they live like they're loaded. I don't think she even likes country music. I never slept with her, although it wasn't for lack of trying on her part. After Lori, I learned my lesson—keep the zipper zipped. Mom kept pushing Julie on me, just like she did Lori, even though I've told Julie I just wasn't interested. I never have been in love, lust, or anything else, with her...I don't know how, or why, she shows up here. I know Hart didn't invite her and I'm sure Ginger didn't, either. She's chased Jack some, too, but he put her in the wind after a date or so. She didn't care for his chewing tobacco.

"I'm sorry I haven't told you any more about her before. I don't like even thinking about her. I was so mad she did that...that kiss, I could have wrung her neck. I knew it hurt you and I should have set things straight right then. I knew it made you mad and hurt you, too. I was hoping it would make you a little jealous, I admit, after she'd done it. But I was so mad myself I knew I'd say the wrong thing at that moment."

"I understand...I can see how she is...I forgive you, love. I love my song, Fred. It's beautiful. You ought to take it to Nashville."

301

"No, I don't want that. It's just for you, doll, your early Christmas present," he said as he held her close. "Just for you." One of the babies kicked hard and they laughed.

## Chapter Twenty-five

*"The steps of a good man are ordered by the*
*Lord; and he delighteth in His way."*
~Psalms 37:23

The next morning Fred walked out to his truck to
find Maybelle in pieces inside its case on the ground.
Someone had taken an axe or something and really
worked hard to destroy his guitar. He had an idea but
kept his mouth shut for the moment. He dialed the
sheriff's office to make a report.

Twenty minutes later a couple of Henry County
deputies came and took tons of photos, fingerprints,
footprints, and the remains of Maybelle, after
questioning Fred, Joy, Hart and Ginger. The deputies
asked for a list of the folks who had attended the
monthly sing, and Hart said he could come up with
that for them.

Joey had barked for a while after Ginger and Hart
had said the last goodbye to all their guests and the
last car had pulled away. Hart had mentioned it to
Ginger, but since Joey barked at every rabbit or fallen
oak leaf, they'd dismissed it. The truck's security
alarm failed to go off as well and he wondered if
someone had stolen his code. He was almost sure
he'd locked the truck, after putting Maybelle safely

inside its case on the backseat. Perhaps he had forgotten to lock it?

The criminal act had broken Joy's heart since she knew how much Fred loved Maybelle. She'd watched him play it many times, as well as the other guitars he owned. The guitar was special and Fred had to be deeply hurt by this.

He'd given the deputies a list of anyone he thought might think of him as an enemy. And as much as he hated to do it, he put Julie Adams at the top of that list. He saw red when he first saw the guitar that had been his prize possession lying there on the ground in pieces. His fists clenched and he wanted to punch something, someone.

Fred also told the deputies about Julie leaving her bikini on the post at his house and the motion camera on the pontoon boat catching her in the act. It was out of their jurisdiction but Fred said he'd contact the police in Eufaula since now he suspected that Julie was behind the whole mess. Joy overheard him telling this and recalled her dream of weeks past and mentioned her own uneasiness of the previous night.

That night she told Fred about her dream and the yellow bikini. She left out certain things but told him enough for him to realize that she had a premonition of some impending occurrence.

"I'm so sorry about Maybelle, Fred. I know how much she meant to you. It was the best sounding guitar I've ever heard," she told him as they sat looking out to the lake.

"She was the best guitar I've ever owned. And she can't be replaced. They made so few of them. I wish to God I'd left her home and grabbed one of the other ones."

"You had no way of knowing, love," Joy said in her soothing voice. "If Julie did it, I hope it haunts her forever. The value was more than monetary. I could see that Maybelle was like your friend…"

"Yes, you are right. I played her many a night and got lost in the sounds, only she could produce. She's irreplaceable. So yes, losing her is like losing an old and much loved friend."

Joy wanted to ask who Maybelle but decided now was not a good time so she let it be. She'd call Hart tomorrow and see what could be done about replacing Fred's precious guitar.

*****

Fred ordered Joy a large wooden floor easel that could hold large canvases since she seemed to prefer the bigger sizes. A designer had bought the floral paintings, asking for even larger pieces, and a gallery had taken the others on consignment. Two had already sold.

Of course, the floor easel came in pieces, with ratchets, pulleys, wheels, and cranks. It was the best Fred could find and he had to get Sol come over to help put the thing together. Fred was good with computers and numbers but not so good with sitting on the floor with pieces of lumber and screws. Or reading directions. (As in not reading).

Sol had been to the house several times, as had Fred's other poker buddies, Art and Nate. Poker night had turned into a cooking night for Joy since all the men did was eat while they played. They played for pennies, or matches, which Joy thought was cute since Nate usually won. No money exchanged hands.

Fred used to spring for pizzas and subs but since his marriage to Joy, he preferred her cooking, so she made homemade chili, club sandwiches and stews. She enjoyed cooking and didn't mind the men having a good time.

Nate was interesting to be around and Sol was Fred's best friend, other than Hart. The four of them were hilarious to listen to as they cajoled each other over each hand.

Joy didn't play. It was too much fun just to listen to as she practiced her crocheting or talked with Mimi on the phone. Tonight she learned the history of the rickety table and was suddenly ashamed of her offer to 'fix' it for Fred. She'd been told that Sol had given the table to Fred. Sol had learned woodworking skills as he served time in prison. He'd made the table and had presented it to Fred one year for Christmas. Sol talked of his time in prison with more sorrow than shame. It was the only low key conversation of the noisy night.

"Hoss beat us big time tonight, Ms. Joy," Nate said. "I usually whup him good, but I think you brought him good luck. That was some mighty fine eating, too. I love that chocolate dessert you made."

The four men had eaten the entire making. Joy had learned to make it while working for Mrs.

Wentworth. She loved chocolate and Joy made the simple dessert often.

"Thanks, Nate. It's something I used to make a while back. Fred loves it."

"What did you say it was called?"

"I never said....some call it Chocolate Delight. The real name is "Sex in a Pan", but I had to change the name because of the lady I used to work for. She loved it, too, but she thought the name was uncouth. Another name for it is "Better than Robert Redford" but she didn't like that name, either," she said and laughed.

"I think you need to be on one of them TV cooking shows."

"Thanks, Nate, but I don't think so. I'm happy right here. Umm...Nate...why do y'all call Fred, 'Hoss'?"

He didn't answer for a few seconds. Joy could see the wheels turning inside his head. *This is going to be good*, she thought.

"You need to ask him about that. I'm afraid he'd deck me if'n I told you," he said and laughed so hard she figured it was a joke of some kind. She'd wondered about it before and just never thought to ask Fred.

Art, Fred and Sol were at the door, bidding goodnight to the other. Nate had lingered longer, helping Joy put dishes and glasses into the dishwasher.

She did ask Fred after everyone had left and he grinned and wiggled his eyebrows. It dawned on her at that exact moment—his nickname did not come from the '*Bonanza*' character, Hoss Cartwright, as she'd thought all along (well, they were both big blonde men—and she had just assumed…duh, darn pregnancy hormones were making her brain foggy.) She should have known that with Fred it was something dirty. The rascal enjoyed watching her face after she asked about it. He had a wicked sense of humor and had a streak of devilment, including telling off-color jokes.

"You could have told me before I embarrassed myself by asking Nate about it. It *is* on your tags." The tag on his Denali read 'Hoss 1' and the tag on his Mustang read 'Hoss 2'. She shook her head. "Nate's probably laughing at me all the way home."

"Yep. I'm sure. I thought you already knew. Or figured it out all on your own, doll."

She wondered if she was the last, no, make that the only, person in town who didn't know the truth behind Fred's nickname. She would never, ever be able to look Nate in the eye again.

"I guess I'm just naïve, Hoss," she said with a definite inflection on his name and walked to their bedroom. He liked the sound of her saying it with her honey-sweet voice. She stretched his name into two syllables. He wasted no time following her.

*****

Joy and Mimi had become phone buddies and Mimi called her almost daily to give a report on the paintings and to check on Joy and the babies. Mimi had bought three large rocking chairs—one for Fred, one for Joy, and one for herself.

Fred also bought her an engagement ring to go with her wedding band. It had three diamonds, a large one, to represent the two of them, united, and two smaller ones to represent their unborn children he'd told her as he presented it to her. He'd given much thought to it and Joy cried when he gave it to her on Christmas Eve.

Joy secretly had talked with Hart and had him searching for a replacement Maybelle. It could not be a new guitar since Maybelle was antique, but had to be one with the same heritage and condition. He'd finally found one, at a high price, and Joy bought it after Hart's approval. Pam and her boyfriend had driven to Tennessee to pick it up.

Hart was somewhat surprised that Joy never hesitated when he'd told her how much the guitar cost. The shop owner was not a haggling man and staunchly stood on his price. The guitar could easily have been in a museum, the man told them. It was the best available 1944 D-28 outside of the Martin Company collection, he said.

Hart had schooled Joy on the 1944 Martin D-28—Maybelle. The 'D' was a 'dreadnought' body style that the C.F. Martin Company made. Dreadnought was a naval term adapted by the guitar industry and used to describe a wide and larger body dimensions of a guitar. The D-28 is highly prized for its booming projection and high tone quality. The wide and deep body produces a tone of great power, especially fine for recording and concert playing.*

Hart had told Joy that Fred's D-28 was almost perfect and had only minor scratches, due to its being stored away in a case under a bed for much of its lifetime. There were other D-28's available, some for half the price but most had been repaired, and although done by nationally known luthiers, Joy wanted the best to replace Maybelle. Joy now knew, too, that Fred had named his prized guitar after 'Mother' *Maybelle* Carter, famous country music singer and musician—a legend.

Three days before Christmas Joy had placed the oversized box under their tree, which was set up in the studio, now dressed with Christmas greenery. If Fred had noticed the box, he had not said anything.

Joy watched his face as he pulled it from its case on Christmas Eve. She couldn't wait another day.

"I know it's not Maybelle, love, but Hart helped me find it. It's Maybelle's twin sister, Hart said."

He examined it thoroughly. The neck felt almost the same, the body was in immaculate condition. No scratches, no damage anywhere. It was in better condition than Maybelle had been when Fred bought her from Nate. There was a leather strap on it embossed with floral scrolling that left a space for a name. Joy wanted Fred to have it stamped with the name of his choice.

"It's…identical to her…thank you, doll. I love it."

He tuned it since the strings had been let down for shipping. He cocked his head as he put his ear close to catch the nuances as he tuned and ran through the chords. It played as beautifully as Maybelle did. No,

310

it wasn't Maybelle. No two guitars played, or sounded, the same. Joy had paid a mint for this one and words choked in his throat. He wanted to scold her for spending such a large amount of money on a guitar, but he knew if he did so, she'd cry over it and he'd regret saying anything.

"Hart found it at a music shop in Tennessee. He knew what to ask for. He and Ginger have been looking since the day yours was destroyed. I knew then I wanted to get you another one. I know I paid way more than you did for Maybelle but I was determined to get it. The store owner said it was played once by a country star from the Grand Ole Opry. You might know his name...", she said and stopped, teasing him.

"Who? It's a 1944 Martin D-28. Same as Maybelle. Not many of them were made during World War II. But lots of country stars play Martins. Hank Williams played one. It's the 'holy grail' for bluegrass players."

"A great guitar player played this one, though. This Martin D-28. Just for one night at a special event in his home. And he died not too long back... he was blind." He'd figure it out in a minute. She'd given him too many clues she realized. The last word was the dead give-away. She'd been enjoying the exchange and should have made him wonder a little longer.

Fred thought for a few seconds.

"No way. Doc Watson?"

She nodded. It was worth every penny just to see the expression on his face.

"The hell you say. The Doc Watson played this baby?" Doc Watson was one of Fred's guitar heroes. He, too, played a style that Fred emulated—flat picking. Once in a while Fred slipped in a bad word. Joy forgave him. She didn't expect perfection. She'd hit her toe on the coffee table yesterday and said a bad word herself before she knew what had happened. It just slipped out.

"That's what the man said. I wrote it all down when Hart found it. I have its provenance."

He loved the way she said 'provenance' with her slow southern drawl.

"And you paid how much for it?"

The rascal was determined to weasel it out of her.

"That's my secret. The price doesn't matter, honey. I have money you know. It was a bunch, but I wanted it for you. I know what Maybelle meant to you."

She wouldn't tell him she'd paid $100,000 for it. And would have paid more. Now she laughed to herself at having the ability to spend that kind of money without giving it a second thought. She might not spend it on herself, but she'd sure spend it on him, or her babies. Hart had listened and watched the shop's owner play the guitar via his computer. A cashier's check in Pam's purse had sealed the deal. Pam had been given specific instructions not to purchase it if it was not as Hart was told. Hart had wanted to be the one to pick it up but work had interfered and Pam had readily volunteered.

"I have a good idea what you spent. You shouldn't have. We could have found another one. It didn't have to be identical to Maybelle. I got a bargain on her. I paid Nate $5000 because he needed money. You paid many, many times that much, didn't you?"

Joy never let on about having money. She seemed unaffected by it. She spent it but made no big deal out of it as some who came into large amounts of money. Her largest purchase had been fourteen thousand dollars for a used car. She came into his life with nine cents to her name and now spent many, many thousands of dollars on a guitar—for him. His love for her deepened and the unselfish gesture brought the sting of tears to his eyes.

"Uh...um....yes, I did." She wasn't going to lie to him. "I wanted you to have a replacement. I would have had Maybelle fixed but the damage was too great."

Joy had cried when Hart had told her that Fred's beloved Maybelle could not be fixed. The neck was broken into four pieces. The inner structure—the scalloped bracing which gave the guitar its superior tonal quality—was in splinters. Even the bridge, headstock and tuning keys were damaged beyond repair. The guitar repairman, a luthier who saw the damaged guitar, said there was really nothing salvageable. The Brazilian rosewood back and sides were broken in many places, the Adirondack spruce top was in a hundred pieces. The sound hole and finger board were shattered. The herringbone purfling—a strip of marquetry trademarked by the Martin company—was ripped away and broken into tiny pieces, as was the binding. Only a hammer or a chisel could have made the marks on the frets and seventy-plus year old guitar. No one could figure how so much damage was done without being heard by someone. A lot of banging and hammering had to have gone on for a while.

Joy mentioned that perhaps the guitar had been removed from the truck, taken someplace, destroyed with some tool, and returned to Fred's truck. Hart had agreed. His framing hammer had disappeared and Ginger swore she had not taken it from the tool belt that Hart always hung in the kitchen. He'd leave it in the truck sometimes but he'd brought it in for a 'honey-do' and the belt was hanging there the night of the sing. Several folks had commented on it after hearing Hart's song. None, including Hart, had noticed whether his framing hammer was missing. He discovered the disappearance the Monday following the sing and reported the information to the authorities. And the fact that their front door was not locked and anyone could have come in and taken the hammer.

The fingerprints on Fred's truck door had turned out to be Julie's. She had not been the least bit remorseful over destroying a valuable and treasured instrument. She admitted doing it, and said she did it to 'get back at Fred for marrying Joy instead of her' and had gotten her idea from Hart's song about his tool belt. She said she'd seen the tool belt hanging on the wall, sneaked in the front door and took the hammer, stolen the guitar later and had gleefully, and methodically, beaten Maybelle into hundreds of fragments before putting all the pieces back into the guitar case, and placing it beside his Denali.

Charges were pending for damage to the vintage guitar, insurance value estimated at a low $15,000, simply because there had been no provenance with Maybelle. Only the word of his friend that his grandfather had bought the guitar, played it very little and put it into a case where Nate kept it himself until he needed some cash a few years back.

"Well, I guess I'll have to kiss you a fifty thousand times then. Let me play on this beauty for a while and we'll see how far we get tonight. I'll let you keep score."

He was in a good mood and Joy felt blessed. Her whole world had changed for the better. She tried to crochet an afghan as he played. Mimi was teaching her and Joy was determined to make the babies a blanket each. Her efforts were less than stellar and frown lines creased her forehead as she held up the tiny pink blanket.

Mimi could crochet a mile a minute and Joy struggled to figure out the stitches and to keep the tension even.

Fred played a selection of Christmas songs and he sang a few. At midnight they went to bed. Joy counted twenty-three kisses before she gave up.

On Christmas Day, Sol brought over a present that he'd been keeping for Fred—a ten-week old black and white puppy. Sol assured Joy that the puppy would have long hair. *The pink bow around its neck was perfect. A girl puppy to grow up with her babies.*

A few weeks later Fred looked at his babies, one with a blue blanket, one with a pink blanket. Both babies were healthy at almost four and a half pounds each but would stay a few days in the hospital since they were four weeks early. They were so small and Fred marveled at the miracle of birth once again. He'd held Joy's hand, flinching as the doctor made a motion that Fred knew was an incision, and was sickened by the smoke from the cauterization. He'd kissed her as they'd shown the babies, one at a time to Joy and Fred, and put each one on her chest for a few moments.

Joy was being stitched up and would go to ICU until her blood pressure stabilized. An emergency caesarean section had been necessary since the babies were putting stress on Joy's body. She'd passed out but fortunately Fred had come home for lunch and found her. She wasn't hurt, thankfully, but it had almost scared the life out of him when he'd seen her on that hard concrete floor. Mimi had been at the grocery store and had just gotten home as Fred was putting Joy in his truck, headed to the hospital.

Fred prayed all the way there. God had brought Joy back to him once.

*I can't lose her now... or the babies, please, God. Take me if You have to take anyone. Please spare Joy and our babies....I'll do whatever You ask of me, dear God, save her...*

## Chapter Twenty-six

*"The joy of the Lord is your strength."*
~Nehemiah 8:10 KJV

Hart and Ginger were in the room waiting for Fred, along with Fred's grandmother. He'd called them as soon as he could from the hospital. Hart and Ginger sped to Eufaula after leaving baby Jimmy with Betty Ruth and Ralph Hinson.

"The babies are okay, and Joy's going to be okay in a day or two," Fred told them. "I thought she was gone one time there, though. Her blood pressure shot up just as they started the incision. They had trouble getting her stable. She'll be in ICU overnight...I don't want her to go through this again. I know she wants more kids, but my heart can't handle another day like this one. We'll have to adopt if she wants more."

They all hugged, and Mimi embraced her grandson, as tears streamed down her face.

"We'll pray for her and the babies, Fred," Hart told his best friend, as he reached around Fred's shoulder. They gathered in a small circle, hand in hand, as Hart openly prayed for Joy.

"Father, we come together in prayer for our dear Joy. We ask for her healing and speedy recovery, and for Your blessings upon these precious babies, and this new family. May their marriage always be based on their love for each other and their children. And we thank You for their friendship. We ask for guidance and wisdom in all that we do. In Your Son's name, we pray. Amen."

Tears ran down Fred's cheeks as he realized how blessed he was to have friends like Hart and Ginger Wakefield. And his precious Mimi.

Frances Grace 'Gracie' Garrett and James Robert 'Bobby' Garrett were named by their father. Gracie, of course was named for Fred's grandmother, who had come into Joy's life and embraced her with love and open arms. The 'James' was in honor of Fred's best friend, James Hartford 'Hart' Wakefield, II. The 'Robert' had been in honor of Fred's younger brother who died at birth when Fred was just two years old and was the child his parents never talked about. The child he'd found out about by accident a few years back at the cemetery when Fred's grandfather had died. His parents wouldn't answer his questions when he'd asked them about Robert. The only comment came from his father who told him, "Let it be. It's best not to speak of it, son."

Mimi had answered Fred's questions and Fred learned that Robert had died after a complicated pregnancy. The placenta had become detached, and Elaine had hemorrhaged to the point of near death. She was unable to have children after that and Robert's death had done something to her mind.

She'd shut down for a while from post-partum depression and grief. Mimi had taken Fred and kept him for months until Elaine had come 'back to life' as Mimi called it. Mimi told Fred that losing Robert had left Elaine cold and bitter, a changed woman who had forgotten how to love again.

Fred had recalled his promise to Joy to move her baby's casket to Eufaula and several weeks prior had made arrangements to do just that. Joy's son would join Fred's brother, where they would rest side by side. Fred bought all the plots next to James' to insure that no one could get them except for family. He had not told Joy about it, wanting to choose the right time to take her there.


Fred rocked his baby girl in the studio/sun room of their home while Joy bathed Bobby. Having twins was a struggle at times, but with help from Mimi, and some hired housekeepers, Joy and Fred were able to manage and still have time to enjoy their lives.

Baby Gracie looked deep into her father's eyes as she grasped his finger and he wondered if the babies were an angelic gift from God, like Joy. Joy had come to him sick and on the run, but instead of Fred helping her, he'd discovered that she had helped him more. God had sent her. He'd told Fred so, and Fred believed it with all his heart. Late one night he'd told her about that occurrence, that quiet, still voice. And Joy believed him and told him that she'd been praying that God would send her someone to love her as much as she had dreamed and wished for, and that

God had answered her prayers in Fred.

She was his second chance at love, and though she wasn't perfect, she was perfect for him. She loved his country music and his rowdy group of poker buddies and made fast friends with his beloved Mimi. His parents were slowly warming to her but Fred had decided he didn't care what his parents, or the world, thought.

Gone are the nights of drinking until midnight and passing out on his porch. Now the porch is a glassed-in room, full of Joy's beautiful paintings. The babies nap nearby as Joy creates and Fred plays. Joy loves Fred's songs and the babies are entertained, and fascinated by their father's music.

Fred's work is easier now. He has a reason to come home, and life is better all the way around. Joy is an angel sent to him on a mission, and their love created two beautiful babies, both with cherubic faces and the curly blonde hair of their doting daddy. Mimi says that both babies are the spitting image of Fred when he was their age.

Money cannot buy happiness he'd learned. And he'd discovered that you can't judge a book by its cover. Joy was so much more than her background and small stature. Her heart was huge, and filled to overflowing with love for others.

Joy is everything in Fred's world and he cannot not imagine life without her. She's made his house into a home, given him a family and love enough to share with all.

Fred tells everyone who will listen, "I am a blessed man."

He rescued Joy and in turn, she rescued him. She brought Fred the gifts of love, of giving, creating, compassion, and more importantly, the gift of joy.

He has come full circle, and now when the rain comes, he is ready to be home.

Is this the end of the story you ask?

Joy and Fred are happy and the grandparents do visit but not often. Mimi lives with Fred and Joy the majority of the time, helping Joy with the babies, and loves to be a part of their lives. Fred bought Ginger's cottage for Joy, and Hart built a picket fence around it and Fred, himself, planted pink rambling roses as his first anniversary gift to her. So you see, dreams and fairytales can come true and Prince Charming *does* drive a Denali.

Oh, you want to know what Fred named his guitar, don't you? (You guessed wrong if you said "Joy". Fred would never, ever, name a guitar after his beloved wife. Besides, that would have been too obvious—ha!) Well, he named her 'Lucille', after the late and great B.B. King's famous guitar. B.B. said that he named the guitar Lucille to remind him never to fight over women. Fred named his guitar, 'Lucille,' because he said he 'liked the name'. That's his story and he's sticking to it.

Hart and Ginger still have their monthly music gatherings where folks from far and wide gather to celebrate the music and food of the South. Ginger's cookbook is a national bestseller and if you listen to country music on the radio you might just hear a song that Hart wrote—a song of the South, and of coming home.

**The End**...or is it? Stay tuned.

(*) information on Martin D-28 guitars from the C.F. Martin Guitar Company and Wikipedia.(By the way, Kurt Russell destroyed a vintage museum-quality 1870's Martin guitar by accident recently while filming a movie. I wrote the scene in this story almost two years before the accident happened with Kurt so I did *not* get my idea from that incident...I swear on Fred's beloved Martin. I actually wrote the prologue to this story, Rain Song, August 14, 2012, for a writers' group assignment, and have been revising and adding since.( This is probably my 10th version of this story. It's the same basic story with the addition of characters, etc. to tie in to Coming Home, my first published full length novel, in which Fred was a character.)

Many thanks to my nephew, Lee Mason Dunn, for his invaluable input on guitars for this book. He is a wonderfully talented guitar player and has a collection as large as Fred's. Lee's are real, though. Fred's guitars were strictly in the little movie that played in my mind while I worked on this manuscript.

Thanks to my manuscript readers, Cheri Lewis, Diane Cook Hallford, and Judy Mull, for catching my numerous mistakes.

A special thanks, again, to Cheri Lewis for

helping me with the Word program and formatting for this manuscript. Maybe I'll learn all this one day, Cheri.

Thanks also to C. Heyward Carroll for the 'use' of his white Denali in this story.

And last, many thanks to my cousin, Catherine Peters Outlaw, for inviting me to her lovely home on Lake Eufaula. She has the wonderful view looking over to Georgia that my character, Fred, has in this story (see front cover photo). She is a wonderful hostess and I thoroughly enjoyed my stay.

For anyone who thinks that Fred is David and Joy is me, you'd be mostly wrong. I will admit that I borrowed from my own personal experiences with art (for example, I won an award in the very first show that I entered) to create Joy, and Fred was created from a composite of folks I know, and those that live in the recesses of my imagination.

It is true that David and I loved to ride the back roads, taking photos for me to paint, but David loved to wander. He always wanted to know what was beyond the bend in the road. We shared the love of dirt roads and wind in our hair, stock car racing, rock and roll or country music on the radio. I miss those wonderful hours and I treasure the time I had with him. David and I took a similar trip (not our honeymoon, though) to Kentucky, Virginia, North and South Carolina, including Kitty Hawk. It was a wonderful trip for us since we left with no destination in mind.

Joy is not a real person, either. However, I do know women who have been abused. I am not an expert on abuse so any mistakes I made in this are strictly my own.


I would like to make a statement to any of you who doubt that God speaks to people as He did to Fred in this story: I can attest to the fact that God does speak to folks. I had an experience after my daddy died and I know that it was God's voice. I wrote about it the morning after it happened since it affected me so profoundly. My daddy had died alone at the nursing home on Mother's Day, May 10, 2009. We were having lunch with my son and his family and had planned to go to the nursing home afterwards. The phone rang, a call from my sis. We hurried but Daddy had died before we could get there. Almost four years later I woke up, 3:45 am, Feb. 3, 2013, and David was beside me asleep. I couldn't decide if I was hot or cold, as is normal with us ladies of a certain age. My thoughts ran to Daddy as I had his afghan over me as extra cover. I got to thinking about how he'd died alone and how much I regretted that fact, how much I wanted to be with him when he died. A quiet, still voice spoke to me and said, "He wasn't alone. I was with him." It was not David's voice. As I said, he was sound asleep. Anyway,that personal experience was a part of why I wrote about Fred hearing God's voice. I believe that He does speak to people. HE spoke to me.

*****

SEX IN A PAN aka Better than Robert Redford
Dessert aka Chocolate Delight
Ingredients for crust:
1/2 cup butter or margarine, softened
3 teaspoons sugar
1 cup flour
1 cup pecans, coarsely chopped (I like them toasted)

Filling:
8 ounces cream cheese, soft
1 cup powdered sugar
2 cups whipped cream or Cool Whip

Topping:
1 package chocolate instant pudding, 4 serving size
1 package instant vanilla pudding, 4 serving size
2 cups milk
1 1/2 cups whipped cream or Cool Whip
1 chocolate bar, grated (Hershey Bar with or without almonds works well)
Directions:
Beat together the butter and sugar. Blend in flour, then stir in the chopped pecans.
Press mixture into a 9 x 13 pan. Bake for 25 minutes at 350 degrees. Cool.
Combine cream cheese, and powdered sugar. Add 2 cups whipped cream.
Pour this mixture over the crust.

Combine both pudding mixes with the milk. Pour over cheese mixture.

Ice with 1-1/2 cups whipped cream and sprinkle with grated chocolate bar.

Chill for at least 4 hours before serving.